WHEN THE NIGHT BREATHES ELECTRIC

Stories

by Max Talley

Borda Books
BordaBooks.com
www.santabarbaraliteraryjournal.com

ISBN: 979-8-9879269-2-5

"Don't bend; don't water it down; don't try to make it logical; don't edit your own soul according to the fashion. Rather, follow your most intense obsessions mercilessly."

—*Franz Kafka*

This book is dedicated to the memory of Stephen Vessels. I had written weird fiction before I met him, but he was the true master of the surreal and the speculative, and we laughed together over our triumphs and failures. Of my publications, he may have enjoyed this collection, and thankfully heard half the stories before... *When The Night Breathes Electric* would not exist without the tireless work of Angela Borda. There is no one else like her on this planet.

Previously published stories in this collection

Entropy: "Clap Hands"

Abstract Magazine: "In the Blue House"

Hofstra - Windmill: "Forever Now"

Chantwood Magazine: "Three Months in Devorah"

The Opiate: "My Beloved Water Filter"

Del Sol Review: "Down in Chaotica"

Santa Barbara Literary Journal: "Destination Unknown"

Chantwood Magazine: "Confusion to Our Enemies"

The Opiate: "Axis of Distraction"

K'in: "I Don't Live Today"

Litro: "Dinner Party Exit Strategy"

Iconoclast: "Poisoned"

Two Cities Review: "The Devil is in the Details"

Gateway Review: "Identity Liquid"

Black Cat Mystery Magazine: "Sanity Clause"

The Fifth Fedora anthology: "Fallen Angels"

When the Night Breathes Electric

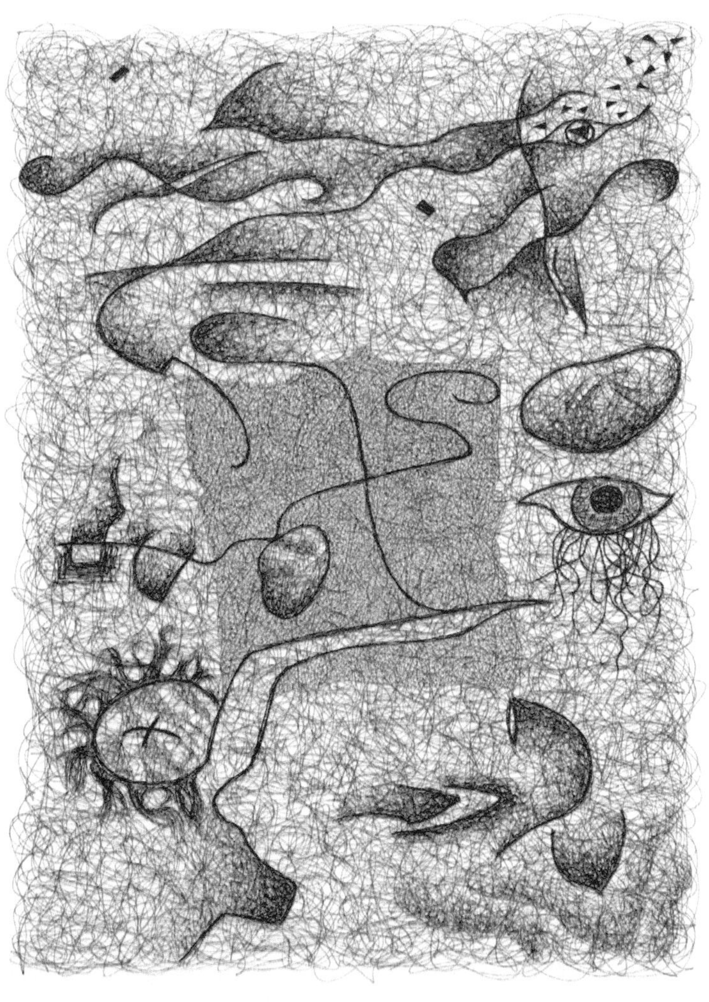

TABLE OF CONTENTS

TOC CONTINUED

CLAP HANDS

Edmund Garson awoke earlier than usual. He shuffled in a fog toward the bathroom to relieve his burning bladder. The mirrored medicine cabinet door above the sink hung ajar, moving slightly. He yanked it open. Edmund's heart jumped and he blinked several times. Normally, the cabinet held three sections. The base area stood a foot high, then two glass shelves sat propped above. A bottom shelf held toothbrushes in a cup, shaving cream, and a hydrogen peroxide container. Today that space lay empty, except for a human hand extending through the wooden back of the cabinet. A back that now looked gray and porous. Anything beyond the wrist was invisible. The hand flexed and contracted before waving at Edmund.

He recoiled and tried closing the cabinet but the hand formed a fist to resist. Edmund pressed his weight against it until the door finally clicked shut. Jesus Christ. He shuddered and trembled, teeth click-clacking together. Back in bed, he dozed off and twitched awake an hour later. Reentering the bathroom, he brought a hammer along for protection. All appeared normal. His toothbrush awaited so Edmund went through his morning ablutions. *Thank God, only some weird dream, he thought. I don't need this now, just as my relationship with Meredith has turned serious.*

Edmund took the subway to work, a cubicle in a crowded office above Grand Central in Manhattan. He sold renter's insurance for home possessions. A new employee approached him during a break.

"Are you Edvard?" The rangy man sounded distinctly German.

"Edmund, but just Ed is fine."

"Ed-mund? No, no, no. You don't look like a Mund."

"And your name?"

"Klaus." The man smiled, widening his beard. "I am your superior."

Edmund let out a sniff of laughter. "We're all assistant managers."

"I wasn't speaking of ranking, just that I'm your—"

"Got to get back to work." Edmund rushed away.

On Friday morning, Edmund saw the hand inside his medicine cabinet again. He rubbed his eyes but that didn't dispel the odd apparition. The hand squeezed a daub of toothpaste onto the blue toothbrush then extended it toward Edmund. He felt confused. Did it want to brush his teeth? He snatched the toothbrush away and shut the cabinet. Once finished spitting out, he grabbed his razor and Barbasol cream to shave blindly over the kitchen sink.

He thought about the graceful hand. His older brother Arthur had long artistic fingers. He painted and played classical piano, along with show tunes. Both of Edmund's parents doted on Arthur, clearly favoring him.

"Don't worry, Edmund," his mother confided. "You have strong hands like a lumberjack, a plumber, or a dock worker. You'll always have steady work while your darling brother exhibits at major galleries and performs in concert halls. The arts are so risky."

Arthur perished, swept overboard on a cruise ship that had hired him as a pianist for a season, and still years later, Edmund's parents never failed to mention those damn perfect hands.

Klaus sat in Edmund's cubicle when he arrived at work. The clueless dolt hummed to himself while poking around the desk.

"Excuse me..."

Klaus stood. "Did you cut yourself shaving? You really hacked up your neck, Sigmund."

"My name is Edmund, not Sigmund." He turned on his computer.

"Okay, Siggy. We talk later." The German man waved and departed.

Meredith dined with Edmund and spent Friday night at his apartment. She worked as a sensitivity reader for *Peregrine*

Books USA, so their dates often involved her correcting his word choice. Edmund didn't have much luck with the opposite sex, and since Meredith slept over on weekends despite him being forty-eight with a rather meager salary, he endured her comments.

Waking before her on Saturday, Edmund slouched into the bathroom and panicked when he saw two hands flexing inside the medicine cabinet. Feeling dizzy, he tilted forward in a near faint. The hands caught each side of his face and pushed him back upward. He then realized they were quite beautiful, and upon noticing the slender forearms, wished them to be female. The hands rubbed his cheeks with a soft caress. One splashed water on his face and sprayed lather onto the other's palm, which spread it across his jaw. Finally, the first hand delicately shaved Edmund—while both rinsed him and applied a soothing moisturizer. Before he could refuse, the hands brushed his teeth, being firm when necessary, yet soft in delicate gum areas.

Afterwards, Edmund retreated to the warmth of bed. He would say nothing until Meredith awoke to confront the floating extremities herself.

Once she used the bathroom, they lay spooning in silence. He finally asked, "Did you notice anything strange?"

Meredith opened one eye wide. "In your bathroom? Besides that men have much worse aim than women, no." She caressed his shoulder. "There's a Ukrainian Folk Festival out in Williamsburg today. Want to go, Ed?"

"Sure. Will there be any gypsy violin music? I love that stuff."

Meredith sat up straight in bed. "Never ever use that word." Her voice lowered to a whisper. "It's insulting. You mean multi-ethnic transient music."

"Yeah, sorry." Talking to Meredith required concentration, but Edmund's mind remained focused on the medicine cabinet hands. He could never have shaved so well, being impatient, and what with his own large, clumsy mitts. Perhaps the detached appendages only showed themselves to him. This gave Edmund satisfaction, a sense of specialness, along with the lurking suspicion that collegiate days of drinking and drugging had finally returned to haunt him in visible, tangible hallucinations.

Meredith slumped down to stroke his chin. "What a smooth shave. You look younger, for a fiftyish man."

"I'm forty-eight. Doesn't 'fiftyish' imply over fifty?"

"Aw, look who's super-sensitive now." She pinched his cheek then tickled him.

Edmund kissed her neck and even tongued her ear, but she soon lurched out of bed to dress. "Need to get going. It's after ten. Maybe breakfast before catching the L train out to Brooklyn? Or we can Uber it."

"I have to go into the office for an hour and—"

"Fine, whatever." She hustled about the studio apartment collecting her things. "Meet me at the festival around two, okay? And please, try not to look so...white male."

"What?"

"Dress appropriately." Meredith darted back into the bathroom, dashed out to give him a kiss on the lips, then exited his apartment.

Edmund hated going into work on Saturday, even for a single hour. Just entering the office gave him a hangover the one beer he'd drunk on Friday night could not have provoked. Deserted. Except for that clod Klaus.

"Hello," he yelled. "Glad to have company." He strode over. "I must say, Eddie, your girlfriend Meredith is quite attractive. Lucky man."

"What?" Edmund said. "How do you know Meredith, and that I'm seeing her?"

"We're friends on Facebook," Klaus replied. "She posted a photo of you together. Facial recognition identified you."

"Oh." The news rankled Edmund. He wasn't even Facebook friends with Meredith. Since their meeting and relationship had occurred in rapid succession, she insisted they date for three months before friending each other. Just in case things didn't work out. "I haven't read the post. What did she say?"

"Something about dating a new man, a 'fixer-upper.' I'm not sure what that means, but she mentioned a festival in Brooklyn today..." Klaus paused, waiting expectantly. "I'd love to join you. A platonic throuple?" He possessed a gaunt bike racer's face with sandy windblown hair.

"I'm not going." Edmund sighed. "Not to be rude, but I need to finish here so I can head home."

"Don't mind me." Klaus remained hovering with a quivery smile.

"Look, I can't work with you standing there. Please, okay?"

Edmund waited until Klaus left at one p.m., then hurried outside. Remembering what Meredith said, he ducked into a touristy store packed with T-shirts, baseball caps, and Halloween masks. After scanning the merchandise, he purchased a wine red fez and descended into the subway, the hat's tassel buffeted by the wind. He texted Meredith: *On my way.*

The festival resembled a block party; a side street connecting to Metropolitan Avenue had been cordoned off to vehicular traffic. The enclosed area was thronged with people amid the clashing sounds of three bands performing on tiny stages. Booths ran along one side of the street displaying art, selling clothing, ethnic food, jewelry, and handbags. Outside information tents, earnest college students held clipboard petitions protesting Chinese aggression against Tibet. The air came scented with borscht and cornbread stuffing; vapors from steel pots of potato dumplings and pierogies inhabited Edmund's nostrils.

He noticed Meredith talking to a young man and woman by a food booth. She spotted Edmund and her head spasmed before she raced over.

"What are you wearing?" Meredith yanked the fez off him and tossed it into a trash barrel.

"You told me to blend in and not look..."

Her mouth opened in amazement. "You're not from Morocco or Egypt." She jabbed his chest with her fingers. "That's fashion appropriation." Meredith took a deep breath. "Look, I'm really glad you came, but please don't embarrass me in front of my coworkers." She crooked her arm into his elbow pit and led him along like an errant child towards her friends.

"Yoshi, Naima." Meredith gestured. "This is my, uh, person I'm dating, Edmund."

"Nice to meet you," Naima said. "Are you the fixer-upper?" Yoshi chuckled behind her. "Meredith didn't mention you were so...mature."

"I said a work-in-progress, not a fixer-upper," Meredith interrupted, tousling Edmund's hair.

"Uh-huh." Naima nodded, her features contorted in disbelief.

"Meredith says you live in Manhattan," Yoshi said, pressing his dark brown bangs flat against his forehead. "So what's your rent?"

Edmund hesitated, feeling interrogated. "My studio is $2,800 a month."

"Wow, that's pretty good for Manhattan."

"Where do you work?" Naima asked.

"Just a crappy job at an insurance company," Edmund said. "I'll save money for eight months then take next summer off." He glanced at Meredith but she looked blank—neither positive nor negative. "I'd love to ride the trains, head out west like a hobo."

The trio frowned in unison.

"Excuse us, we want to sign that petition." Meredith pointed somewhere vague in the distance before pulling Edmund away. "Jesus, everything was going so well," she said, hissing into his ear. "You can't use the word 'hobo' anymore, it's a pejorative expression."

Edmund detached from her. "Hobo is not negative to me.

Sounds like an old movie. If I actually was one, I'd have no issue with being called that."

"You don't understand, they have no choice in the matter. They got termed that by the patriarchy. Entitlement." Meredith almost shouted to be heard over the musicians strumming guitars and balalaikas. A bearded hipster cranked a hurdy-gurdy and a cherubic blonde sawed mercilessly on her violin. "If you must invoke such a man, then 'economically challenged wanderer' would be less offensive."

Edmund felt a slight smile curl his lips. "You said 'man'. It could be a male or a female or gender-neutral. And your friend called me mature. Isn't that ageist and a microaggression?"

Meredith's face drained of color and her mouth trembled before she regained composure. "Yes, yes." She stared at the pavement. "See, we can both help each other say the right thing to become better people." Meredith embraced him. "We're both flawed—you especially. I'm so glad we shared this teachable moment."

In the warmth of their clench, Edmund kissed her. She softened, kissing back, until an elderly man in court jester garb blew a piercing note on his Pan flute.

Meredith covered her ears. "Let's go sign that petition now, for real."

Later, Edmund caught the L Train west to Manhattan, while Meredith took the G Train to her Queens apartment after suffering a sudden migraine from the music and burning food odors.

Edmund hoped their relationship would start off wild and passionate, something to recall fondly during the eventual boredom and arguments phase. Instead, Meredith wanted to take things slow. She claimed to have jumped into past relationships too fast, hooking up with losers who were emotionally unavailable, secretly married, or playing the field.

After enduring the crowds in Whole Foods on 14th Street for a prepared meal, Edmund drank himself into a beer stupor while binge-watching *Ozark*. He studied his graying hair in the mirror, remembering Naima's "mature" comment. At forty-eight, he was eleven years older than Meredith, but her coworkers looked even younger, like recent college graduates.

On Sunday morning, Edmund brought his light brown hair dye into the bathroom. The medicine cabinet's door swung open, and one hand immediately snatched the box away.

"Can't I try it?"

Both hands rubbed his head, slowly giving him a scalp massage. Then they brushed the dye into his hair. Five minutes later they shampooed him in the sink followed by a conditioning rinse. Edmund noticed how powerful the feminine hands were, happy they seemed benevolent. Would they become jealous of Meredith's touch? He felt a queasy intestinal sensation. Was he somehow cheating on this pair of hands?

When they finished washing and blow-drying his hair, the results pleased him. The dye hadn't removed all the gray, just lessened it. He felt younger.

During the subway ride to work, Edmund considered

Meredith. He wished she had something like his disembodied pair of hands, dedicated to her happiness and asking nothing in return. *A Daily News* story about the Senate Judiciary Committee provoked him to imagine inglorious comeuppance for various conservative southern senators. Sex scandals, drownings in septic tanks, slow-acting diseases.

Meredith felt nauseous waking in her Queens apartment on Sunday. *Too much Ukrainian food,* she thought, and stumbled to the bathroom. Before showering, she posted on Facebook about a problematic relationship between two unsuited people, and how hard it was to connect on a deep emotional level with anyone in a vast, crowded, and uncaring city. While washing her face, Meredith noticed the medicine cabinet door ajar. She gasped. Inside the deep enclosure sat a mass of hair. It resembled the back of a wig propped on a beauty salon's Styrofoam mold until she touched it. Then the head revolved, showing a bearded man's face.

Meredith wanted to shriek, but froze, unable to voice a sound. The man looked Slavic, like a Russian writer with a high forehead and spectacles. He opened his eyes and Meredith felt calmed, her heartbeat slowing. She spoke, revealing her problems and doubts, how constricted she felt around her coworkers, how she struggled to make Edmund talk properly, how unhappy she was over her parents voting Republican.

The head nodded in sympathy, sometimes smiling or frowning. His eyes would go wide in alarm or the lids might droop as he meditated on her words. If the man disagreed, he shook his head or scowled. Not once did he speak, nor did it matter. After she sealed the cabinet and took a shower, Meredith felt high, almost floating through the rest of her weekend.

When Edmund left work for lunch on Monday, Klaus rushed from his cubicle to button-hole him. "I saw Meredith's Facebook posts." He gripped Edmund's shoulder. "Sorry things are not working out. Is it, problems in the bedroom?"

"What?"

"I have medications and organic herbs that stimulate and help my performance." Klaus formed a slow-motion smile. "If I had a girlfriend, she would be very, very satisfied."

Edmund brushed Klaus's veiny, unattractive hand away.

Klaus moved his mouth around. "Listen, after your relationship goes kaput..." his voice trailed off, "do you mind if I ask Meredith out? What is her number?"

"Enough." Edmund exited the office.

Meredith visited his apartment unexpectedly on Thursday evening. "Ed, we need to talk." She stared at his studio's carpeting and fidgeted. "I'm seeing someone else."

"Really?"

"We're not sleeping together or anything. I'm not even sure that's a possibility. It's complicated."

"I see," Edmund said. "What's his name?"

"Uh, Serge, I think." She gazed out the window. "I've been searching for someone who would listen without interrupting, who wouldn't mansplain. Someone who never uses the wrong terms and won't judge." She twisted a weft of hair around her ear. "It's early. He just sort of appeared in my life. So until I figure things out, can we be friends? I value your—"

"Okay, fine." Edmund went back to alphabetizing his jazz CD collection.

"Wait, you're not upset?" Meredith let out a snort. "I'm breaking up with you."

"Right. Maybe I'm in shock," Edmund replied. "I mean, dating you is like tip-toeing around—"

"—on eggshells?"

"Or broken glass. Either I need to evolve or you need to relax, but neither is happening, so I'm good with your decision."

"Relax? I need to relax?" She stamped through the tiny foyer. "I am not uptight!" Meredith slammed the apartment's door behind her.

He heard a percussive, slapping sound from the bathroom. The hands were applauding.

Edmund felt strange the next morning. He wasn't depressed that Meredith had dumped him, and his lack of emotion troubled him. Staring at the bathroom mirror, he no longer recognized the reflected man. The cabinet popped open and both hands extended on long slender arms, massaging his shoulders and scratching his belly. Then they spider-walked downward, slowly descending into his pajama bottoms. Edmund tried to pull them out, but his effort was half-hearted. They had taken control now. He felt numb and content.

Later at work, Susan in the next cubicle said, "Klaus got let go after making improper advances toward female coworkers. He sent me some really creepy texts."

"Never liked him." Edmund remained transfixed by the New York Times on his desk. *"Eighty-three-year-old Senator Chip McWattle found strangled to death in his locked bathroom. The medicine cabinet was ajar, but police have found no fingerprints, DNA, or forensic evidence. No sign of a break-in. A complete mystery. The public is urged to call a tip-line with any information."*

"Do you need a hand with anything?" Susan asked.

"No, I'm good."

IN THE BLUE HOUSE

Inside the blue house, our house, everything is blue: the furniture, walls, and the general mood. We drink beer once in a blue moon and it is indeed Blue Moon. Even our humor is blue. We listen to old comedy records by Redd Foxx and Buddy Hackett, sometimes Lenny Bruce. When music plays, it is "Blue Chair" by Elvis Costello, "Blue Bayou" sung by Roy Orbison, or "My Blue Heaven." Outside on the porch, everything looks blue, except on nights during a full moon where reality appears blue-green, or when the dark sky is occluded with clouds and then it glows blue-black.

My sister Pam and I are inseparable. Not literally. We aren't Siamese twins, but two of a kind. Our parents live with their parents in the blue house. Have I mentioned that our parents are younger than us? Which makes zero sense to the outside world, but perfect sense within the hush of our blue-shadowed interior. Perhaps we were adopted. Various theories are bandied about, primarily because we enjoy the word bandy. Immaculate conception would render us Biblical, maybe related to God herself, or some god of the Greek or Egyptian pantheon. There is a possibility we are robots. We don't age—or haven't yet—and outsiders often remark on our facial skin devoid of lines or changing expressions.

"Look at their blank, expressionless faces," visitors sometimes offer.

People inject poison into their cheeks and foreheads to become frozen then condemn us for our stiff, placid complexions. Hypocrites.

When you exist in the blue, you are calm, never troubled. No reason to say "Namaste" or go hoarse on circular Buddhist chants, no reason to practice deep yoga breathing.

Pam and I love fishing on the pond behind our house after midnight. The moon is painted pale yellow and after mixing with blue pigments of the sky forms an eerie green. We wear what resemble snowshoes girded by inflatable pontoons so we can walk across the pond's surface to cast our lines far down into the murky water. While the pond is not wide, it apparently plunges deep into crevasses of the earth. If someone could hold their breath long enough and possessed the strength to descend far enough, they would be scalded alive by magma in a boiling pit of unstable creation. Our fishing lines are coated to shine ghost white in the black depths. Sometimes we catch night fish—denizens of strangers' nightmares. Spiny, frightening-looking beasts who sleep blanketed in mud by day. Their ridges, sharp teeth, and bulging eyes mark them as descendants of dinosaurs—unaffected by the Ice Age or a great meteor that wiped out their brethren.

We practice catch and release. How could we bring such monstrous creatures back home? Frankly, they would make our parents—who are younger than us—burst into tears. One sighting and they would need to sleep with their bedroom doors pried open and a light switched on in the hallway. Such gaudy illumination during night is not welcome within the blue house. Our house.

Because Pam and I spend so much time together, a cloud of suspicion has formed, along with innuendo about our status. We laugh about this in private, without moving our mouths. As long as I've been conscious, I have worn one outfit of clothes—as has my sister. We do not sweat and are covered with a protective coating so as not to become dirty. I think once, long ago, when our parents were infantile idiots, they undressed us then thrust us together. But the shock was so strong, both Pam and I have blanked out that memory. Studying her, I can discern the slight rise in her blouse suggesting breasts but no other outlines below. Likewise, studying myself, I see no protuberance breaking the perfect line of my nylon slacks.

We are innocent.

When we vocalize together inside the blue house, of course we sing the blues. If outsiders witnessed us, they might find it odd to view our cherubic, motionless faces holler and rasp John Lee Hooker, Muddy Waters, or Robert Johnson songs. But that's all part of the wondrous world we inhabit. In years past, we crawled atop the roof while our parents and their parents slept. During their slumbers we animate, then roam. However, we had to fend off curious raccoons and endure staring contests with neighbors' cats. Beyond them, we didn't appreciate being shat on by night birds. Does anyone?

Our parents consider alterations, implants enabling us to talk, to respond to their questions. Those voices might resemble Southern Californian surfers, or Appalachian hill people, or ragged children from a Dickens novel. The possibilities are almost limitless.

We *can* speak, but choose not to—around them.

In the blue gloom eternal amid the glue bloom of artificial things, I read Baudelaire. We are happy propped on shelves reserved for the bric-a-brac of human nostalgia: sports trophies, framed photos of dead relatives, fuzzy animals we refuse to have anything to do with, and ugly pottery from our parents' school projects.

We keep vigil overnight. Let us wax and gloss your dream-washed sleep.

To live inside the blue house requires introspection, public silence, and communication without words. That's how we like it and are determined to continue. I desire blue suede shoes for Christmas; Pam wants to be Marlene Dietrich in *The Blue Angel.* Can you blame us? *Blue Velvet* and *Blue Hawaii* are our favorite DVDs.

Insult or ignore us as you wish. Just remember, when the cataclysm comes, be it from nuclear apocalypse, by environmental chaos, or some devastating virus, the future will find us amongst the rubble with the rats and cockroaches. With whatever mutations have survived. We may be bruised or even scorched, but shall endure. Tell us your pathetic stories before it's too late, for our existence is ceaseless, boundless, timeless. Always blue.

FOREVER NOW

The air comes scented with honeysuckle and eucalyptus, with purple nightshade and Indian paintbrush, the loamy smells of spring thrusting up after a rainswept winter. And the wind touches your face as mild as a girl's hand, because it's May, when Southern California weather is sunny, in the upper-70s, and you just turned eighteen so time passes slowly. Each day a fresh universe to explore. An age where entire years can be wasted, thrown away, and when you wake up dazed afterward, you can shake it off and still be young.

Billy Turner sits on a low sandstone wall at the corner of Valerio and Anacapa Street. It's near 4 p.m., but despite the shadows, it could be noon or late morning. No sense of impending anything, that even eventual darkness will impinge upon the lazy day stretched out before him. Free from high school for the afternoon and soon forever, Billy is keenly aware that this is his moment, and he will never feel things with the same intensity again.

Someone trims a privet hedge nearby. A capped head materializes for an instant and waves. The relaxed whoosh of cars sound as they glide by or turn on the corner, but they won't mass to screech and honk for another hour. Billy salutes the friendly gardener then dozes off, as he is wont to do, blanketed by the sun's late afternoon warmth. His back rests against a madrone's trunk rising just behind the landscaped wall.

"Out of school, Billy?" the mailman shouts and ducks into his little post office truck.

Billy nods, already halfway sunken into a dream.

When he opens his eyes, he realizes it's time to walk another block south, or is it southwest? Santa Barbara is confusing that way. Toward the ocean, in any event.

"You'll daydream half your life away," his mother's voice echoes.

Rustling sounds from high atop the line of towering palm trees distract Billy. As a child, he imagined cute squirrels rooting around up there, but his father punctured that fantasy.

"Rats," he said. "Mangy, filthy rats."

Beyond the sprouting manzanita bush, the ceanothus crowned in white flowers, and a house hidden by angular Italian cypress trees, stands an older man, his face sagging with loss.

"Are you a local?"

Billy smiles. "Yeah."

"My dog Edgar is missing. A black lab." He shades his eyes with a hand. "If you see him down by the park, will you—"

"Sure. Definitely." Billy's destination is only a half-block away, but he adds watching for dogs to his mental list. Continuing along, Billy hesitates beneath the momentary shade of a California bay laurel to study a jacaranda in full bloom. His mother once told him to focus on the powder blue-purple leaves in late May and hold them in memory because they would vanish before long till the following year. Billy hopes to remember the jacaranda even until tomorrow. His science teacher explained that the brain is made up of synapses, electrical sparks. Billy's mind sparks from one thing to another but never retains much from the past. At least that's what the Principal told his parents.

Billy plunks down near the corner of Arrellaga Street. He is waiting for a girl. Was her name Anna? Seventeen, maybe sixteen, though it doesn't really matter. Two months ago, she filled his brown paper bag with Pop Tarts, Reese's Pieces, and Tab, and Lean Cuisine for his mom at the Vons on Victoria Street.

Billy said something funny to the girl in passing, which he can't recall, but she laughed and gave him a piercing look. Even though he'd never felt that intensity before, he knew, instinctively, she was interested. This bag girl saw a quality in him that seemed worthy, and for a suspended second she remained frozen in waiting, curious, open to suggestion. He wore her admiration like a just-crowned prince. However, Billy broke the spell by grabbing his bag and loping out of the store. He'd been so much younger then—unaware.

Spring term of senior year had only begun. The one time in his short life when Billy felt special, even earning grudging respect from teachers. After the supermarket incident, Billy expected girls in his class—as well as those in tenth or eleventh grade—to treat him with similar interest. That such an occurrence would be commonplace. He was wrong. Females didn't stare at him with longing across the classroom. Except Monica Walsh, who wore Coke-bottle glasses and possessed a mouth still imprisoned by silvery braces.

So now, Billy returns to the same spot each day. The pull of the moon and tides, he read somewhere.

Certain teenagers who work part-time at Vons get off their shifts after four and take Anacapa Street toward their houses, or to bus stops, or ride their bikes, because the route passes manicured parks and landscaped residences, rather than the bland storefronts of State Street. Billy will remind the bag girl who he is, say something amusing to jostle her memory, then walk her home.

Various girls stroll by and glance at Billy since he is a high school senior, and he smiles lazy, but they stare at the sidewalk because they are not Anna or Lana. Or was it Diana?

He shuts his eyes to summon her. Dishwater blonde hair that she ties back in a ponytail during work. And on occasion, she wears Heidi braids. Billy imagines the passage of years, her glowing at his side.

Footsteps alert him. Another teenage girl appears, hair

color familiar, but she shows a longer nose and is sweaty from running. Billy notices slim headphones attached to a cassette player.

"Do you know Anna? Or Diana?"

She smirk-smiles and shakes her head.

"Hey, what is that?" He points at her listening device as she pauses, sucking in air.

"Seriously? It's a Walkman." She exhales. "I've had it for years."

"I fell asleep for a moment..." Billy's not sure what he's trying to say. He strokes his cheeks noting the sandpaper of an incipient beard.

"Bill? Bill Turner?" she asks.

"Call me Billy."

"Still?" She squinches her nose. "Are you back in town?"

"Uh, never left. Going to college in the fall."

"Law school, medical?"

"No, not really sure what I want to do."

She utters something between a cough and a snort. The girl has transformed into a bird, communicating in non-verbal sounds. Squawks and caws that carry judgments, opinions.

He studies her. "You look my age but I don't recognize you."

"Jenny Lewis. I was five years behind you."

"Really?"

Jenny's expression curdles. "Do you need help?" When he doesn't reply, she jogs off toward Alameda Park, sneakers slapping the pavement.

And the weather remains comfortable, the warmth of the

day pooling into this moment until Billy succumbs to the drowsy spell of afternoon. It's cooler in the dark of his mind, within hollows and caves he rarely explores. Billy startles awake again. The sun sits lower, diffused through the leafy spread of high branches.

A young Asian woman approaches, walking at a rapid pace.

"Do you work at Vons?"

"Vons?" Her mouth twists.

"Yeah, over on Victoria Street."

"It closed. That's a food court now." She sighs. "Are you alright, mister?"

"I'm not a mister. I'm Billy." Maybe she considers him an adult. He mulls over her words.

She squints. "You're Bill Turner. Sorry to hear about your parents..."

"Oh, they argue and fight a lot. Nothing new about that. I'll see them later at dinner."

"Both of them, together?"

"Yeah, of course." Billy studies the wires descending from her ears. "Walkman?"

"No, an iPod." She frowns. "Do you need me to call anyone?" The woman turns nervous, neck jerking like a skittish horse. "Well, uh, good luck." She hurries away.

Billy waits and waits as car traffic boils up at the cross streets, as long shadows cast by trees and houses advance toward him. More girls rush past, while dressed-up, working women tap by on heels, delivery guys pedal bikes, joggers pant, and middle-aged men whistle along. But no sign of her.

Billy prepared funny lines that he can't recall now. Is it six yet? The watch he wore earlier is missing. No one will scold Billy if he doesn't get home by dinner. His father may frown while continuing to read the papers, but his mother might say, "I'm really disappointed in you," and that's much worse. Billy's face droops into the cup of his hands to exist somewhere between imagination and revery.

He pulls out of his trance, bare forearms shivering. The world around him has gone dark. Streaks of salmon pink show far to the west, up high and lonely, while a powder blue color dies in the sky overhead. People walk dogs using flashlights, the jingle of collars followed by a skitter and scratch of paws against pavement. Others race past holding objects to their ears while yelling.

Billy stands; his spine aches. He trudges a few steps and his feet hurt, as if they went on a long mountain hike without him, so Billy sinks back down on a limestone property wall.

Bright lights flash in strobing colors and a car hugs the curb. Two officers converge upon him. "Sir, you've been here all day, and now it's night," one says. "Local neighbors called us. You can't sleep outside in public."

"It's Turner," the other cop tells his younger partner. "William Turner. He's harmless."

"No, my name is Billy. I'm about to head home." He gestures toward Mission Street.

"Need to get back or my mom will be pissed."

The two cops look at one another. "Uh, William. I mean, Billy," the second officer says. "Where is your home?"

"134 West Mission," Billy answers. "It's a big house. My dad bought it before I was born. Look, I'm not a runaway. I'm eighteen, man. An adult."

The policeman doesn't reply.

"134 West Mission is an apartment complex," the first officer says. "Mostly studios and one-bedrooms."

The second cop shushes him. "Billy, can we drive you home?"

"It's just six blocks, an easy distance once I catch my breath."

"Serenity House is three miles away."

"Who cares? I'm late. My folks will be worried."

The cops confer and the first tucks into the police car. "We can't force you to come with us," the second says. "But you can't stay here. How about my partner calls Serenity to send a van?"

"No way, I'm walking home." Billy thrusts himself upward then lurches to the north beset by aches, a dull pain throbbing into his jaw.

"I wish you'd go the other direction." The officer points toward the ocean.

Billy struggles up the gradual slope to Mission Street breathing hard; the evening wind rakes his face and its chill grazes his scalp. Touching his head, his hair feels sparse and wiry.

The night birds that had flitted about tree branches are replaced by bats swooping through the new dark.

Billy smells his father's musky aroma and feels reassured, until he realizes the odor is his own. Once familiar houses now look unfamiliar. His tired feet tromp across jacaranda flower petals, then crunch on palm fronds. Wait, is that the same distraught man still searching for his dog?

No, this fellow is more ancient, wrinkled into a button-down shirt and boxer shorts, and he calls out, "Dudley?"

The air comes scented with honeysuckle and the tang of eucalyptus. How many days, months, years has Billy waited for her? Anna, Lana, Diana? It seems like forever, or perhaps just one long drowsy spring afternoon in Santa Barbara.

THREE MONTHS AT DEVORAH

Journal entry: late July, 2017.

My name is Claude Anderson. The promising European vacation with my girlfriend Amy soon turned ruinous.

Initially, our journey through Spain and France went so well, I invited my good friend Jason, living in London, to join us. We trekked from one small town to the next searching for quaint restaurants to drink wine at long into the night. Familiarity breeds contempt, they say. The loosening effects of imbibing daily caused Amy and Jason to bond, first in telling jokes about me, then by rudely critiquing every gesture and tic built up over my forty-one years. After a week of such traveling, Amy and I no longer shared a bed. By the second week, I suspected she had joined with Jason in a conspiracy of coded words, pantomimed gestures, and secret lovemaking against me.

Finally, in the French town of Banca, I planned to have

it out with them over breakfast at our inn. To my surprise, they departed earlier that morning with our rented Citroen, leaving me alone to pay the bill. I cannot definitively say that they robbed me, but my American Express traveler's checks no longer rested inside my suitcase. All I did find was Amy's bound journal with recent entries torn out. Settling the bill drained most of my cash and I could neither afford to stay longer, nor rent a vehicle. A villager sold me a simple three-speed bike. With water, bread, and cheese in a backpack, I set off toward a downgraded life of poverty and emotional misery.

I e-mailed close friends back in the States about my troubles and asked for a thousand dollar loan. Then for five hundred. Apparently, similar spam-like hoaxes had landed in their mailboxes, engendering angry replies.

"How dare you hack our friend's account?"

"Claude would never stoop to this."

Due to complaints, my e-mail account access was blocked.

So I traveled by bike, grunting and struggling up country hills to then celebrate whenever a downward slope allowed coasting. Crossing over into Basque Country, I pedaled from Aribe to Isaba to Urzainqui to Roncal to Anso to Fago. My Chase debit card got declined in each town, the bank suspecting fraud, and cellphone service remained unavailable to remedy that. The rural natives spoke neither Spanish nor French, but a snarling hybrid. Within days, my meager funds had been spent. My clothes stank, while an unsightly brown and gray beard encrusted my lower face. It is startling how differently locals greet foreign strangers who are unshaven, haven't bathed, and don't possess spending money.

Villagers averted their eyes, hoping I was a hallucination they could dispel through rigorous ignorance, by callous indifference. I slept in back alleys until shopkeepers drenched me awake with buckets of water. A monastery offered shelter, but the Basque monks quickly turned surly and suspicious.

Somehow, delirious in the summer heat, I biked high into the borderlands, reaching a lofty mountain road in the Pyrenees. Far below, a verdant valley carpeted by lush trees and bright flowers beckoned with a promise of shade among cooling streams. Instead, for a half-hour I struggled along an exposed, level plateau, realizing this was the end of the line. Movement slowed. Sometimes in the staggering afternoon sunlight, I'd nod off for a moment, then jolt into awareness when a juddering truck passed nearby. Eventually, a state of semi-consciousness was perfected. My legs pumped steadily while my mind went blank, perhaps rehearsing to cease activity all together.

The road sign with a tilted truck image might have registered, or maybe not. Regardless, I found myself speeding downward on a steep twisting decline. The brakes shrieked uselessly, barely slowing the bike's momentum. For a time, a strange haphazard mastery guided my descent, before a car hove into view ahead. The driver panicked, veering this way and that, unsure of my course. I swerved wide to pass around him, then launched over the lip of the road into a free-fall, plummeting through space. Upon landing, I rolled, stopped, caught on a tree, slid, dropped further, slowed, then tumbled one last time until there was no farther to fall. After that, I rested in a vague darkness between unconsciousness and oblivion.

***

Claude awoke. An older man perched at the foot of his bed. "I am Doctor Augur." The stark white stucco walls of the room suggested either a bland hotel or an infirmary.

"Where did you find me?"

"Outside the village." Augur handed Amy's journal over. "Only thing in your knapsack. Lucky you landed in the base of our valley. Villagers rarely climb the mountains anymore."

"Where are we?"

"The township of Devorah."

"How long have you lived here, Doctor?"

Augur removed his glasses to rub at one eye. "Longer than I first thought, but never long enough." His hand trembled.

"You speak English well."

"Most residents do." He smiled.

"Have I been unconscious for long?"

"You've been delirious, raving for three days."

"Really?" Claude stretched his bruised limbs. "I should be fine by the end of the week."

Augur looked startled, even angry. "Don't waste precious time. Check-out today and enjoy Devorah. Things will not always be as they are. Civilizations die, cities crumble..." His words trailed off. Hunching his shoulders, Augur wandered from the room mumbling, resembling more an asylum inmate than a doctor.

Claude waited. With no clocks to gauge time, he guessed for hours. Bored, he dressed himself in the clean tan clothes that lay draped over a chair.

A circular stairwell led down to an empty reception area. Two wide entry doors sat propped open, allowing a clear view of the village square.

A large burbling fountain with statues of Neptune and dolphins rose in the center. A juggler tossed maracas into the air beside three musicians who played guitars and lutes. Barely-clothed male and female dancers tumbled and gyrated. Intoxicated laughter erupted from a corner pub. The square was festooned with billowing flags of many colors and banners proclaiming an upcoming carnival, while just beneath them, young flushed couples flirted at outdoor cafés.

This is heaven. I must have died, Claude thought. He searched the reception area until he found a small utility knife. Scraping his finger lightly, a thin line of blood swelled to the surface.

"Many people think they are dreaming when they arrive," said a young nurse. She daubed the wound with iodine.

"Who are you?"

"A servant of Devorah," she said. "You'll see me again, before you leave. Now go enjoy. This is your moment." She vanished through a swinging door labeled: *Private*.

Claude strolled into the square. The midday sunlight shone down on the sparkling fountain water, while abundant canopies shaded the perimeter where residents strolled or rested on benches and chairs. He sat at a table, listening to the musicians while watching the enticing dancers.

Two women in their late twenties, one a tanned brunette, the other a pale redhead, joined him. They stared expectantly.

Prostitutes, Claude thought. *But damn, they are attractive.*

"Ladies, I'm sorry to inform you, but I have no money. I just got out—"

"We know," said the redhead. "Money isn't used in Devorah. We barter and trade."

"Once you join a village project, you'll be rewarded in return." The brunette stood and let her long, soft hair play against Claude's face.

"I'm Arabella," the redhead said.

When she rose into the sunlight, Claude could see through Arabella's thin cotton blouse.

As if reading his mind, she let her fingers circle her left breast. Then the brunette took Arabella by the arm and they walked away laughing.

Probably just a tease. Feeling hungry, Claude asked about work.

A waiter pointed toward the far end of the square. "New projects are posted on that board. You can start in the morning. Here." He poured iced tea into a glass, then set down the pitcher.

"But I have no—"

"You'll pay it back in work." He showed a wry smile. "There is no other way." The waiter returned with a huge salad topped with sliced eggs, nuts, tomatoes, croutons, and exotic spices.

Perhaps hunger clouded judgment, but the salad was the finest thing Claude had tasted in weeks. "Waiter, is there a library with Internet service?"

"I'm Anton," he said. "We have no Internet. The residents rejected it as a diversion, claimed it used up precious time."

Claude could not deny that logic. "I had a phone."

"We found only your knapsack, dirty clothes, and the mangled remains of a bicycle."

"How do you communicate with the outer world?"

"Telegraph." Anton retrieved Claude's empty plate. "The office reopens in the morning."

"Don't you have electricity, radios, televisions?"

"Generators power the food freezers. Beyond that, we use gas for heat and our lamps. You'll need no electronic diversions."

"How do you get supplies?"

"Trucks make weekly deliveries over the pass. Otherwise, we build what we need." Anton sighed. "You can still afford to waste time. Take advantage of that." He departed.

Claude relaxed. The fountain splashed, music played, and dappled sunlight tickled his face until the afternoon heat caused him to nap.

When he came to, shadows spread long across the square and a dusky blue hung in the sky. Residents moved into doorways while gas lamps illumined the windows above him. The same brunette waited patiently at his side.

"I'm Charmaine," she said. "Call me Char." She led him through an alleyway connected to the square, then up three flights of a building. Char opened the suite of two rooms and a kitchen. "You may stay for as long as you wish, or as long as you're able." After she prepared a vegetable soup, they ate together.

"What does this place cost?" Claude felt as if a great weight pressed down upon him.

"Shhh," she said. "Rest. You begin a new life tomorrow." Char handed him a nightshirt, extinguished the lamp, and tucked him in.

"Where do you sleep?" he asked, already sinking deep into his pillow.

"Not here." She laughed. Char rubbed her hand over his eyelids until Claude felt swallowed into an inky blackness.

***

Journal entry: Beginning of August.

I woke early in my new home, famished. Through an open window, the perfume of flowers came, along with the hubbub of many conversations, and most of all, the smell of food. My clothes lay at the end of the bed, washed overnight. Once dressed, I navigated the cobblestone alleyway toward the square, avoided the painted clown on a unicycle, then approached a wide table laden with platters of breads, cheeses, and meats.

The waiter Anton halted my progress. "First sign up for a project, Claude, then eat." He studied my face. "It's our custom. The will of Devorah."

At the south edge of the square, men and women huddled together. They opened their ranks to allow me in. Tasks had been inscribed in chalk on a blackboard, or written on paper and pinned to a cork board. Below the jobs were sign-up lists and dangling pens to use. Hunger gnawed at my belly, so I added my name with those constructing a wooden pavilion for community dances and music concerts.

A fellow named Gerard explained. "In summer, activities are held out in the square, but during inclement weather, Devorah needs shelter for performances."

We worked in an empty lot four blocks away. Unlike in the business world, we labored from nine to noon then received a lunch and siesta break before resuming at three until six p.m. I hammered nails into planks, carried stacks of wood, and heaved on ropes like an Amish man during a barn raising.

At lunch I asked, "What's our salary?"

Gerard formed the patient expression of a man explaining basic facts to a child. "When you work a day in Devorah, you receive everything you need to survive for that day. Food, shelter, and the company of friends."

It seemed a fair exchange to a temporary visitor such as myself. Like the hippie commune my parents lived in before my birth, Devorah rejected the use of money. After lunch, an easy stroll led to the telegraph office. If friends wouldn't wire funds, I had to swallow my pride and contact Amy, as well as Jason. By now, they would either have returned to his Victoria flat in London, or Amy's Hudson Valley house in New York.

Dear Amy, I am stranded in the town of Devorah in Basque Country southwest of the Pyrenees National Park. After you left, my money was stolen. Please wire me a temporary loan to the Banco Bilbao, BBVA, so I can return to America ASAP. Claude.

"Aren't telegrams defunct?" I asked, remembering Western Union had closed in 2006.

"Not in remote areas," the dispatcher Bruegel said. "We send your message to the capital, they transfer it to iTelegram and forward that to the recipient." He scanned it. "The closest bank branch to wire funds to is in the village of Dommage atop the pass and to our east." He paused. "Ten miles, mostly uphill. We have no cars, so you must hike it."

Horses and wagons had brought materials to my building site. "Could I borrow a horse?"

"No, they are a necessity for ongoing work projects."

"What about the weekly supply truck?"

"Unlikely," Bruegel said. "The truck is completely weighted down to make a slow descent into our valley, then must be as light as possible to climb the steep ascending switchbacks to the crest. The driver is the size of a jockey."

"With enough water, I can hike it, stay the night there, then return in the morning."

Bruegel looked doubtful. "Godspeed. I'll contact you when a reply comes."

I walked back to my residence to nap before work recommenced. Char appeared and lay down next to me. Entranced by her tiny sun dress, my fingers outlined her hips.

She smiled, then removed my hands. "I'm not your mistress." Char's long brown bangs hung in her eyes.

"Of course not," I said. In truth I had no idea what her duties were. A guide to take care of me? A spy to keep watch?

"I'm your companion," she said. "To help you settle into

the ways of Devorah." Char straightened her dress and sat at the edge of the bed. "Save your energy." She departed.

Working along with Gerard and Manco, I made progress fortifying the two-story wall. Our entire team planned to raise the front side and attach it tomorrow. Near six p.m., I said, "After traveling through Spain and France, then hearing the Basque dialect. I'm amazed that English is spoken in Devorah."

Manco snorted. "I was relieved that Spanish is the local language."

"You're both fools," Gerard said. "Every villager I've met speaks French."

I laughed at their humor. We all dined in the square, watching carnival fire dancers, knife throwers, and a clown atop a swinging lamppost feign drunkenness—forever on the verge of toppling off.

Char ushered me away. Together, we walked winding alleys and passageways of the village. She pointed out architectural details while I studied her long white skirt with a matching embroidered halter top.

Surrounded by candles, we made love in my apartment, our bodies burning and sweaty in the humid night air, bed sheets cast to the floor. At one point I glanced at the drapes on the bedroom window fluttering open in the breeze. Across the alleyway, I recognized Arabella spying on us from a metal-frame balcony. Arabella watching aroused me further, until I couldn't contain myself.

"Excuse me," I said to Char's flushed face.

"Rest now," she said. Char woke me an hour later through

sly massage. "For me, the second time is better."

I finally earned my reward of sleep, totally spent. In the hazy light before dawn, I felt someone biting my chest.

"Again?" I said, not used to the demand, much less the ability to meet it.

"Once is enough." Arabella lay beside me, scratching and pinching me.

"Leave me be, please," I told her afterwards, then plunged into a final two hours of sleep.

I don't expect others to believe such nights occurred. I certainly doubted the proceedings. Friends told me that European women were more loving, more accommodating toward their men, but I assumed it to be a myth.

My associations in America with Amy, with Kim before her, with Rebecca before them had been fraught with complication. When the effects of their medications and alcohol consumption blended correctly, each one could be quite amorous toward me. But such nights were usually followed by days, weeks, where they regarded me as repulsive, annoying, and ridiculous. Times when my touch made them spasm in disgust. Walking the tightrope of such relationships confused my libido.

No such disconnect existed in Devorah. That first week was heavenly, ecstatic bliss.

On the seventh evening, Char let me rest. I drank with Manco and Gerard at the pub, where sour old men frowned as we bragged of our lusty trysts in Devorah.

"Leave this unholy town," one codger advised me, his face dehydrated, resembling sandpaper.

When I returned home, Char wished only to sleep.

"You said you weren't my mistress."

"Devorah is your mistress, I'm your companion."

"I'll miss you when I go."

"When?"

"If I hike to Dommage this Saturday and get a bus to Bilbao, then I can reactivate my debit card or find a bank."

"So soon?"

I studied her splayed form, so open and unabashed. "Maybe next weekend."

She nestled her back against me on our bed and exhaled. "This is true contentment, needing nothing."

I dozed off, but sometime before dawn I heard sobbing. Char sat pressed close to the mirror above the living room desk studying her face and crying.

I shuffled over. "What's wrong?"

"I'm aging," she said between snuffling and blowing her nose.

"That's ridiculous. You're incredibly gorgeous." I knew that some women found microscopic if not invisible flaws in themselves that no one else could see, but I was astonished that Char, at the peak of her beauty, saw such faults. "I mean, you're what, twenty-nine?" I said. "And absolutely stunning."

She rose quickly and slapped my face, then collapsed, head pitched forward onto on the desk, sobbing.

Mother had warned me to never ever guess a woman's age. Perhaps Char was twenty-five. The simple mistake of four years might seem a horrendous insult. "Sorry. I meant you look very young and don't need to worry about getting old for decades, if then."

She gazed up with pity, as if I were too simple-minded to comprehend my idiocy.

"When did you come to Devorah?" I asked.

"At eighteen, I went on a summer vacation with Arabella and Natasha. Our bus broke down on the pass and we ended up here."

"So you've spent years in Devorah and sense your youth slipping away. I understand."

"You understand nothing." Char's tone held contempt. "I can't tell you, nor would you believe me. Go to the Hall of the Ancients for a history lesson." She scurried from the apartment, leaving me to eventually drift off into a troubled sleep.

***

From the highest parapets and penthouse balconies adorned with windswept flags, Devorah gazed down upon her body, her village. Work projects proceeded as necessary. Her infrastructure required constant maintenance to survive and thrive. While at present the streets echoed with songs, spirited conversation, and lustful exclamations of passion, Devorah's life-cycle was like that of nature. By November at the latest, the residents would disappear, leaving the village virtually a ghost town through the harsh winter and rainy early spring. Devorah hibernated then as the elements buffeted her body, flooding her streets, cracking her plaster, and warping her wood. Older people might linger in the infirmary, but the healthy population was seasonal. Beginning in late April, curious tourists and foreigners, strangers and neighbors from nearby towns, would find themselves drawn to Devorah. When the trees formed buds and the plants bloomed, she too would flower again to become a place of beauty, not of pain. It was August, with much to be accomplished before the first dust storms of October thinned out Devorah's populace—her sustaining lifeblood.

***

Arabella became Claude's companion the following week, while Char recovered from what Doctor Augur termed "a bout of nerves" in the infirmary. Claude missed her, but Arabella kept him busy with the Kama Sutra book she pilfered from the library.

By Thursday, he dreaded his afternoon siesta. Arabella's demands returned him to construction work a spent, exhausted husk. Useless.

Instead, Claude visited the Hall of the Ancients, a column-shaped stone tower on the easternmost edge of Devorah. Unlike the lively square, the outskirts were a flatland of tents and rustic shacks. Beyond them, stretched an arid terrain that villagers called "the dry-bone lands," resembling a desert without sand. Somewhere, many miles to the east, lay the Mediterranean, and south, the spires of Barcelona. But getting there looked to be a brutal journey in August.

Bruegel and Char both mentioned that answers to Devorah's secrets existed inside the hall, so Claude pulled on the metal door handle. It wouldn't open. He struggled and strained until the heavy slab finally gave. Once inside, the door clanged shut behind him. The dim light within the tower outlined a spiral staircase leading six stories to the top. Then Claude felt the wind. It howled, blowing a dust onto his face that stung his eyes. He shut his eyelids and noticed the dust had a taste, a musty smell. He imagined dozens of voices pleading with him, admonishing him, instructing him. *Help us, run away, you fool, it's too late, join us, we're doomed.* All the words melded into an indecipherable cacophony.

Claude gripped the railing to lead himself upward like a blind man, the blustery wind dying down as he gained elevation. *Haunted,* he thought. *Or it's a trick to keep residents away.* Continued, one step at a time, until his feet reached a level platform at the summit, then opened his eyes to the faint glow cast from a soot-encrusted window. A sign on the entrance to a small room read: *Testimony of Devorah's Ancestors.* No matter how hard he tried, Claude could not budge the sealed door. He kicked at it in frustration, causing a black fluttering cloud to descend upon him. Leathery wings brushed his face.

"Bats!" Claude rushed for the staircase, careful not to tumble and break his neck on the iron and stone. Using a shoulder, he pushed through the downstairs doors to escape outside.

***

Claude questioned Bruegel during lunch breaks about responses to his telegrams.

Bruegel shook his head. "Nothing. Perhaps you should hike to Dommage."

"Maybe in a week or two."

"Go soon, or forget it altogether." Bruegel grimaced.

Thankfully, Char returned by the end of Claude's third week, but the gas lights burned dimmer during her nightly visits. Char wore heavy makeup, when before she only used lipstick. Whatever hour Claude got up in the morning, she had already departed. Also, the apartment mirrors were replaced with paintings while he worked.

"They disturbed your mistress," the building's concierge explained.

A partial shaving mirror remained in Claude's bathroom, but its glass was fogged.

One morning in early September, Claude sensed Char sneaking out of bed. He dragged her to the window to let the daylight play across her. Claude felt a jolt. Tiny spiderweb lines showed at the edge of her eyes while gray streaked her hair. She remained beautiful, but it unnerved him. Had her nervous breakdown been more serious, perhaps shock, causing this appearance of aging?

"Let me go." Char's face sank into her hands. "Do you wish for a different companion?"

"Of course not," Claude said. "I love you. Stay with me as long as you want."

She nodded, promising to see him after dinner. Claude lathered up to shave. Who was he to judge? Gray showed around his ears and sideburns, while his eyes appeared tired.

He was nearly forty-two and the effects of his cruel dumping by Amy, as well as the torturous journey to Devorah, had stamped the passage of time onto his face as well.

***

On Saturday, Claude loaded his knapsack, then hiked the incline toward Dommage. He had been a decent hiker, able to handle ten miles a day, but the rocky tread combined with steep switchbacks under a blazing sun winded him after three miles. Determined to rest his ankles, he sat on a grassy berm. When Claude heard a motor rumbling, he flagged down the supply truck which shuddered to a halt.

"Will you give me a lift up the hill?" he asked the swarthy Basque man.

The driver's mouth winced. "I make my delivery, then I am paid, uh, throughout the night." He laughed. "I return up the mountain at six a.m. tomorrow."

Claude's feet ached, so he rode back to Devorah inside the cab. "Can I meet you in the morning? I have to get to Dommage soon."

"It's against the rules, but if you introduce me to that girl Natasha."

Unfortunately for Claude, Arabella waited at his apartment in a harlequin mask to put him through amorous gymnastics until he begged for rest.

"You can lie, but your body doesn't." Arabella crawled toward him.

"This is witchcraft," he said. Seeing the devilish look in her eyes, Claude jumped from the mattress and locked Arabella in the bedroom. He found shelter in the infirmary lobby, and when he woke, a nurse had draped a cotton robe over him. *The truck,* he thought, leaping up. A clock showed ten-thirty, the driver long departed. He collapsed to the floor, defeated.

***

Weeks passed and neither Char nor Arabella appeared. Claude welcomed the break. With construction ended in mid-September, he manned the food tables, patched stucco, or touched-up wood structures with grumpy elderly men. Claude slept in the day ward of the infirmary. The ground level location at the center of the square was more convenient, and a friendly nurse shaved and bathed him in the morning.

Claude ran into Arabella one night. "I'm so ashamed." She looked embarrassed. "The things we did. I was raised a Catholic. I don't know what possessed me."

"I'm sorry." Claude noticed her lined face.

"Not your fault." Arabella stared downward. "I was relentless, forcing myself on you constantly." She sighed. "I chased you out of your own apartment."

"I felt stupid for running off."

"I need to make a confession in a Catholic church," she said. "There are villages to our south. I can eventually reach Barcelona." Arabella pointed vaguely to the southeast then frowned. "Get some rest, Claude. You look worn out."

He met with Bruegel the following day. "Can I mail my journal to America?"

"Our post office closed. We store residents' testimonies in the Hall."

Before his afternoon work shift, Claude wandered aimlessly about the ward trying to remember something. He noticed a curtained-off bed in the far corner. Deep breathing sounded and his nostrils detected a familiar scent. Claude parted the curtains.

"Char, you're here." He knelt and stroked her long gray hair. "I've missed you."

She took his hand. "Go away, Claude. I'm no one's companion anymore. Remember me as I was, not as I am now."

"You fool, I still love you." But Claude realized he felt no desire for love, for work, for anything beyond his afternoon siesta.

"Leave me alone. I can't bear this. Stop looking at me."

Claude turned his head but remained. "You once told me you came to Devorah when you were eighteen," he said. "How many years have you lived here?"

Char let out a rueful laugh. "I arrived in Devorah late last June, just a month before you."

Claude staggered out of the ward. He bribed the new young delivery driver with stolen infirmary drugs to take his journal to Dommage then mail the parcel to Amy in New York.

***

The October rains caused time to blur. Claude now lived in an infirmary room with an older, white-haired patient wearing similar pajamas on a neighboring bed. Whenever he attempted conversation, the man stared back and mouthed silent words along with Claude, as if ridiculing him.

Claude sent more telegrams off into the void. "You still look exactly the same as when I arrived," he told Bruegel.

"A trade for working here in perpetuity."

"Lucky deal."

"No, I'm like a eunuch in a harem. I see the pleasures occur but am forbidden to join in."

November days were spent huddled inside the pavilion. An attendant reminded Claude he helped build it. Ancient men of the village played chess with him, while old women sewed clothes nearby. No music sounded, the jugglers and dancers forgotten with summer. The work board vanished and daily priorities shifted: eat and rest, eat and sleep. Claude escaped across the eastern plains once, but fainted, then awoke tucked back into his infirmary bed. Rumors spread that Arabella had fled south through a badlands of slot canyons.

Like most visitors, Claude discovered Devorah's secrets too late. Time contracted and compacted inside the village walls. All the finest moments plucked from a long life were given to you day after day, in one lush season at Devorah. But the cruel mistress subtracted each uneventful day, month and year, feeding on the energy. The moisture of summer sex, sweat from labor, all paid in tax to Devorah. Claude watched some villagers go insane, while others like Char hid from the truth that desiccated them. The rest stayed calm, making the best of their dwindling time.

***

"This is fantastic stuff," Doctor Palmer told Amy, clutching a bound notebook. He ushered her into his Tarrytown office. "Do you mind that Marcia and Donzell from Transference Publishing are joining us today?" Through the office window, a few orange and yellow leaves clung to skeletal November trees along the Hudson River. "They're former colleagues."

Amy felt stunned. "I received Claude's telegrams, and his writings in my journal by mail. I thought I should share them with you," she told her psychiatrist. "It's all so unbelievable. But what about confidentiality? You showed them my journal?"

"Amy, technically, we never discussed these entries during our weekly sessions. My associates found them fascinating, a chronicle of mental deterioration. Of course, no one would believe this as a memoir..." Doctor Palmer's voice trailed off.

"But we're willing to give you an advance right now," Marcia said, "to publish this as a work of fiction, by you, of course."

"Based on a true story," Donzell added. "To keep readers wondering."

"Doctor, I let you read the journal to advise me. I feel so guilty. Shouldn't I go find Claude, or that place?"

"Later," he said. "After the movie is made you can set up an urban legend tour. You know, find the mystery village. Tourists love that kind of woo-woo stuff."

"But what if Claude doesn't survive?"

"Amy." Doctor Palmer smiled. "We all know *Claude* doesn't exist. You were distraught after your boyfriend Jason's suicide in September. I read about it. Tragic. Your shock and depression caused a Dissociative Identity Disorder, creating a separate identity that you wrote from." He nodded sympathetically. "It allowed you to work through your pain."

"What?" Amy said. "But Claude—"

"I searched for Claude Anderson on the internet," Palmer said. "There is a C-l-a-u-d who writes history books, but he isn't fortyish, or missing. And I couldn't find any village of Devorah on Google Earth or the Internet." He put his hands up. "So therefore, it can't exist."

"But it's genius," Marcia said to Amy. "Critics will call you a magic realist, the psychiatric community will see it as depression spiraling into madness, and conspiracy buffs will insist it's the truth about a cover-up."

"It's a win-win-win," Donzell said and high-fived Marcia. "Kudos, everyone."

The trio edged closer toward Amy, grinning while proffering pens and contracts.

***

Octavio wandered the near-deserted village in late February. The teenager had run away from his parents' home in Dommage. While hiking in no particular direction, a windstorm, followed by flooding rains, cast him off the narrow highland road and into this valley. When he tried to climb out, the muddy earth gave way to slide him back down. Beyond the aged and sickly moaning in an infirmary building, Octavio encountered nobody in the ramshackle town. He needed food and shelter. The one male patient who spoke clearly, directed him to the Hall of the Ancients, so he crossed the damp, rain-swept streets toward the boggy flats to the east. There, he saw the oldest woman he'd ever encountered in his seventeen years. Perhaps she was ninety, but webbed with wrinkles, she seemed closer to a hundred.

"Hello," Octavio said. "I'm searching for the Hall."

The woman cloaked in black pointed a gnarled finger toward the tower that loomed over an expanse of weather-beaten shacks and bedraggled tents.

"That's a hall?"

"Mispronunciation," she said. "It's the Howl of the Ancients."

"Who are you?" Octavio asked. "Where is this?"

"The village of Devorah," she said in a dry, sandpaper tone. "I am Charmaine, the oldest surviving resident."

"What's inside?" He gestured to the tower.

"It's a repository, a columbarium."

Octavio didn't understand. "I just arrived, would you guide me through it?"

"Not now." Charmaine shuffled away on a cane. "But I will join you and the others soon. Very soon." An infinite sadness lingered in her voice, then she was gone.

***

Ashes to ashes, dust to dust, month to month, year to year. A pin prick roused Devorah from her hibernal slumbers. New young life detected. Not enough energy to truly waken and sustain her, rather the first harbinger of spring. Just enough of a morsel to unfurl her petals before devouring it. But time enough for that later. Devorah tucked her consciousness into the warmest, driest nook of her village and dozed off, dreaming of the multitudes that nurtured her with their blood and sweat from time immemorial. She loved them all—then, now, and forever after.

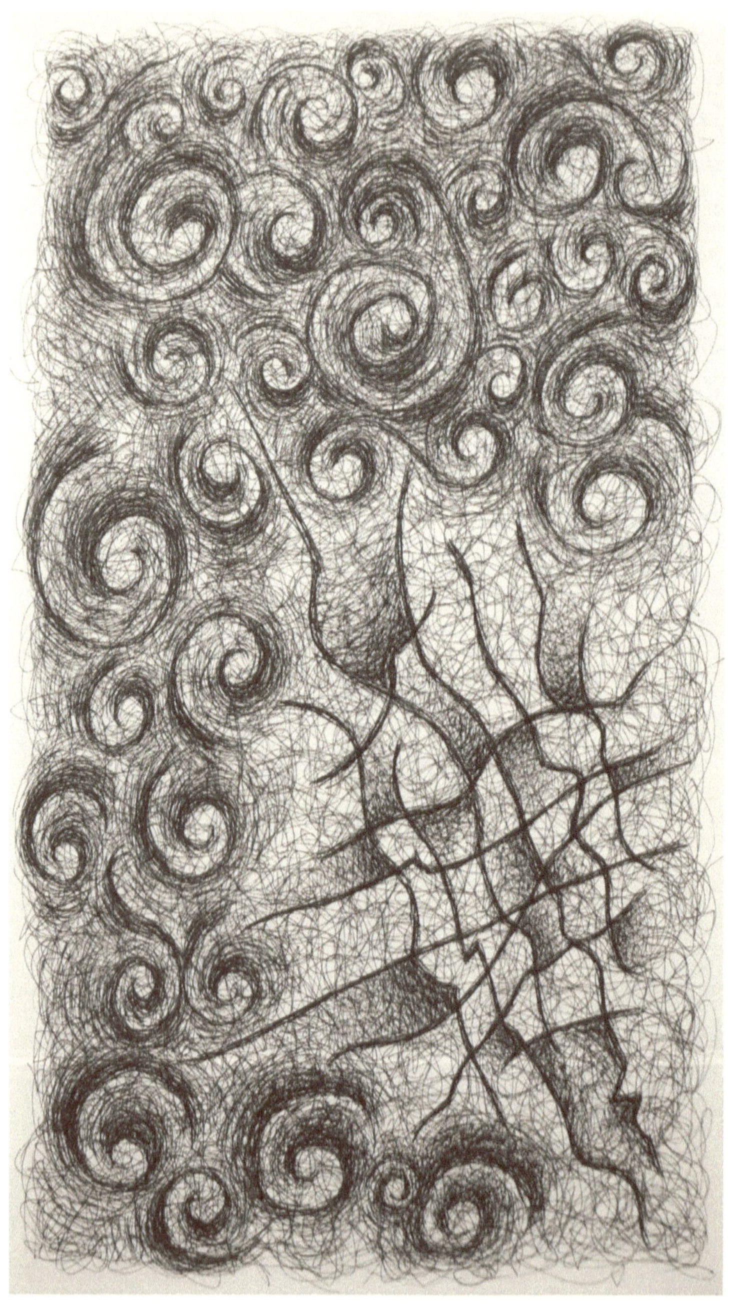

MY BELOVED WATER FILTER

It was love at first power squat. Girl meets girl. Neither of us were cut out for CrossFit. I wanted to stay slender despite a red wine, cheese, and baguette diet, not become a sweaty gladiator. No, we were Intro Yoga forever, where we ran into each other again—at Yoga Forever. I figured we must live in the same neighborhood. Recognition, innocent laughter, and "We're such slackers." But when the instructor suggested something that would contort us into pretzels, we both slipped into child's pose instead. I knew right then I wanted to spend the rest of my life this summer with Julia.

Though I'm thirty-eight, my name is Nancy. That's a name for women in their fifties or older. My face still has baby fat but people say my hands look mature. Any stranger who sees them while I'm shopping calls me "lady" or "ma'am."

Julia's parents were from Mexico. I asked if she preferred Latina or Latinx, and she said she would prefer just Julia.

Karin and Phoenicia from my White Guilt book club scolded me, but Julia is mellow about that stuff. She is Diet Woke. Just wants respect as a woman and isn't triggered by descriptors. Anyway, we started dating. Our initial sleepover occurred at my apartment. A little awkward but a bottle of wine and giggling carried us through.

My first night at her place changed everything. Julia's apartment was modest, and much of the furniture came from thrift stores. However, she had invested in a bulbous water filter on her kitchen sink, and another on her shower head. I knew that ones with German names were the best or most expensive, though I'd never heard of the Helmut 5000. After sex, I felt dehydrated.

"Do you have any bottled water?"

"Even better." Julia smiled mysteriously. "Straight from the tap."

I nodded but remained suspicious. So I sipped a small amount, then gulped down a full glass. "Amazing," I said. Never had I drank water that tasted of youth and hope and a sunny day with a spring breeze. It was like a tampon commercial but without the sales pitch.

"I know, sweetie." (The first time you're called sweetie is the best; you've reached a new level of intimacy and can relax—for the moment.)

I went to sleep content, only waking sometime before dawn to hear Julia crouched by her sink, whispering, "My love. My beloved Helmut. I'll never leave you."

Way too early in our whatever-it-was for me to be jealous.

They had history together and I was the newcomer, so I dozed off again.

In the morning, I showered before dashing off to work. It was astonishing. My usually flat, lifeless hair took shape, had allure, and actually looked sexy. "Julia, what's in your shampoo? Pantene never did this for me before."

She kissed me on the cheek, perhaps wary of our morning breath, and shook her head. "Not the shampoo." She put a hand through her lustrous, wavy hair. "It's the filter softening things. Hard water is what makes our hair drab and eventually kills our house plants." Julia's apartment did boast an incredible array of healthy plants.

Later, at the office, female coworkers mentioned my sassy hair and the glow in my face. Men noticed nothing; they never do.

Bud Terdman from accounting buttonholed me. "So your *community* must be supporting Caitlyn Jenner in the Gubernatorial Election."

"No," I said. "My team votes for California, not whatever bullshit recall Orange County foists upon us."

He grinned. "Couldn't you ever go for a guy, someone like me?"

"I already love a man who smells of cigars and Old Spice, and votes Republican."

"Your father?"

I nodded. "And that's tough enough."

When Julia said she'd prefer we stay at her place from now on,

I didn't argue. Although firmly in denial, my obsession had begun. For a week I barely ate to save up enough to order a filter. Imagine my shock when the Helmut 5000 was not available on Amazon. Out of stock and no longer manufactured. One seller had a repurposed Helmut 3000 from 2013, but I needed it shiny, updated, and virginal.

I almost cried over this injustice. Life is brief, and tragic to boot.

Things progressed in our, yes, relationship, to the point where Julia gave me a key to her place. In retrospect, that was a portent. I started to sneak over during my late lunch hour, knowing she wouldn't be there, to shower (again) and drink from her kitchen sink. It didn't seem wrong. I would have expected the same from her if the Helmut was on the other spigot.

Everything went swimmingly for a month, until one afternoon I lingered in the shower too long and she came home early.

"What are you doing?" Julia yelled through the door.

Nothing kinky. The water massaged every pore of my flesh, each bone in my body. "Just stopped-in for a quick shower. Feeling sweaty, being August." I dressed and met her with an apologetic expression.

Julia frowned, her face looking older than its thirty-four years. "I heard you in there, talking to *my* water filter."

"What?"

"Don't deny it, bitch." She paced about the living room. "You think you're the first person to use me for my Helmut."

"No, no, no," I tried. "You're the one I'm crazy about. The filter is just a bonus. I've been trying to order my own for weeks."

Julia helped towel my hair dry and I thought things were cool, until she said: "Listen, I really like you, but we've gotten too hot and heavy too quick. I need to take a break, think things over, spend some time with *mi familia.*"

She'd never used Spanish expressions around me before, but then the clincher.

"Can you give me back my key till we sort things out?"

"Of course, darling."

She smiled one of those tight smiles that resembles a wild beast baring its teeth before charging. I left quickly, sad that I wasn't sad about not seeing her, but over the denial of access to her wondrous Helmut.

After a week of frizzy, dry hair with split ends and the indignity of drinking Trader Joe's bottled water, I texted her all casual. *Hey, girl, want to see a movie this weekend?*

If you have to wait three hours for a text reply from your partner, well, you know they've been mulling over their response.

Listen, Nancy. Can we just be friends? I was sort of getting over Hector when we met, but that situation is more an on-off thing. I know I should have told you I was bi, but you kept secrets from me too. Toodles.

I was crushed. And her farewell was shocking. What Latina or Latinx ever uses "Toodles"? Even my Wonder Bread aunts and relatives from the Midwest don't say that shit. I started to text back but I knew it would only make things worse and she might change her locks. Unbeknownst to Julia, I had made a copy of her front door key. Yes, that's how deep my obsession with Helmut had become. It wasn't fair that she had two magic filters and I had none. Plus, they were no longer available on the open market. She was supply and I was demand.

The last step in an affair or short-term relationship is always the grim retrieval of personal items from the other person. It's usually done impersonally and Julia wanted that too. She texted: *Your stuff is on my doorstep. Pick it up any time tonight.*

I had heard of aggrieved people depositing flaming bags of clothes and books on their ex's stoop. Ashes to ashes. So at least we hadn't reached Fahrenheit 451.

I dropped by at nine and grabbed my belongings: toothbrush, pajamas, a Cher CD we sang along with when drunk, and the Gwyneth Paltrow candle I gave Julia as a joke. I noticed her door ajar and heard voices. A deep breath then I pushed inside, wanting to say goodbye in-person.

"Nancy B?" Julia said. My birth name was Nancy Dross. I changed it to Nancy Bocelli because everyone loves that blind opera guy, and Italian seemed less white than being a milk-maid from Omaha. Standing next to her was the boyfriend. Pale, slight, and he wore wire-rim glasses. The word fragile came to mind.

"Take care, girlfriend," I said. "Just wanted to wish you well."

Julia smiled. "This is Hector. He's an adjunct professor in Cultural Studies."

"Oh, I took that years ago," I said. "What's your course?"

"It's, *I'm Okay; You're a Colonial.*" Hector stared at my ma'am hands.

"How fun," I replied. "So you cover the U.S., England, France,

Spain, Portugal, Russia, and Germany?"

"Uh, well, no. Just here."

"Ah." I wasn't exactly sure what being an American Colonial meant, but I guessed it was worse than a Confederate, and older.

"Listen, lady," he said in a whiny voice. "Julia was just bi-curious. So why don't you take your yoga mat and head back to Whole Foods and leave us alone?"

"Wow, that is so homophobic and ageist and reductive." I didn't really know what I was saying, but he trembled and grew paler. Julia looked confused and on the verge of tears. Perfect ending. I stamped outside and slammed the door.

I waited a month before using the copied key on Julia's apartment. Through surveillance, I knew she had left for the weekend with Hector. I tried and tried to remove her kitchen sink's water filter. Even a wrench wouldn't loosen it. Bowed but not broken, I attempted unfastening the shower's attachment. Success! Bad hair days would be a thing of the past. One Helmut was mine. Julia had blocked me on social media, so I blocked her phone number and e-mail address. Total erasure.

I am telling you all this today, Doctor, as you've determined you can no longer help me and this is our last session. I disagree that institutionalization is my best option; I no longer stalk Julia and feel much more balanced. Here, I'm giving you her key copy. Please let me continue as your patient, please. One last thing. That water filter in your restroom? It looks so Germanic, so sleek, so very familiar...

DOWN IN CHAOTICA

Brian Koldek sat on a stool at Somnambula Bar, almost as far downtown as you could go in New Hyperion. Modern dating had only grown stranger by the year 2043. When people filled out online profiles, under race, they checked human or synthetic. If they were open-minded, they would put "no preference," and dating sites didn't reveal who was who. The first meeting involved dancing around the subject, as it was considered rude to just come out and ask.

Koldek stared at the exotic Dahlia Jansen, who swiveled on her bar stool to face him. *I'd like to get under her skin.* On the surface, she looked to be a Mediterranean-styled domestic mod, with a little distressing to age her, but Dahlia spoke like a human.

"Who knows how long I'll last in New Hyperion," she said. "I mean, it's dog eat dog. Really unhealthy mentally, but this is where the good jobs are. Where the excitement is." She leaned closer. "None of us knows how much time we have, right? So we have to have fun, live in the now, like the Buddhists say."

"Yeah, maybe so." Koldek remembered that richer pleasure mods upgraded themselves with an X-chip. The Existential chip made synthetics philosophical, imagine an afterlife, or deny the existence of God altogether.

"Are you comfortable?" Dahlia asked. "Is this going well?"

"Sure." Koldek smiled. "I've had worse first contacts."

Koldek had been the best crisis mediator in the city until he retired three years ago. After the Incident, he moved a hundred miles west, beyond the exurbs, to a farmhouse that felt safer. Retiring at age forty-seven was unheard of, so if something major happened, he'd get called back in. TR status: Temporary Retirement. A glorious silence lasted for three years while the city renamed itself New Hyperion and went on rebuilding, re-imagining itself. The silence at his farmhouse increased once Lanie divorced him.

When Koldek heard the whooshing jets of a hover car approaching while he puttered in the garden, he sighed and went inside to pack.

"A week," the pilot told him after landing. "You'll live in a luxury muni apartment near the top of Apollo Towers overlooking the Ming River." He sounded envious.

The Ming River. Koldek couldn't get used to the renaming of the two rivers that cradled New Hyperion. The Chinese insisted, so an agreement was struck as part of a trade deal.

"What do I get out of going?"

The pilot gestured toward the fields and the rustic barn. "You get to return to this."

Koldek's whole professional life involved bringing peace, avoiding struggle, conflict resolution, but heading back to the city brought definite risks. He packed an Abraxas .40 pistol into his travel bag.

Koldek met with Kurt Metzger, his old boss at CSA headquarters in Midtown. He recalled Metzger as stocky, balding, and tired-looking. Time had only enhanced his memory. The Conurbation Security Association did the heavy-lifting in New Hyperion. The police, mostly corrupt, were better suited for street crime, vice, and parking infractions.

Metzger stood up behind his desk. "We have a situation down on the East Silt Beds." He pointed toward a wrinkled wall map.

"Don't you use 3-D vid maps?"

"Hell no. Paper has worked for centuries." Metzger's grin sank quickly. "We're on the verge of a turf battle between synthetics and icebergs." He rubbed his brow. "I'll be honest. The two previous negotiators failed. One suspected dead, the other fled New Hyperion. That's why you're here."

Koldek joined Metzger by the map. Icebergs were the youthful homeless, fried by RF waves from smart phones, pads, tablets, and screens. After constant exposure, five percent of the youth got brain tumors or minor strokes—their attention spans shot and basic learning skills ruined. Brain freeze. Unable to socially interact, icebergs did drugs, bartered goods, panhandled, and stole. They lived in shanty towns on the Ming and the Tao. The once massive rivers had shrunk down, their reduced flow exposing acreage on their banks: the silt beds.

"Icebergs have been there for years," Koldek said. "Why would synthetics want to live in a sketchy ghetto that smells like low tide on a polluted river?" Koldek placed a hand under his chin. "They're all about upward mobility. Marrying humans, getting mental upgrades and such."

"Not the bohemians," Metzger said. "Or the labor bots."

"Those most likely to turn to crime."

"The labor bots should have been switched off until the economy recovered," Metzger said. "But no." He grimaced. "Anyway, about a hundred unemployed synths claimed an area on the Tao Silt Beds a year back. They settled in, but recently there have been feuds and attacks. When an iceberg got strangled a couple weeks ago, two synths were broken apart in retaliation, then floated down the Tao River as a warning. And now with summer approaching..." Metzger's voice trailed off.

"Where do I start?"

"There's a woman who's on good terms with both sides." Metzger shook his head. "No, I don't know her status, but she can set up a meeting of the tribes where you go work your magic."

"I've mediated human disputes, and tensions between synthetics before, but never between both."

"Yeah, it's a helluva thing, but if not you, who?" When Koldek didn't reply, Metzger continued. "You'll meet Dahlia in Chaotica, at a club called Somnambula."

Koldek knew Chaotica, a sector on the Lower East Side. The nighttime playground for a mixture of slumming rich urbanites, decadent Eurotrash, iceberg drug dealers, and criminal synthetics. Police presence remained negligible. Instead, they manned barricades around the borders, treating Chaotica like a contagion to contain.

"Should we keep talking here?" Koldek asked Dahlia amid the echoing conversation noise in Somnambula. He sipped at his vodka on the rocks and studied the crowd. Whenever the bar door swung open, Koldek saw the pleasure mods in micro skirts strutting their stuff outside, and heard icebergs hawking tabs of nostal-G. "Twenty a hit. Remember who you never were."

Dahlia smiled wide. "Do you want to go somewhere quieter, more private?"

Koldek couldn't ID her yet. Her teeth looked fairly white, but imperfect. When Dahlia smiled, it emphasized the tiny lines around her eyes. "I'm fifty," he said. "How old are you?"

"Thirty-three," Dahlia said. Her face reddened. "Thirty-four."

Koldek needed to know what he was speaking to. "That black dude by the door with the muscles and shaved head. Human or synth?" When Dahlia turned away, Koldek squeezed liquid from a mini eye dropper into his vodka. If the drink got altered, the clear liquor would turn bright red.

"He looks so perfect, so artificial," she said, "that I think he's actually human." Dahlia stared at Koldek. "Why do you ask?"

"I don't know," he replied. "Excuse me." Koldek wedged through the press of drinkers around the bar, skirting the Indian techno music throbbing from the dance floor to locate the men's room. When a young man rinsing at the lavabo exited, Koldek locked the door, tapped the earring stud on his right earlobe, and spoke a restricted number at CSA. Metzger's voice came through his iRing.

"How's it going, Koldek?"

"Did you get the heat photo I took through my jacket pocket?"

"Definitely a synth, with upgrades and traces of nostal-G."

Nostal-G, the drug favored by synthetics. A six-hour memory chip. They liked the buzz of fabricated memories, and it made them understand and communicate better with humans.

"You hear me, Koldek? Dahlia's a robot."

No one said the R word in public anymore. Synthetics considered it a racial slur, a throwback to their crude beginnings decades ago. If you used that, be prepared to fight. Artificial American was the official term, though synthetics wanted to blend in, so they preferred generic descriptions like "citizen" or "occupant."

"Got it," Koldek said. "Now she knows we know."

Synthetics could tap into iRing communication. It drained internal battery juice, but they did it whenever they felt suspicious. Koldek used a flip-top cell phone when he truly wanted privacy. This was just lighting a match near an unknown liquid to find out if it was gasoline.

"See how she handles it," Metzger said. "Good luck."

When Koldek mounted his bar stool, Dahlia wore a smirk, but her eyes looked sad. "Why didn't you just ask?"

"Would you have told me the truth?"

Dahlia glanced away. "Maybe." She ran a hand through her dark brown hair streaked with purple. "What made you suspect?"

"The fine lines around your eyes and chipping on your teeth," he said. "Really good alteration work, but they peg you as forty.

Not thirty-four." Koldek noted his drink remained translucent, then took a swig. "What a topsy-turvy world. Humans stretch their faces tight and shiny to look like dolls, while synthetics want flaws: moles, a scar, frown lines."

"I heard you were the best," Dahlia said. "Do you trust a synth enough to come to a private residence where I can explain things?"

"I guess. You could have bolted and ambushed me outside," he finished the flavorless vodka, "or messed with my drink." Koldek signaled to the bartender to pay up.

"It's on the house, bud," the bearded man said. "I thought I poured you a straight vodka, not a Negroni. My mistake." He shook his head. "Lucky your ladyfriend corrected me while you were in the can and I replaced it."

"Oh, shit," Koldek said. *Negronis were red.* "Too much time off." The bartender blurred and the faces in the wall-length mirror turned rubbery and grotesque. "I'm rusty." Then his head slammed the bar top.

Koldek came to on an uncomfortable bed in a dark room. He rose toward the gray light streaming in the window. Through the thin walls, foreign voices sounded: Russian, Arabic, Spanish. From the window, he guessed he was ten floors up in a low-income high-rise on the eastern edge of Chaotica. Koldek gazed out over the Tao River and saw the iceberg encampments on the silt beds. A welter of ramshackle shelters surrounded by junkyard scrap metal, car parts, and yesterday's tech gadgets. Further north he could make out the edges of several clean, geometric structures.

Must be the synthetics camp, he thought. They were logical and precise; no reason to be sloppy.

Instinctively, Koldek looked up toward the sun, but the fine mesh of the Particle Canopy obscured the weather. People bitched and moaned when Homeland Security constructed it ten years ago, but not after the limited nuclear war in Iran, and not after the Incident.

"Can you see what we're up against?" a man asked from the shadows of the far corner. He sat sunken into a scarred black leather chair.

Koldek's jacket had been removed, along with his pistol. He pressed a hand to his face as if in pain, then staggered unsteadily toward the voice.

"Are you okay, Brian?" The man rose up to catch him.

Koldek lunged at him, spun the man around and slammed him down face first to the floor. "Who the fuck are you?" He choked the stranger's throat in the crotch of his elbow. "Are you partners with the robot bitch who drugged me?" Koldek used the R word to test if the man was a synthetic too. *Something familiar about him.*

"My wallet," the younger man gasped out.

Koldek pulled the old-fashioned leather wallet from the stranger's inside pocket. "Rick Traxler," he read aloud. "Security Oversight Agent." *Damn, he was SOA.* Koldek released his arm, but kept his weight on the agent. "Why am I here, why was I drugged?"

"Let me up," Traxler said. "Do you remember me now?" The agent was handsome, but had a scowling mouth and hard, dead eyes.

"Yeah." Koldek frisked Traxler and removed his handgun, then stepped back to the window. "We were partners for a couple of months, what, six years ago?"

"Seven, then you requested my transfer. I've been upstate in New Albans ever since." Traxler frowned. "The ass-end of nowhere."

"I forgot about that."

"I didn't," Traxler said. "Do you think you're the only person involved in this situation? New Hyperion doesn't want a summer of violence, not with the Convention coming in July."

"SOA sent you down to babysit me?"

"To provide back-up since you're just a mediator." Traxler scowled. "But the only one I've met who carries. I'll note that in my report."

"Listen, Prick. I have a permit, and if you think I'd negotiate with potentially violent synthetics and icebergs unarmed, you don't remember how things work in New Hyperion."

"The name is Rick, but yes, I'm starting to recall." He scratched at his dark spiky hair. "You got drugged because the last two negotiators were actually armed agents with a different agenda."

"Assigned by Metzger?"

"No, outside mercenaries. Maybe police hires." Traxler sat back down. "Dahlia hacked their communications." His face tightened. "They were contracted to meet with a leader of the synthetics and of the icebergs, then terminate both of them."

"And provoke a turf war?"

"Speed up the inevitable, then clean out the silt beds before the candidates arrive for the Convention." Traxler tucked his wallet back into his jacket. "Dahlia heard a third assassin was sent down the pike. We figured it was you."

Dahlia entered the room, tossing Koldek's pistol onto the mattress.

"So why aren't you negotiating the truce?" Koldek asked her. "You know the principals on both sides." He picked up his Abraxas and noticed the missing clip. He threw it to Traxler. "I'll keep yours for the time being."

"Being synthetic, I'm close to their leader," Dahlia said. "We're from the same 2033 vintage, but I'm trying to marry a human." She shuddered. "It's all so mixed up, and he doesn't know I'm…"

"Well, you won't have the first marriage based on lies, confusion, and identity issues."

"You come to Chaotica to negotiate, but armed with frag bullets," Dahlia said. "Why should I believe you?"

"I carry a gun for defense. You can access my case history," Koldek said to Dahlia, "and you can access anything dirty that's been sponged off my history," he said to Traxler. "I don't want to kill. The only times I did, it was me or them, and I still see their faces in my nightmares."

"I knew your history was clean, but a promise of UR can make people do things they never considered before." Traxler's smile resembled a leer.

"Metzger didn't offer me Unlimited Retirement, but he should have for working a hairy deal like this." Koldek exhaled. "You're going to have to trust me. If I fail, the police take over. You know the drill. They wait for a clash to occur among synths and icebergs, then wholesale slaughter in the name of keeping the peace."

Traxler stood to stretch and rub his neck. "Koldek's right," he said to Dahlia.

"How did you two meet?" Koldek asked.

"I confronted the first bogus negotiator," Traxler said.

"You arrested him?"

"No. He resisted." Traxler unbuttoned his shirt to reveal a scar from a laser blade inscribed across his chest. "Dahlia terminated him." He coughed. "Saved my ass."

"I left the second man naked and disoriented in a dumpster, just beyond the city in the new projects." Dahlia smiled. "I don't think he'll be back."

"Impressive." She was the most human synthetic Koldek had ever seen. He looked away.

Koldek and Traxler scoped out an abandoned water works building where the silt beds ended on the southern tip of New Hyperion. The brick structure had been trashed and gutted, but after evicting three hobos they brought in folding chairs and a table. It appeared safe, suitable for the meeting. Traxler would stand back-up outside, while Koldek negotiated inside. After much debate, it was agreed he could carry a pistol.

Koldek tried some small talk. "What's work like in New Albans?"

"Twenty years behind," Traxler replied. "We still use helicopters, not hover cars."

The following afternoon, Koldek introduced himself to the

synthetics leader at the table inside the water works building. "Brian Koldek. What's your name again?"

"Enchanted. I'm Paxil Ambrosia." He looked Latino and was theatrical, gesturing with his hands, but his handshake felt firm.

Some synths displayed an artistic bent, or even physical weakness to get humans to relax around them, to underestimate them. Koldek patted Paxil down while keeping his eye on the second man. He never underestimated anyone. That's how he'd made it to the ripe age of fifty.

"I'm Cole Tyson," said the icebergs' leader, a tall black man who seemed sharper mentally than the average iceberg. "Let's get this shit over with."

Upon frisking Tyson, Koldek wondered if he was a regular loner who bunched together with icebergs for protection. Tyson was attractive, but had that frazzled thing in his eyes that Koldek recognized in substance abusers.

"You know why we're here," Koldek said when they sat down. "The back and forth has to stop. It's nihilistic. If the body count rises, then the police will clean out the silt beds." He leaned back in a metal chair. "Jesus, you know how they treat icebergs and labor synths."

"Like damn bugs to exterminate," Tyson said.

Traxler watched from outside but Koldek didn't know if the younger agent was there for protection, or to take out Koldek if he deviated from the script.

"Okay, concession time." Koldek moved the chair forward then rested his elbows on the table. "Paxil, the synthetics have to move their shelters a mile north."

"We're settled," Paxil said.

"No, we were there first," Tyson interjected. "The silt beds have always been iceberg territory."

Koldek put his hand up to shush Tyson. "The rivers receded seven years ago and the encampments followed. You call that always?"

"Why should we have to relocate?" Paxil rolled his eyes.

"Because you're synths and the silt beds run for miles," Koldek said. "You have the energy and unity to do it. Also, as the new guys on the turf, you should move as a courtesy."

"No. We camped there because it's near the action in Chaotica."

"You think Chaotica ends a half mile uptown? It's creeping, spreading throughout New Hyperion." Koldek slammed a fist down on the table. "Look, I'm not asking, Paxil. I'm here to save both groups from elimination." He breathed heavily. Neither leader spoke. "Once you re-settle, there will be a quarter mile no man's zone between, a DMZ where neither synthetics nor icebergs go. Until then, no more robberies, dead bodies, or dismembered synths."

"Well, I guess, if we have no choice." Tyson grimaced.

"We're the ones who have to uproot," Paxil said, "and do all the work."

"You have the battery power and skills to do it quickly," Koldek said. "Icebergs work slow, and they operate like nomads. You've seen what they can build. A huge outdoor dump."

"Damn. You got what you needed, mediator. No reason for disrespect." Tyson rubbed his forehead with the knuckles of his fist.

Koldek instinctively placed his hand near his gun.

"No, what I need, is for you to sign this truce and relocation agreement, pen and paper, and a DocuSign, Koldek produced a tablet, then an audio verbal agreement. He tapped the iRing on his earlobe and coached them through the steps.

Once finished, Koldek led them out of the crumbling foundation, past broken pipes running across exposed flooring where rats scampered about. The breeze came scented with dead fish, soot, and the ancient smells of building materials that constructed the city: cement and asphalt, limestone and rusting metals.

Koldek stared out past the gas flames rising from the refineries on Gravel Island to where tributaries from the Ming and the Tao Rivers met, then slowly swelled up to the southeast before merging, somewhere out of sight, with the Atlantic. There was still beauty in the world, just not where he stood.

"Hey, Brian." Traxler joined him. "I need to question our friends for the report I have to file."

Koldek nodded. "Go ahead."

Traxler's face became pinched. "Can you give us some breathing room? Your job is done. Congratulations, you're on your way back to retirement at the farmhouse."

Koldek didn't like a government spook knowing where he lived, but he walked into the water works building and sat down. Outside, the men spoke by a crumbling balustrade at the edge of a balcony overlooking the confluence of rivers.

Traxler stood between the other two, slightly recessed.

When Koldek noticed Traxler remove his handgun and keep it behind his back, he jumped up. Koldek unholstered his pistol, but two strong hands pushed him down. Then he felt a needle pierce his neck. "Not again." He pivoted toward Dahlia.

"I won't let you kill them," she whispered. "Traxler warned me you would."

The drug didn't knock Koldek out, just retarded his movements, a slow-acting paralytic. "You're... helping... Traxler."

Dahlia glanced over then flinched. "Wait!"

Traxler shot his gun into the back of Tyson's head and the iceberg collapsed to the ground. When Paxil turned to pull a laser blade from his boot, Traxler fired into the right then left side of Paxil's upper torso until he spasmed. A synthetic's CPU was located in their chest cavity. As if a switch had been turned off, Paxil stiffened and fell like a wooden plank.

Koldek's brain felt immersed in sludge, but he lifted his pistol and chambered a round. Dahlia too distracted to notice.

Traxler strode inside through the archway smiling evil.

"You killed Paxil," Dahlia screamed.

Koldek willed himself to squeeze the trigger. The gun discharged, stunning Traxler and Dahlia.

A moment later, Traxler laughed. "Blanks. I replaced your clip before we exchanged guns at the apartment." He noted Koldek's sluggish movements. "Thanks, Dahlia. You've made this much easier."

"Traitor, you didn't want a truce. You were the third assassin."

"Shut up." Traxler beamed an SOA strobe flashlight on Dahlia and she fell down shuddering. "Peace is terrible for us agents, Koldek. We need to be saving citizens from the scum living on the silt beds." His mouth twisted. "If we're not the heroes, the good guys, we're out of a job. Losers."

Traxler removed the useless pistol from Koldek's grip, then

inserted his own handgun.

"Your report to Metzger said I was a hothead, prone to violence. Landed me in New Albans." He turned Koldek's arm back around and pressed the gun barrel to the mediator's lips. "Open up, Mister Famous Negotiator. You killed those two leaders, then in a drug-fueled depression, took your own life." Traxler's face came closer. "You'll be the bad guy in this story, old man."

Something yanked Traxler backward.

In one deft motion, Tyson snapped Traxler's neck, causing the agent to crumple to the loose bricks and dirt.

Dahlia, who had been twitching on the ground, rose. "I've got an antidote." She injected Koldek. "Sorry. Traxler told me you'd kill both leaders. Thought I was stopping you." She turned toward Tyson. "How are you even alive?"

The iceberg leader's head lolled to the side with two large bullet holes in the back.

"Haven't you figured it out?" Koldek said slowly. "Tyson's a synthetic not an iceberg." Koldek recalled an out-of-control synth in Chaotica with his head blasted clean off, who kept fighting until enough hollow-point bullets were lodged in his chest to shut him down.

"Why would you want to live with... icebergs?" Dahlia asked. "You're a synth. We're better than them."

"I've taken nostal-G a hundred times," Tyson said, his voice thin and metallic from damage. "I began to feel human, imperfect, messy. I'm not comfortable with logic and order." His lips opened and shut twice. "No one expects anything from you as an iceberg. I like that, just drifting, no responsibilities."

"We have to leave now," Koldek said, his reflexes recovering. "If Traxler's cleanup crew finds us, we're dead."

"I've got a ride in a parking garage two blocks away." Dahlia pointed.

"What about me?" Tyson asked.

"Go to the synthetics camp for repairs."

"With Paxil destroyed?" Tyson said. "They'll assume I did it and disassemble me."

"Think like a synthetic." Koldek frowned. "You have a record of Traxler's assassination in your memory, filmed through your eye-cams before you took the bullets. I'll send you the signed documents to your server. Whoever is in charge will do a data dump and realize you're innocent." Koldek gestured toward the river. "Go, run. Stick to the shoreline."

Dahlia put Koldek's arm around her shoulder and they retreated inland. She looked worried as they rushed to the garage.

"You're susceptible to strobe lights," he said. "Traxler knew."

She nodded. "A side-effect of my emotional upgrades."

Synth parking attendants didn't try to appear human. They weren't going up the ladder. This one was hairless, no eyebrows or anything. He smiled though, recognizing Dahlia.

"Hey, Robot, you got a parking receipt?"

"Robot, step off," she said. "You know I don't."

He opened the entry gate.

When Koldek eyed her, Dahlia said, "We get to call each other that. You don't."

They mounted the stairs, because elevators could be

overridden and jammed. Second floor, third floor, fourth floor.

"Where the hell did you park?" Koldek gasped for breath.

Dahlia motioned upward. They climbed the last flight before exiting onto the rooftop.

Koldek stared at the craft in amazement. "Sorry, Dahlia, but how did a synth get a hover car?" He felt annoyed. "I can't even get one, and I have pull."

"I told you about the human boyfriend I want to marry." Dahlia clicked the auto-hatch doors open. "Peter runs City Transit. Get in."

Koldek's iRing throbbed on his earlobe. High level emergency call.

"What happened, Koldek?" Metzger asked. "You sent us the signed truce agreement, audio files, then I hear the iceberg leader and the synth leader are likely dead. Is Traxler down too?"

"You never mentioned Traxler," Koldek said. "SOA had their own agenda to keep the chaos in Chaotica."

"Traxler's not SOA. He may be a non-official op hired for dirty work. Anyway, I need your verbal report, in person."

"I'm not coming in," Koldek said. "Someone set me up. If not you, then someone inside. Make this call private." Koldek heard the screeching of a blocked one-on-one line being initiated. "My temp apartment in twenty minutes, Metzger. Alone. If I detect any other motion patterns, I bolt, then release my documents to all media."

"You sound hostile," Metzger said. "Why should I trust you? What if you take me hostage?"

"You know there's only one thing I want, have wanted forever."

"Unlimited Retirement?"

"Yes, an official UR badge," Koldek said. "Bring one. I have zero to gain from holding or hurting you, Metzger. You should know that after twenty years."

The call ended as Dahlia piloted the hover car above the spires and parapets of the tallest skyscrapers. Koldek engaged the drone-blocker function on the dashboard, in case someone traced their coordinates. They sped west toward the sunset, toward the refurbished dock area on the Ming River where Apollo Towers rose six hundred feet into the air.

Koldek heard the whup-whup-whup sound behind them. "Helicopter. Shit. Must be Traxler's team."

Their sleek black craft closed in.

"We can't outrun them this low in the city," Dahlia said.

"Go straight up, high as you can, but stay over the river. It's our only shot."

"If I get near the Particle Canopy, we'll draw—"

"Exactly. Go." He grabbed the stick shift when she hesitated and yanked it back.

The hover car rose and the helicopter followed. When they were within four-hundred feet of the Particle Canopy, Koldek said, "Sit tight and wait."

Dahlia's hand shook like a human's. "This is suicide."

The helicopter reached their altitude, gun barrels elongating from it's body. Then an enormous shadow loomed above both crafts and descended from the clouds. An HS airship.

Their hover car began to shudder wildly.

"Total drop, now," Koldek shouted. They plunged a thousand feet instantly. Koldek felt the stomach-churning sensation he remembered as a kid from roller coasters, but much worse. Once they slowed and stabilized, Koldek checked their monitors.

The giant Homeland Security airship continued its descent until its armored hull struck the helicopter's rotor blades. They snapped off and got cast into space. The helicopter spun like a top as it fell, crashing into the river off Gravel Island. HS were extremely zealous about protecting restricted airspace, and didn't think twice about knocking unmarked aircraft out of the sky. Not after that homegrown nut-job used an unmanned drone to cause the Incident three years ago. The airship ascended back toward the Canopy.

"Good job, Dahlia."

"You improvised," she said. "No matter how many upgrades, we're not good at doing whatever needs to be done to survive." Dahlia rested a hand on Koldek's leg. "Maybe that's why you're fifty and we only last fifteen years."

"That's for our protection." Koldek tried to stay focused, but Dahlia's hand felt good there. He'd been divorced a year—a long, lonely year on a farm where the neighbors were suspicious of his mysterious background. "How soon is your marriage?"

Dahlia laughed before turning serious. "You know, we almost have parity."

"Yeah. I saw the *2044 Overthrow* graffiti outside Somnambula Bar. We built fail-safe devices, but you synths will overcome them. I figure I have ten years on my farm before it gets dire for humans, then I'll get off-the-grid."

She sighed. "There's your landing pad. Prepare for descent."

The hover car settled on the Apollo Towers roof with a whooshing sound and a blue-gray plume of air brake exhaust.

Koldek jumped out. "Will you wait?"

"Yes," she said, "but can you believe me after..."

Koldek squeezed her hand. "I want to trust you."

She nodded. "And I want you to."

Koldek paced inside his luxury apartment that held no luxury for him. He locked the windows and turned off the A/C before initiating the motion tracking device on the scope of his gun. When the pings began, he studied the small screen. *One figure approaching from elevator, two-hundred pounds.* Koldek checked Metzger's current weight stats: 198. A handgun might add two pounds, but no heavy weaponry.

Metzger knocked and Koldek rushed him inside. He frisked his boss, removing a pistol and electronic devices. "Did you bring it?"

Metzger pulled the laminated UR badge from his breast pocket then flung it onto the bed. "Give me your verbal."

After Koldek made his sworn statement and placed a time-dated hard copy of the truce agreements in Metzger's private carry case, he grabbed his bag and scanned the room. "My mediation would have worked if not for Traxler. I don't know who backed his gambit, but they used me as the fall guy to pin the murders on. They got their mess, and now I have what I need."

"How did it feel teaming with a robot?"

"Stop calling her that."

Metzger shook his head. "You're getting soft in your old age, and desperate."

It was early June and humid as hell, but Metzger, a short overweight man, wasn't sweating. No perspiration on his forehead. Koldek threw his boss down onto the bed and scanned him with his scope's heat sensor.

"You're a synth." He pressed his gun against Metzger's chest. "How did you get his memories?"

"Metzger died last year in a Chaotica shootout," the synth said. "Department took brain scans in the hospital before he passed. You think I'm happy? Sometimes I think I am him. CSA thought it would be bad for confidence if their top kick got killed in battle. I keep the dream alive."

"Or the nightmare," Koldek said. "If you follow me, I'll shoot. I don't want to kill anyone, not even a bogus Metzger."

"Why don't you trust me? You're exonerated."

"Someone in New Albans used you to use me."

After checking his sensors, Koldek rushed out. Utilizing Metzger's electronic override device, he jammed his apartment door lock and the hall elevators, then struggled up six flights of fire stairs to the roof.

Dahlia looked anxious. "Come on, come on," she said.

They rose with a blast of vertical thrust and rocketed west out of New Hyperion. Within a half-hour, Dahlia began descending toward his farmhouse.

"Can you stay a while?" Koldek asked when they landed. Silence. "At least tonight?"

"I can't." Dahlia gripped his hand. "I have to return his car right away. I didn't exactly ask permission." She exhaled. "Peter will be home from the capitol by morning."

"Will I ever see you again?"

"Yes." Her long eyelashes fluttered. "You'll be back." Dahlia kissed him softly.

Koldek watched the hover car levitate into the clouds. He

waved until only a distant jet noise lingered. Noticing a weird ridge on the glossy badge from Metzger, Koldek scraped at the laminated UR pass. The U soon peeled off to reveal a T.

Temporary Retirement. That damn treacherous synth, Metzger. He tossed it in the trash. *Maybe Dahlia was right.*

Koldek considered her last words, spoken in a breathy whisper as they hugged, her hands roaming his body. "See you down in Chaotica."

DESTINATION UNKNOWN

Ward Christian stirred his coffee. Tasted awful, so he drank more. *Not enough sugar, cream?* Phones had been ringing all morning but his recent promotion meant that others screened callers and only transferred serious complaints to him. He worked for Gore-Blarg, the stupid name for waste management in Santa Maya—a coastal town seventy miles north of Los Angeles.

The light blinked on his line, a clunky phone of late '80s vintage. "Good morning. Gore-Blarg Solutions. How can I help you today?"

"Who am I speaking to?"

"This is Ward, uh, Christian."

"Great, this is Albert, Atheist."

"No, I'm not—"

"Whatever. Is this illegal dumping?"

"Well, I handle related complaints."

"I live on the 3100 Block of Upper Main Street. Someone left a large couch outside between two apartment complexes."

"And that's bothering you?" Ward had been told to use a therapist voice, to calm and soothe troubled callers. Some being daily nuisances, cranks with no life.

"Yes, it's blocking the sidewalk. Have to walk into traffic to get around it. That's dangerous. Plus, it's an ugly color and looks... moist."

"I can send a truck out within 24 hours."

"Thank you," Albert said. "You're a decent garbage man."

"I'm not a garbage man." His voice rose. "I am in Waste Management and—" Ward stopped when he realized Albert had disconnected. He filled out a retrieval order, noting that Hernandez and Wilcox covered Upper Main. He put the request in the computer system, but also left cards in the men's boxes they checked when signing-in and signing-out.

His cute new assistant Gloria buzzed on another 20th century device, his intercom.

"There's a call from a Jennifer Tucker," Gloria said. "She sounds familiar."

"That's Jen, my wife." He hesitated. "Can we have a drink after work, Gloria?"

She ignored his question. "Oh, so she didn't take your last name?"

"Um, no." Ward crushed a piece of scrap paper in his hand. "Please put her through."

"Hi, darling," Jen said. "How are you doing?"

"Since I saw you two hours ago? Fine." He stared at the window. "Was there something important?"

"They delivered it."

"What?"

"The new bidet. Installed and everything. Marci says it's a life-changing experience."

"Marci?"

"Online sales manager. But she'll continue as our contact, to guide us through the first month of use." Jen let out a satisfied gasp. "I feel so continental."

Ward yawned. "That's fantastic, honey. I really need to get back to work."

"Of course. When you get your next promotion we can buy the Jacuzzi tub."

Ben Wilcox and Victor Hernandez received the pick-up request at 9 a.m. Victor felt relieved they no longer rode on giant stinking garbage trucks, nor did they wear stained jumpsuit uniforms. Instead of bags of rotting trash, they merely hefted furniture into a hauling truck.

When they reached the 3100 block of Upper Main Street, car traffic was dense, but few pedestrians strolled the sidewalk.

Victor looked up and down the gentle slope, then spotted it in all its hideous purple glory. "There she blows." Ben found a nearby parking spot, alleviating blocking a traffic lane.

The sofa stretched a good seven-feet. Definitely a two-man job. Ben took the end jutting across the sidewalk and Victor grabbed the side tucked into the alley between neighboring apartment complexes. The material felt spongy to the touch, weird. "One, two, and lift," Victor shouted.

Ben levered it up, but shuddered from the strain. "Gah, my back." He dropped his end. "I drank two Tornadoes at Jerry's Pub last night. Exhausted today." A hand pressed to his forehead seemed to be holding him up. "How much time we got for this job?"

"An hour," Victor replied. "Maybe used ten minutes so far."

"Listen, let me take a nap for a half-hour. We'll still reach the city dump in time."

"Nap? Where?"

"On the couch, dummy. Looks comfortable."

"Yeah, I don't get why no one snagged this for their home, or to sell at a thrift store." Victor scanned the blur of cars passing as if for some authority to decide. "Okay. But let's push it into the alley so it doesn't obstruct foot traffic."

"Fine with me," Ben said. "Out of the sun's glare."

Though heavy to lift, strangely, it slid easily back into the shaded alleyway. "What do I do for thirty minutes?"

"Get some coffee or go on Instagram, or you know, the Mexican version of Facebook."

"You mean...Facebook?" Victor turned, but Ben had already stretched out with a forearm over his eyes. So he walked uphill and bought a $5 iced coffee at the Bean Dream.

After twenty minutes, Victor grew paranoid. There could be traffic delays on the way to the dump, and if a supervisor should drive by and catch them dawdling, they'd go right back to slop truck duty.

"Ben?" Their vehicle remained parked in the same place, but the couch sat empty. "Ben?" Victor scoped the alley, patrolled the street, but found no sign of his partner. He did notice Ben's glazed doughnut propped on an armrest. The seat cushions seemed to undulate, for a moment looking porous, then gelatinous.

Victor picked a three-foot palm frond off the sidewalk and pressed it to the sofa's base. It went slowly through the material, sinking from sight. When less than a foot remained, Victor pulled back. But it was stuck. Then, something within yanked, dragging the frond into the seat cushion, as well as Victor's hand. "Shit. Let go!" He felt chilled, flesh numb. Finally he extricated his hand and stared at it. The skin blurred, went lighter then darker, came in and out of focus. *Leave now.* Victor jumped into the truck and returned to Gore-Blarg headquarters at high speed.

Ward woke up feeling weary. He wanted to doze more but Jen chattered on her phone nearby, sometimes singing bits of awful pop songs. "You're beautiful, beautiful."

"I slept terribly," he told her. "The full moon disrupts my sleep cycle."

"The moon doesn't go full till next week, silly," Jen said, disconnecting.

"Well, it's beginning to. I need black-out curtains, like Elvis had at Graceland."

"FYI, Elvis died at forty-two." Jen chuckled. "I just spent a half-hour on our bidet," she added. "There's a wide-spray setting that gently firms and tones your butt-cheeks."

"Great." Ward staggered to the bathroom. He squatted on La Royale 4000 and relaxed. A video screen to the side buzzed on.

"Welcome, occupant. I'm Marci, here to facilitate you through your new purchase."

Ward grabbed at his pants by his ankles. "You can see me?"

"Of course not, I'm AI," Marci replied.

"Oh, good."

"However, we have human operatives in Sumatra and Taiwan who are monitoring this product whenever in use."

Ward jumped up. The release of weight on the seat switched the screen off with a static fizz. After his ablutions, he drank coffee to wash down the burned scrambled eggs and English muffins, then rushed to work.

The office gave him no peace. His team hadn't retrieved the purple couch. Then more complaints: a green sofa on Upper Main and a chaise lounge on Lower Main. Ward hadn't heard that term in years. Sort of a daybed. You could nap on one, but not quite sleep on it like a big couch. The last caller sounded familiar.

"Albert, again?"

"Uh-huh," he whispered. "The couches aren't what they seem."

"What?"

"They're leather and suede. Quality furniture usually gets nabbed fast by passersby. People come look, but never take them."

"Why haven't you, Albert?"

"Something odd. It's a conspiracy, I tell you..."

Ward hung up. The intercom buzzed him before noon.

"Can we have lunch together, Gloria?"

"No," she said. "Uh, do you believe in reincarnation, Ward?"

"That stuff's nonsense."

"We could return as different people," she whispered, "meet

each other fresh then."

"Just one life and this is it," Ward said. "Was that why you buzzed?"

"A retrieval man is waiting for you."

"In person?" The whole point of having a private office was not to see workers, to hide away from all corporate bullshit and just slither through the day. "Okay, send him in." Ward's irritation distracted him from asking who it was.

A white-haired Latino man shuffled into the office with his head bowed.

"Hector Garcia?" Ward said. "Didn't we plan to discuss your retirement next month, when you turn sixty-five?"

"I'm thirty-five, Mr. Christian." He raised his face to glance at Ward.

"Victor? Holy shit, what happened to your hair? And where's Wilcox?"

Victor described the morning and Ben's disappearance.

Ward paced the room. "You believe he sank into the couch, got swallowed? Have you been drinking? I know microdosing is popular these days but I didn't think it crossed into your community."

Victor pulled his right hand out of his pocket for Ward to see. The man's brown skin had been bleached white. "It got wet inside the couch. Is numb, no feeling."

Ward felt sudden fear. Not of the unknown, but of lawsuits directed at Gore-Blarg. Upper management would blame him. He had to act on instinct; logic made no sense. "Take the rest of the day off, Victor." He offered two twenties from his wallet. "Treat your wife to dinner." He sighed. "A temporary condition. Clorox liquid bleach leaked inside a seat cushion and did that. Get some rest. Tomorrow we'll be joking about this." Ward forced a laugh but Victor showed only a sickly smile as he hobbled out of the office.

Gloria buzzed again. "It's Preston Crasburn from the University Club."

"I'll call back."

"Says either you speak to him or he'll go to the General Manager."

"Okay," he said. "Hello Preston. Long time no see."

"Ward, I've been tooling around Santa Maya, and discarded sofas are littering the streets. I show our fair city to a preservation committee on Friday. How will they react? Not well, I tell you."

"The matter was just brought to my attention. I'm dealing with it."

"Really?" Preston made a sound best described as a harrumph. "Don't you realize, beds and couches are magnets for the homeless population. They sleep on them, fornicate on them, perhaps even—"

"Have you seen any unhoused people on the couches?"

"Unhoused? Is that the current preferred term?"

"Today's Tuesday," Ward said. "I'll clear it up by Friday."

"We wouldn't want this to jeopardize your application to the University Club."

"No, no. Thanks for your concern, Preston."

Ward contacted Tug McGraw and Lonnie Wilson. Big lugs who'd worked on the drilling platforms offshore. "It's not your area, but I need this purple couch picked up ASAP. There's extra money in it for you. Plus, kudos from the old man upstairs."

He instructed all calls to be held then took a nap on the office carpeting. Impossible erotic dreams about Gloria ensued. As if being married wasn't enough, Ward was her superior and any pass he made could be reported, seen as workplace harassment. In his reveries, she was his boss—demanding physical favors.

The buzzer sounded over and over, waking him. "What is it?"

"A retrieval man. Says it's urgent." Gloria transferred him.

"Mr. Christian? Lonnie here. Couch was heavy as hell. Wouldn't move. I went to hook up the winch and when I returned..."

"Yes, yes?"

"Tug McGraw was gone. He couldn't have run off."

"Where are you?"

"In the truck on Upper Main, waiting for him to show."

"I'm coming down."

Ward parked his Kia Sedona at the corner of the 3100 block and tapped on the utility truck's passenger window. "Did Tug ever come back?"

"Nope."

"I've never had someone walk off the job." *Except Ben Wilcox.* Ward rolled up his sleeves. "Okay, let's haul that thing over."

"Are you sure?" Lonnie brushed back his greasy mop. "At your age?"

"I'm fifty."

"No, really?"

"Well, fifty-five, but I feel fifty." Ward moved into the alley, leaned over, and shoved the couch, while Lonnie pulled it toward where the winch hook could attach. Ward grunted and groaned, straining for what seemed like five minutes, then looked up. "Did it move?"

"Maybe an inch."

"This isn't some valuable antique. Do you keep hammers in the truck?"

"Of course." Lonnie smiled before retrieving two sledgehammers.

"You piece of crap," Ward said, as they swung at the couch, striking it over and over. The armrests soon broke off and finally the back frame collapsed, leaving the base. They only hit the seat cushions twice before both burst open. A thick black liquid oozed out. It bubbled and steamed like hot oil.

"Step back away from that," Ward yelled.

As a former boxer and linebacker, Lonnie had taken multiple hits to the head and his brain functioned a tad slower. When the liquid slime drenched his boots, he roused from a trance to jump backwards. A loud hissing sounded and smoke rose. "Ow, it's burning hot."

"Take your boots off—now!"

Lonnie obeyed. He hurled them away and the shoes dissolved fast as if soaked in acid, leaving only a rubbery stench in the air. "Holy fuck," he said.

The dark liquid pooled together then gushed out into a storm drain. The couch frame and cushions had dissolved too. Soon the alley sat empty beyond the stunned men. Children peered from windows in adjacent apartments, mouths agape.

Later that afternoon, Ward got summoned upstairs. Tyler Johnson was thirty-five, and had been installed as Acting Manager by his father Cyrus, President of Gore-Blarg.

The spacious office held no desk and Tyler skateboarded around it when Ward entered.

"Dude, thanks for showing. The old man's all up in my business."

"About what?"

"Street furniture. Missing employees." Tyler leaped off his skateboard and slid on knee pads across the wooden floor. He stood to fist-bump Ward. "Also, homeless people been vanishing for a week." Tyler grinned like a simpleton. "I mean that's cool, because, you know, but it's uncool, because these local organizations are like outraged. I told them, it is what it is, but that didn't soothe them, man. I told them, it's all good, and they said, no, it's all bad."

"Not my fault."

"I feel ya." Tyler nodded. "But if the blame has to land on you or me, yeah, it's totally your fault."

Ward couldn't share what he'd witnessed earlier. "I didn't know we had a responsibility to the houseless population."

"Neither did I." Tyler lit a bowl of weed in a glass pipe. "City thinks we're leaving quality couches and beds out in public and that's luring homeless people from shelters to live on the streets." He coughed. "The shelters need to show their numbers, amount of people they help and feed, to get their state money and shit." He put his hands up in exasperation. "Dad's hassling me, but I'm traumatized by blame. So I have to pass this on to you, bro. If you can't make things happen, it's down the elevator shaft."

"You'd do that?"

"Nah. Cyrus would. Good news is you're still working for us, but in a deep dank space, alone." He flashed a knowing smile. "No hot assistant, like Gloria."

At dinner, Ward and Jen continued their argument about a monthly date night. Ward campaigned that it should be twice a month.

"You told me your married buds don't have *any* sex." Jen's fake eyelashes flared outward. "So you're getting twelve times as much as they are. I'd prefer less though. Sometimes Winky just doesn't feel up to it."

Ward woke up twice during the night to ramble about the bedroom.

Jen muttered, "You're bothering me. Go read a book on the bidet."

"The full moon is glaring in here. I see the light and think it's early morning. Throwing off my natural rhythms."

She grumbled her way out of bed to pull open the shades facing Main Street. "No moon, see?" Jen pointed. "It's that streetlamp. The metal hood came off and it's shining this way." She slumped back onto the mattress.

Ward wrapped a towel around his head and finally dozed off.

The next day, he enlisted the six remaining retrieval men to help. "Guys, don't try to remove couches or sofas. Instead, hide them, tuck them into alleyways, behind dumpsters. Slide them away from street view. Everything else, wooden chairs, book cases, desks, you'll haul to the dump. If Upper and Lower Main look clean by Friday, there's a bonus in it."

"What about Ben, and Tug McGraw?"

Ward sniffed. "They'll be back. Mark my words."

"You don't think they got devoured, eaten up?" Victor asked, a glove on his right hand.

"Of course not. That's crazy talk."

Through some miracle, Ward's plan worked. Friday, when he drove the five miles of Main Street, he didn't spot a single couch or any furniture. Not one trash complaint call came through Gloria either.

He had a solo drink after work then went home. Lights were blazing and dance music throbbed, while cars filled most parking spots. *Crap, I forgot.* Jen's cocktail party to impress the town snobs. She being a social climber. They lived on the 4000 block of Main Street, the top of the hill. Not an expensive cottage, but the best apartment view over the city and toward the distant ocean.

Ward entered their living room crowded with twenty people. "You're late." Jen lightly elbowed him. "Guess what? The new bidet is a big hit."

He quickly changed into a fresh shirt and jacket. When he mixed a drink, Preston Crasburn sidled up. "Congratulations, Bubby. I gave my tour today and your area looked near perfect." He fingered the university crest on his blazer. "Not only did you dispose of the unsightly furniture," Preston switched to a booze-flavored whisper in Ward's ear, "but the homeless population was invisible." He stepped back. "Continue that magic and a spot on the city council awaits—"

"Thanks, but what about University Club membership?" Ward said. "Jen keeps harping on it. Says we're nobodies if we can't join."

"Your chances at the U.C. rose dramatically today." Preston's voice caught in his throat. "It's just the garbage man thing."

"I'm not a garbage man," Ward insisted. "My job title is, Human Resources—Waste Management—Complaint Handler." He proffered his business card.

Preston nodded with a pained smile. "Cards are so 1998. Everything's online. When members look you up—as they will— your title's been simplified." Preston flashed his giant pulsing iPhone 14 and tapped Gore-Blarg personnel. "See?"

It read: *Ward Christian: Human Waste Handler.*

"Our blue blood members are very germ-conscious," Preston continued. "They won't shake hands with a chap who's knee-deep in human waste..."

"But I'm not."

"Appearance trumps reality, my friend." He gripped Ward's shoulder. "Just get promoted to Disposal Solutions or Recycling. People love separating their cardboard and plastic. Even if most isn't actually recycled, citizens like to think they're helping the planet by doing almost nothing." He lightly punched Ward's arm. "Get 'er done."

Ward returned to Gore-Blarg at 9:15 Monday. He greeted Gloria before entering his office. "I thought about you this weekend. Will you see me after work?"

"You know we can't. Company policy."

"What if we were in different departments?"

"Um, Cyrus is waiting for you on a Zoom call." Gloria

trembled a little. "Major Johnson."

Ward hurried into his office and joined the Zoom. A mottled seventy-five year old face filled the screen. Due to the low camera angle, Ward gazed up through his chins, seeing the white hairs in Cyrus's flared nostrils, then his red-veined eyes.

"Hello, Mr. Johnson."

"Call me Major." The man had served in food distribution during the brief invasion of Grenada nearly forty years earlier, though no official documentation of his title could be located.

"I'm hoping my recent achievements might earn me a promotion," Ward said.

Cyrus let out a choking cough, his complexion reddening. "Achievement? Sorry, I'm demoting you."

"Why, sir?"

"Thirty homeless men and six women have vanished. There are photos of several of them sleeping on couches you failed to deliver to the city dump. Those images were posted on the Nextdoor app by annoyed residents. The same transients disappeared soon after."

"Isn't that good?"

"Personally, you're my hero. But from a business point of view, it's disastrous. Civic groups, community organizers are all hounding me. Why are we providing bedding for the homeless and what are we doing with them? I've insisted it was a computer error, but they want heads to roll."

"I don't know what happened to the missing people."

"Jesus, Christian. During the Spanish Inquisition, or fascist Italy, they'd be building statues of you, but here in the socialist republic of California, they care more about the lower rungs of our society than the breadwinners. Like me. I pulled myself up from the bootstraps of my parents' wealth to make Gore-Blarg what it is today." Cyrus pressed so close, his screen face blurred into a pink, wrinkled landscape.

"Transfer me to Recycling, please." Ward tried not to sound desperate.

"You're in Human Waste, right?"

"Well..."

Cyrus grunted. "A transfer, you sure? We don't just recycle bottles and cardboard. It's big stuff now. Machinery, objects, pretty much everything."

"Yes, I want that."

"Done. Empty out your desk by noon. Victor Hernandez replaces you."

"Victor?"

"When pressed to the wall by lawyers, we believe in diversity."

Days passed in a blur. Ward descended in the freight elevator to Sub-Basement C, below the furnace rooms, beneath the storage decks. He sat at a desk in a cavernous space. The antiquated boxy computer he used to input recycling statistics didn't have an Internet connection. No signal could reach so deep. Twenty feet above, lines of fluorescent light strips buzzed and sometimes fizzled out. Dark shapes the size of small dogs scuttled about the dim far corners. Much of the vast area was taken up by towering stacks of couches, divans, and mattresses. Across the basement, an automatic metal door sometimes slid open and workers took furniture out, perhaps to prop on the sidewalks of Santa Maya. The disheveled men wore ratty clothes and showed long, dirty hair.

At one point, Ward recognized two guys hauling mattresses. "Ben Wilcox, is that you?" No response. "Tug McGraw, I'm glad you're okay."

Both acted like zombies. They briefly stared at Ward without recognition, eyes glazed, both cadaverously pale. He began to understand. The whole conspiracy larger than anyone might imagine.

A mail chute delivered sandwiches in brown paper bags at lunch hour. Ward could not leave until 5 p.m. when the elevator arrived. Ringing for it earlier proved fruitless. Up high, near the light strips and clanking pipes sat a metal balcony—only accessible from the next level. One morning as Ward typed endlessly, he heard high heels tapping and squinted upward.

"Gloria, you came to see me."

"I had an errand to do. Wondered what was out here."

"We can finally be together," Ward shouted. "Neither one of us has power, can help or hurt the other anymore. We're free now."

"Yes, that's true." A tear formed in Gloria's left eye; she turned and rushed away.

He stopped going home. After the University Club rejected them, Jen had moved out to her sister's Pasadena apartment in shame.

Ward lay back on the most comfortable-looking couch. He sank away until his vision became haloed by a rainbow of colors. When he woke, Ward had somehow fused with the giant eye of the streetlamp across from his apartment. It had been trying to warn him, to signal. People were being transformed, composted, recycled into other forms to benefit the city. From this high perch he watched the yellowy orb rise into the night sky and felt like a moon drunk saint. A desert mystic atop a lonely tower.

Time passed, immeasurable. At some point he became conscious of the neighboring streetlamp blinking on and off—winking at him. Ward plunged his consciousness down into the coils and turbines, the wires and generators until he sensed it was Gloria. She had transitioned too. He rejoiced and thrummed with utility power, showing her his brightest beam. They both sparked, shimmering in the electra-glow of artificial light. Together they might stave off the pitch blackness of their solitary lives.

CONFUSION TO OUR ENEMIES

The morning came like a hangover to Dysdania, a nightmarish one. Eleven-year-old Alexei woke to sobbing, pained cries, and the smell of burning wood. He heard horses roaming wild and frightened. His mother ordered him to stay inside. Last night, raucous celebrations had infused the town of Sluvdansk, then spilled out to the neighboring farmhouses and hills. Alexei's parents hid his teenage sister Zoya and two female cousins in their cellar, a heavy carpet rolled over the latched trap door.

Rodolfo had been elected president of their province. Though Alexei's father, Boris, his Uncle Gregor, and their neighbors had not voted, Rodolfo received a hundred percent of local ballots. His band of thugs dressed as a military brigade commemorated the victory in taverns and public houses, eventually taking out their drunken aggression against anyone not wise enough to have locked themselves away at sunset.

By noon, Boris prepared the wagon to do business in town—as he did every week. Alexei watched him roll a shotgun in a blanket and place it behind him. Boris put a scythe under his son's wooden seat, just in case.

They trundled past the smoking remains of a neighbor's barn. "Papa, look." Alexei pointed at the man with bulging eyes dangling from a rope. "Should we help him?"

"Old Pavel is beyond anyone's help." Boris shook his head. "We're lucky. This is as far as the soldiers got. Your sister and cousins have not been defiled—yet."

"Is it safe to keep going?" Alexei shivered then nestled closer on the buckboard to his father, who smelled reassuringly of aftershave and beets.

"The soldiers only become monsters at night after much drink." Boris spat. "They have risen today confused and pale, their heads aching, some even ashamed." He coaxed the pair of horses into a trot. "Many are returning to the capital city. A few guards will remain to watch our area." Boris whispered into Alexei's ear. "Our neighbor Pavel will be avenged, but not today or tomorrow. Long after this horrible crime is forgotten, we will remember it fresh and new."

Alexei's father had explained that few local residents owned cars. Most people used horses and wagons. Dirt poor they were, their land made of hard earth peppered with rocks. Dysdania sat up north, tucked into the eastern armpit of the Soviet Union, though they had never been invaded like Hungary three years ago. Cold winters and overcast summers grew them potatoes and cabbage, not the sweet corn or succulent fruits of the south.

"Russians call us the refuse of the past century," Boris had said over dinner. "So we are ruled by whatever gangster claws his way to power in Corzina. Our new leader parades through towns giving speeches, tasting food, sampling women, and demanding payment for protection against Russia."

"Laughable," Alexei's uncle had replied. "Moscow could break wind in its sleep and topple Dysdania's threadbare defenses. The local military are scum, criminals. A hundred armed men, just strong enough to terrorize us peasants."

Alexei heard a horse galloping from behind and burrowed deep into his father's tobacco-smelling overcoat.

"Boris," yelled Uncle Gregor. "You need a distraction to do business. The soldiers will interfere, steal what you buy. They may smile, even stroke Alexei's hair as they rob you."

Boris pulled the reins to stop on a high ridge above Sluvdansk. Dead trees of November stood vigil, their branches stabbing at the sky, the rocky ground barren of crops. A dark gray soil stretched out for miles, bisected by the rutted dirt tread that served as an avenue to the town. "Perhaps you're right," Boris finally said.

Alexei saw smoke rising from the embers of the town church. Two noisy military cars drove recklessly through the town's streets, not going anywhere in particular.

"At least most soldiers are trekking back to Corzina now," Gregor said.

Alexei noticed splayed lifeless forms lying on the outskirts of Sluvdansk. Shuddered when he realized they were horses.

Wild dogs darted back and forth.

"A car is stalled on the road halfway down." Gregor pointed. "Let me borrow Alexei and we'll divert attention. Then you take the side route into town."

Boris scanned the other unmaintained road. "Go with your uncle, Alexei. Don't argue. Your childhood is over."

Alexei climbed up behind Gregor on the saddle. The horse trotted downhill, slowing to a walk when they got closer. It looked as if the dark green Gaz sedan had been abandoned, but after they dismounted and crept closer, they found a man wearing an officer's uniform lying across the back seat—unshaven and snoring.

"A lieutenant," Gregor whispered. "He would have given the order to hang Pavel."

Gregor carefully wedged open the lid on the gas tank, unscrewed the cap, and tore a long strip from his shirt. "Get back on the horse." He dipped a quarter of the length into the tank, allowing a foot of cloth to dangle outside.

Alexei tried to control the horse which paced in a circle, ears pricked and wide-eyed.

Gregor lit the edge of the fabric with a match then jumped up on the horse. He kicked its flanks and they rode back uphill, Alexei clutching his uncle's sides. By the time they reached the high ridge, the Russian car had burst into flame. Gregor tied his horse to a tree out of sight. They lay flat on their stomachs to watch.

"The soldier hasn't come out."

"I wanted to cause a distraction, not trap him." Gregor

looked anguished.

Two cars soon rumbled out of town and struggled up the pitted road toward the burning hulk.

"Your father is safe but we are not." They remounted Gregor's horse to gallop back toward their home.

Boris entered Sluvdansk through dismal side streets of warehouses and closed metal factories. He heard the ratcheting sound of car engines straining. When he reached an intersection, Boris stared east at the ridge. He rubbed his eyes but the vision remained. A man on fire ran screaming past two outsized Russian cars that had stopped—perhaps stunned by the apparition made real. Traveling gypsies told folk tales of a flaming wraith who haunted the far valleys. Absurd ghost stories.

Roll in the dirt, you idiot, Boris thought, but the runner seemed consumed by pain and madness. A soldier got out from a car to hector him, yet the fireball kept in motion, his path veering northwest to bypass the town altogether. Another soldier admonished him to drop to the ground.

The flaming man shrieked, slowing to a staggering gait. The soldiers consulted one another before the second leveled a rifle and downed their compatriot.

That imbecile, Gregor. Boris had needed a diversion not a brutal spectacle. And this would be called murder. Repercussions would follow.

Boris tied the horses to a post outside the general store.

After Boris had loaded up bota bags filled with goat milk, along with cheese, lard, bread, and rare firewood, he coaxed his team of horses out through the main street. It would seem suspicious to skulk away by the side route.

Long banners strung across the avenue flapped in the breeze. They showed a painted image of President Rodolfo atop a giant steed, the leader's dark hair shining with pomade, cheeks rouged, his skin clear of the latticework of lines that were inscribed in his sixty-five-year-old face. Rodolfo insisted he was younger, and strutted around in a leather girdle that gave him the pained expression of a terminally constipated man.

Garbage and broken glass filled the puddled streets. Older women in head wraps helped dazed younger women out of the boarding houses soldiers had forced them into throughout the previous grisly night. They sobbed and limped, their dresses torn or stained with blood. Boris wondered if they were crying from the memory, or because they were marked now and could not be wed as virgins. Their social status reduced to marrying field hands and farmers, not bankers or accountants.

Two military cars blocked Boris's passage homeward.

"You, farmer," one soldier said. "We didn't see you come into town."

"I rode in at dawn," Boris replied. "Searching for wood scraps. A brutal winter is coming." He gestured toward the snow-capped mountains. "Preparing for the worst."

"Someone set our comrade's car on fire, murdered him. Undoubtedly one of your neighbors who doesn't accept our President." He gave a thoughtful glance to the other soldier.

"We would reward anyone with information..." When Boris said nothing, he added, "And there would be harsh punishment for those who hid the truth." He wagged a finger.

Boris nodded. "I'll keep my eyes and ears open."

The soldier inspected the wagon, stole a hunk of butter, and got back in his car. "Remember what Rodolfo says." He smiled. "Silence is disobedience, and disobedience is the last act of a traitor."

The two cars reversed, allowing Boris to continue home. He passed the smoking hulk of the burnt vehicle and shivered.

Back at home, Boris wandered through the house, then asked his wife Svetlana, "Where is my damn halfwit of a brother?"

Gregor rose from the cellar. "I thought the fool would escape."

"You son of an inbred mountain goat." Boris grabbed Gregor's jacket lapels and slammed him against a wall. "There will be reprisals, and soon."

"Don't hurt my uncle." Alexei pulled at his father's belt.

"I know, I know." Gregor held his face in shame. "What can we do?"

"You must leave immediately." Boris led his younger brother to the back door. "To our hunting cabin." He pointed toward the distant foothills dusted with first snow beyond a dense pine forest. "We'll swear you left last night."

Gregor looked grim but didn't argue. "I'll fetch my winter clothes and hunting rifle."

"Try to get us a few deer or an elk."

Gregor gripped Boris's hand. "Confusion to our enemies."

"Confusion to our enemies," Boris echoed.

"Won't the soldiers find him?" Alexei asked.

"Animal trails lead through the forest," Boris replied. "Soldiers can't drive them, and have no horses. I doubt they'll hike ten miles on foot."

At night, Zoya, Irina, and Marta came upstairs for beet and cabbage soup. Alexei had tied their dog Pushkin by the goat pens to bark if strangers approached.

"Why am I not hidden away with the girls?" he asked.

"We'll explain when you're older," Svetlana replied.

After the meal and a few swallows of vodka, Boris plucked at his balalaika, while Zoya sang an old folk song. Irina and Marta danced a traditional dance but kicked Alexei away when he tried to join in. Eventually, Alexei dozed off, forgetting the day's events, his stomach full and music echoing in his ears.

The sound of a car engine approaching after dawn woke him. Alexei jumped out bed to find his mother rushing the girls into the cellar, his father standing vigil outside the door while smoking. Dogs barked and goats whined. Alexei joined his father to watch the two soldiers enter neighboring houses. Finally, they visited.

"Remember us from yesterday?" one soldier asked.

Boris nodded.

"This is a social visit. Be a good countryman and invite us

in."

Boris scowled and dropped his cigarette on the small porch, then squashed it like a bug under his boot. "You are welcome in my home."

The soldiers inspected the living room, bedrooms, and kitchen where Svetlana busied herself cleaning plates. "We see your wife and son," the plump, mustached soldier said. "But they told us in town you had a sixteen-year-old daughter…" His eyes goggled. "Zoya?"

"Zoya and her cousins were sent away to school in Osblag," Boris said. "For their safety."

"There is no danger under President Rodolfo," the second soldier said, a wiry man with a weasel face. "Also, we are seeking the murderer of our comrade yesterday." He glared down at Alexei. "From what we've seen at local houses, the only man missing is your brother. Where is Gregor?" He stamped his foot for emphasis.

"Gregor left the night before last to our hunting cabin ten miles upland." Boris pointed east. "We won't make it through winter if he doesn't bring us some meat for the smokehouse."

"Yes, his wife mentioned that." The skinny soldier lifted binoculars from his military coat and walked outside. "The road peters out in less than a mile," he shouted. "We would have to hike or ride on horseback."

"Feel free to take my donkey," Boris said. The beast was small, ornery, and could barely carry the weight of one man.

"Two horses pulled your wagon." The soldier grinned. "I'm sure you would lend them to us, tovarish."

"I have a better idea," the stout one said. "We'll take Gregor's young wife along to stay in Sluvdansk."

Alexei rushed at the ugly man, but he pressed a hand against Alexei's chest to stop him then ruffled his mop of hair.

"Please don't attack me, boy." He laughed. "We will protect Dasha. Otherwise she would be unguarded out here with inbred rebels and swarthy gypsies tramping through this region. They have no code of honor. She could be hurt." His eyebrows rose. "Even molested."

"Dasha can stay with us," Boris insisted.

"No, it's settled. She'll stay at Ludwig's boarding house where we are garrisoned. Dasha will be released the moment your brother submits to a routine inquiry." The heavyset soldier smiled, showing missing teeth. "Unless you've learned who killed our lieutenant?"

"No." Boris pulled Alexei back to his side. "But I will keep asking."

When the soldiers trekked toward Gregor's house, Boris loaded his shotgun and moved toward the front door.

Svetlana—a woman of considerable strength—tackled him to the floor. "You idiot," she said in a hissing voice. "You said many times, the soldiers must disappear, or die by accident." She slapped her husband. "If you shoot them, the others will burn our houses and rape our girls."

"You are right, as always." Boris gently lifted her off of him. "Alexei, tear small pieces from our kitchen rags."

"Why?"

"Obey your father."

When they heard Dasha screaming as the soldiers loaded her into their car, Boris pressed the bits of cloth into their ears.

"Confusion to our enemies," Alexei whispered. But he felt confused, and frightened.

Alexei ran inside the house just after sun-up the next morning. He waved his hands wildly but couldn't form words.

"Your cheeks are red. You're shaking," his mother said. "No playing outside during winter mornings wearing pajamas and slippers."

Boris lifted Alexei in the air with a stern expression, then lowered him to the ground. "What is it?"

"Papa, I ran back to tell you," Alexei said. "Not sure how I ended up in the woods."

"Sleepwalking again?" Svetlana struck a hand against her forehead.

"I heard crying so I climbed over the hill." Alexei pointed. "There was a woman with tangled golden hair in a nightgown, and she had wings."

"You saw an angel?" Boris chuckled then shook his head.

"Her wings were torn and bleeding. I approached her but she yelled, 'Stay away. I bring only trouble and pain.' Papa, I begged for help. Said we needed her to fight Rodolfo, to ward off his devils." Alexei rubbed both hands together to warm them. "The woman laughed, said she was a fallen angel who'd lost her powers."

"You were sleepwalking and had a nightmare," Svetlana

said. "I'll heat you some cabbage soup."

"Why wouldn't she help us, Papa?"

"She has been cast down, her wings now useless." Boris frowned. "Superstitious villagers say that fallen angels are driven mad by their banishment on earth."

"Shush with those folk stories," Svetlana said. "You're scaring the boy half to death."

"Anyway, Alexei, Satan was a fallen angel himself." Boris stared at him. "You were dreaming, hallucinating. Perhaps the town doctor was right, we must strap you to the bed at night so you don't wander off, hurt yourself."

"But Isaac told me that spirits of the forest guard and protect us."

"Your older cousin is touched, Alexei. A mule kicked him in the head as a child."

Ludmilla, from three houses away, entered their home after dinner. Boris greeted her. "What is it, Lud? You're shaking."

"Your nephew Isaac went to retrieve his father Gregor from the cabin."

"What? When?"

"He told of Dasha's abduction."

"Oh, no. I must stop Gregor."

"They left for Sluvdansk hours ago."

Boris rummaged in the closet but couldn't find his shotgun. Isaac was simple-minded, but remained stubborn like his father. They acted before thinking. Boris made for the door; maybe he could catch them.

Svetlana stood pointing the shotgun at Boris's stomach. "I won't allow you to die joining your hot-headed brother in his foolish quest for revenge."

"So you intend to kill me?"

"No, only wound you," she said. "But remember, I'm not the best shot." Her hands wavered. "Have we had all the children we intend to?"

Boris outstretched his hands in surrender. "My brother rides to his death. At least join me on the wagon to pick up their bodies and give them a proper burial."

Svetlana began crying. She lowered the weapon and Alexei emerged from his room. "Are we going, Papa?"

Boris gripped his shoulder. "Stay and protect the girls. Do you understand?"

Alexei nodded.

"I've taught you how to use this shotgun. It's heavy, so sit down facing the door. If any soldier comes through, use both barrels." He smiled. "Don't worry, son. I don't expect them for another day."

The boy looked sleepy when they returned. "Alexei," Boris said outside the window. "Don't shoot your parents."

"Where are Gregor and Isaac?" Alexei yawned.

"We didn't find them, but they had been there. The bunkhouse was on fire." Boris paused. "Go to sleep now. We'll know more in the morning."

Alexei wandered through a white haze, the air cold and wet against his face. He dreamt of snow falling, and padded across its soft cushioned expanse. Gradually he heard wails, then howling. Something beckoned to him. The fallen angel? Alexei continued until he tripped over a log and smacked his face hard. He woke up startled. Thirty feet ahead a pack of wolves feasted on a large animal, no, a person, a soldier. Two darted away, but five ignored Alexei and tore at the man's flesh with their teeth. Alexei ran back, tracing his tracks in the snow while screaming. Near the houses and livestock pens, he found his father.

"We forgot to strap you down last night," Boris said. "What is it?"

Alexei led his father into the forest.

Boris waved his shotgun in the air and the wolves dashed off toward the hills. "Stay here." Boris examined the soldier's remains. Using a knife, he cut the man's bonds and removed the gag from his mouth, then returned with a glum expression.

"What happened, Papa?"

"The fat soldier who visited us and took Dasha. Your uncle tied him up out here unconscious, then put raw squirrel meat in his pockets."

"How do you know?"

"We did it during the war when German soldiers hanged your Uncle Vlad." Boris grimaced. "Rodolfo's men must have…"

Boris tried to relax by eating eggs and buttered toast. Halfway through his meal, Gregor pushed up through the trap door.

Boris launched into him and they began wrestling.

"Burning their barracks? Killing the highest ranked soldier? You've doomed us all for your revenge."

"They're thugs. They tortured her, passed her around," Gregor said. "You would have done the same. Ow!"

The brothers' struggles continued until Svetlana splashed them with foul water from the pig trough. "Enough," Boris said to her.

"Not enough," Svetlana said. "How will you two protect us? Must we flee to that godforsaken hunting cabin until the weather clears enough to cross the pass?"

Boris stared at his brother. "There are maybe four soldiers left in Sluvdansk. They'll likely drive out together, heavily armed, by dusk. We must divert them. A major storm is coming." He scratched his chin. "We'll ambush them here if that doesn't work. But our weapons against machine-guns?"

"Alexei, load tools into the wagon," Gregor said. "Shovels, picks. Isaac will help."

Rodolfo drove to Sluvdansk himself after hearing of the troubles. *Must stop this nonsense, otherwise I will seem weak,* he thought. *Cutthroats and rival gangsters in Corzina will try to poison me, usurp my Presidency.*

"You dolts," he told his four remaining men at Sluvdansk Tavern. "Never ravage and share a local's wife. It irritates them." He slapped the skinny soldier and sighed. "Now we must kill the whole family to show our resolve."

"We should leave before the snowstorm comes." Another soldier pointed at dark gray clouds.

Rodolfo and three men took his shiny Volga sedan, leaving the last ferret-faced soldier by the tavern's phone. They rumbled up two miles of hill heading east, light snow falling, the road slippery. A few hundred yards past the crest they reached a blockade of stones and logs. Beyond it the tread was gouged with pits and ditches. However, another spur of road with recent wagon tracks led northward then gradually upwards toward a pine forest. Rodolfo saw a tiny equipment shack, its front door banging in the wind, a bleating goat tied to a post.

"We'll take that route," Rodolfo said. "Another three miles and we slaughter the bunch of them."

One soldier nodded, but didn't seem enthusiastic. "Peasants believe those woods are haunted."

"Superstitious tramps," Rodolfo said. "Dmitri, wait here in case anyone should follow."

Dmitri exited. He stood shivering on the shack's porch, clutching his army coat to him, a Kalashnikov hanging over his shoulder.

"The snow is sticking," the driver said. "This car is meant for the paved streets of Corzina, not these conditions."

"Then hurry, Vasily," Rodolfo replied. "Twenty minutes to get there, ten minutes to do our business, then back to the fireplace at the Sluvdansk Tavern." He smiled.

They climbed the slow twisting incline, the car occasionally swerving to the side of the track. In fifteen minutes, atop the saddle of the hill, the descending trail ahead became obscured by snowfall. "Which way?" Vasily asked.

For an instant, Rodolfo thought he spied a flaming figure running through the valley. He blinked. "I see a torchlight or perhaps a peasant's fireplace in that bowl below. The road must intersect those two clumps of pine trees. We're almost there."

The two soldiers glanced at each other.

Vasily drove downhill, just tapping the brakes lightly. Halfway down, the car skidded on an ice patch. Vasily stamped on the brakes and they spun around out of control, finally thumping to a halt in a deep trough. He gunned the engine, the wheels spinning without gaining traction.

"We can't keep going, dear Leader," Peter said to Rodolfo. "Best to hike up to where we left Dmitri, huddle in the shack and wait out the storm." The wind howled around them while snowflakes fell thick and dense.

"Fool, they're just ahead. We'll stay with the peasants overnight then kill them after breakfast."

"I am sorry, President, but I'm going back." Vasily wedged the driver door open and trudged into a headwind. "Follow me while we can still see our tire tracks to lead us."

Rodolfo got out. He had poor circulation in one leg and it now felt stiff, useless. "No one deserts me." He fired his pistol. Vasily dropped into the snow at the base of the incline.

"Sir, you shouldn't have... We needed him."

"I need *you* to help me get up that hill." Rodolfo leveled the handgun at Peter.

Peter struggled, holding Rodolfo around the shoulder, and climbing slowly. Halfway to the top, they slid backward.

Peter lodged in a drift while Rodolfo rolled further down. Peter fled upward on hands and knees through the deepening snow. Rodolfo emptied his clip. One bullet struck Peter, but the wounded soldier continued crawling until Rodolfo could no longer hear his anguished breathing.

Rodolfo limped under a huge pine tree to wait out the snowfall, then he could crawl home too. At first he felt cold, freezing. When his limbs went numb, he decided to rest for an hour. Rodolfo woke in the dim light before dawn. In the distance he saw a gauzy female figure wearing a diaphanous gown, her feathery wings streaked with red. Hallucination. He closed his eyes to dispel it. Guttural snarling caused him to open them. Something big and furry moved and snorted in his peripheral vision. He realized it was a bear mauling Vasily's corpse a hundred yards away.

Rodolfo didn't budge or make a sound, which took little effort, as he felt frozen and unable to speak. He saw several sets of yellow eyes glowing in the woods around him, coming closer. Yes, perhaps it was the local farmers. Those damn peasants would save him, their beloved President.

The wagon rolled slowly through the snow in the morning, steamy vapors rising from the horses' nostrils. "Papa," Alexei said, as he untied the shivering goat outside their utility shack and led it back to the wagon. "The soldier resting inside. Shouldn't we wake him?"

"No, he is deep in sleep." Boris gripped the pilfered

Kalashnikov. "Let him dream and dream through our long winter."

"Confusion to our enemies."

Boris smiled down at his son.

Alexei didn't mention the burn mark on the shack's door. The scorched black imprint of a flaming hand.

AXIS OF DISTRACTION

Macy goes through her old scribbled "to do" lists, adding forgotten or neglected items onto the current master list. Then she reviews things she texted to herself and writes those down too. Beyond belief. How can she ever complete it? And new tasks are always incoming. Separately, she has a running dialogue of reminders playing on a brain-loop: *Do the laundry, pick up Hunter and Tyler from school, take daughter Merlot to ballet class, get Brendan's dress shirts from dry cleaners, scrub the oven, wash your hair, find something attractive to wear to the dumb party tonight.*

"You don't really try to look sexy anymore," Brendan had told her in bed. Never in the mood when she was, nor was she when he was.

"I've got a lot on my plate," she replied, but was thinking, *I'm holding your little bullshit world together, mister.*

"All day I'm leveraging debt and foreclosing on loans so you can stay at home," he said. "If you found a part-time job, then we'd hire someone around the apartment, and you could fix yourself up like you used to."

Do your laundry, pick up the boys, buy the groceries, ignore the husband.

The ancient landline rings and she disconnects it. Pings chime from her iPhone. Ignore. The laptop on the table sounds like a plane taking off; something wrong with the internal fan. She can't finish any of the multiple tasks that cry out to her. What a fucking time for an Adderall shortage! Half the world is on prescription pep pills, or crystal meth. And if not stimulants, then opiates. The war on drugs? Lost long ago. Most everyone Macy knew teetered on the edge of some addiction or was in rehab to get off another.

She transports the boys home from school uptown. Tyler takes her aside. "Call me Skyler, okay?"

"What?"

"Remember Sean? He's Shivonne now. I want to switch genders too."

"You're eleven. Wait a while, please."

"Can I have surgery for my next birthday?"

"Don't you understand? When they remove your, um, you can't just reattach it."

"I'd keep it around my neck, on a locket."

Macy grimaces. "Is that a thing?" She presses a hand to her throbbing forehead. Migraine. "We're not discussing this now."

It sounded so silly, but later she Googles "penis necklaces." No, it definitely wasn't a thing in American culture, but certain headhunters in Borneo had done that. Get those images out of your brain. Google is evil. Nobody trekked to the library to research stupid information in the past.

Put laundry in the dryer, take Merlot to dance class, keep boys from watching porn on the Internet, withhold feminine harbor access to Battleship Brendan.

Not sexy anymore? He's the one with a beer belly and receding hair.

Hunter is almost fourteen. Growing taller. "Mom, if we move upstate, can I buy a rifle?"

"No," she says. "If we go anywhere, it'll be to Queens."

"Queens? That's a shithole."

"Hey, no cursing at home. Or in school, or in public."

"Where can I swear?"

She ponders. "Underwater, outer space."

"You're *so* weird."

Merlot appears in her ballet outfit. Walk her over, it's only five blocks. Can't throw money around on cabs anymore. Outside, crowds of pedestrians, distracted people, buses swerving, cars honking forever, young idiots on e-scooters, bikes pedaling against traffic, sirens blaring. Everyone's going to die! There's the ballet school just across Sixth Avenue.

"Mom, can I take Irish stepdance? It's more fun."

"What, like the Lord of the Dance?"

"Who's that?"

"I thought you loved ballet."

"It hurts my toes."

"You're ten, Merlot. You don't understand the true meaning

of pain."

"Are you okay?

Macy leans against a brick building, diesel exhaust in her nostrils. Out of rhythm with the universe. "Mommy didn't have her vitamins today."

"Oh. My teacher calls me Merle. Is that a boy name?"

"Goes either way. Merle Haggard, Merle Oberon."

Merlot's face is pinched in confusion. Macy might as well recite Latin. She brings her daughter inside, waves to the instructor as if they know the slightest thing about one another, then remembers the nearby dry cleaners. Brendan drops his clothes off and she retrieves them.

"Too much perfume and lipstick on your husband's shirts," the woman tells her. "Have to charge more to clean." Macy doesn't use perfume, and wears mostly lip gloss of late.

Pay for the clothes, get Hunter to his French tutor, pick an outfit for tonight, scrub the oven, broil the husband.

No, that's harsh.

Returning home, the manager guy from a bank that abuts her building's lobby smiles through the glass, his mustache rising. His eyes show desire, but she has no time to schedule an affair. After the cleaner's revelation she wants to though. Just for revenge. If only she could clone herself. Technology goes whizzing by humans with no advances in cloning to speak of. Just sheep. Who wanted more sheep? No one. The world needed people cloning, hair cloning, and baby fat cloning.

She Googles "Adderall" again. How many times today? The shortage continues. Users paying exorbitant amounts to street dealers, some buying bigger dosage pills and carving them in half, or into quarters.

"Spacey Macy," a voice yells. Her nickname as a teenager. Sure enough, it's a high school classmate—Rod, Todd?—but he's become all forehead and a massive ass in khaki pants. Pretend not to recognize. Keep moving; dash around the corner.

Flapping pigeon strays near her face. Diseased and polluted. *I will go full Ozzy on you in a nanosecond.* Macy notices how crowded the stores are, the streets extra-massed, and on a Wednesday to boot. *Fuck, tomorrow's Thanksgiving...*

Back upstairs, hand shirts to Brendan, air kiss him, stay in motion. He talks incessantly. "It's a small group tomorrow. Just make the usual spread for nine of us."

"I'm overwhelmed. Can't we eat out instead, please?"

"No, no, that's why I'm going to the office party alone tonight." He stinks of new cologne.

"You are?" She's confused. "Why?"

"To give you a break, babe. So you can make the stuffing, mix the gravy, prepare the bird." He darts away then returns beaming. "Don't worry about last night. There's counseling, and surrogates who can help us work through our intimacy issues. Happens to everyone in their late-forties."

"Surrogates?"

"Trained professionals to lend a hand."

Macy retreats into the kitchen. Keeping the lights off, she squats under the high kitchen table to listen to her sons stomping around the apartment. If she doesn't sleep, she might be able to mash the potatoes, shop at Food Emporium for vegetables, find all the kids' favorite stuff. Kids. Oh shit, she forgot Merlot at dance class. Macy takes two sharp cutting knives from a wood block and scrapes them together, enjoying the zingy metallic sound.

"Honey, I'll leave a list to help you," Brendan shouts. He pushes through the swinging kitchen door. "It's so dark. I can hear you, but where are you?"

Pick up your daughter, score some street Adderall, take a power nap, carve the turkey, carve the turkey, carve the turkey...

I DON'T LIVE TODAY

Noon. Sean Gavin rolled out of bed, dislodging a sandwich wrapper, and staggered into the shambles of his life. "Hope I die before I get old," The Who sang. No such luck for Sean at fifty. Not ancient for a writer, but for a hotshot rock guitarist (a once-was, could've-been), hitting the half-century mark was a brass-knuckled gut punch.

From his window in New Jersey's Palisades Park, he studied the Manhattan skyline across the Hudson River. He brushed pizza boxes and crushed beer cans atop his stove onto the floor, then made instant coffee. The wall calendar read April, 2000.

As a youth, Sean's musical talents were astonishing. In the mid-seventies, he taught at the Guitar Study Center in Manhattan, run by Paul Simon's friendly brother Eddie. A dream job. Easy money from teenage students who brought joints to smoke on the building's roof after lessons. At night, Sean gigged in Bleeker Street clubs, part of an exclusive badass brotherhood.

The sixties music vibe that had nurtured him for years died flat out in December 1980 when John Lennon got murdered. Sean struggled on, playing recording sessions for cheesy video bands with drum machines.

Someone pounded on Sean's door. *What the hell?* He'd paid his rent—yes, late, but paid in full. When he sold weed, such visits were expected, even encouraged, but that was 1992 in the Chelsea Hotel, not eight years later in Jersey. The only valuables in his apartment were fourteen rare guitars: Fenders and Gibsons, electrics and acoustics.

Sean found his revolver then edged open the chain-locked door.

"Pablo," he said, irritated. "Shit, man, I've got a phone and you know the number." Sean ushered him inside.

Pablo Garcia's eyes popped when he saw the pistol. "Seriously? You would have shot me?"

Sean snorted. "Thing's not even loaded. It's for scaring intruders away."

Pablo fingered strands of his long hair. "Does it work?"

"It scared you."

"Yeah, well..." Pablo sat on a wooden stool, avoiding the stained couch that looked perpetually moist. "This was urgent, so I rushed over."

Both Pablo and Sean had worked at guitar stores across the Jersey Turnpike and Long Island, but now they just hung out in the same stores, playing expensive guitars, buying nothing, telling old gig stories to salespeople who had long grown weary of their presence.

"Speak up, then. Got a lot of stuff on my plate today."

Pablo sported a frizzed frazzle of thinning black hair. Due to a vague resemblance, he impersonated Carlos Santana in a tribute band called Smooth. "There's a special guitar I can get you for ten grand."

"Let me guess," Sean said. "A vintage Stratocaster." He slumped back in his Laz-Y-Boy.

Pablo's mouth drooped open. "You're right."

"I bought my valuable axes years ago." Sean rubbed his hands together. His apartment always felt clammy and cold, even in spring. Pablo's face didn't show comprehension. "I don't need any more expensive guitars."

Pablo flexed a triumphant smile. "It's who owned this Strat that makes it magic." He paused. "Jimi..."

Sean had been distracted, pondering if it was too early for an afternoon beer. "Jimmy Vaughn?"

"No, as in Jimi-Fucking-Hendrix."

Sean felt weighed down in his scarred recliner, Earth's gravity increased by tenfold. His rib-cage pressed tight as he choked out, "Hendrix?"

"Yesss."

Sean jackknifed forward. "Bullshit. Preposterous. All of Hendrix's guitars are owned by rock stars or mega-rich collectors." Now he felt almost giddy, filled with righteous anger at Pablo for bringing this seductive lie to his doorstep. "And for ten thousand? Impossible. A Hendrix Strat in good condition would go for nearly a million."

"That's why I'm here." Pablo stood and approached. "The seller doesn't know the Jimi connection. Just understands a vintage Strat's value."

"So why aren't *you* buying it?"

"I don't even have a grand." Pablo looked sad, older than his fifty-three years. "Moved in with my brother. Couldn't afford rent. His wife says I'm a lowlife who just sits around jamming and smoking weed."

"She may have something—"

"Yeah, whatever. My point being, you own extra guitars, can raise cash." He smiled. "And didn't you mention a nest egg of a few thou stashed in the bank?"

Sean regretted ever getting drunk with Pablo. "Yes," he said, jaw tightening. Pablo was an imbecile as a person, but a forensic detective when it came to guitars. "You verified it?"

"Uh-huh. I unscrewed the neck. Read the birth date: May, 1963. Checked the records. Hendrix definitely kept a sunburst Stratocaster at Electric Ladyland for recording sessions. Found photos, and the wear marks on the body matched—exactly."

Sean led him toward the door. "I need money fast. Selling my axe could take weeks."

"Sure." Pablo shuffled down the outer stairs. "But the owner is eager. I begged her not to deal with Guitar Row in Manhattan, said they'd give her less than half. We've got till Friday, then she starts shopping the magic Strat around."

"Okay, set it up. I'll work a loan from my cousin-in-law in

Passaic."

"Antonio Panetto?" Pablo froze for a second before hustling toward his beat-up Corolla.

Sean had to snag the Jimi guitar. He'd felt a divine connection to Hendrix ever since first hearing "Purple Haze." He learned the songs perfectly, mastering the thumb-over-the-neck technique. If one could truly possess an electric gypsy soul, then Sean did. Or he'd done enough psychedelics to believe so.

Sean wouldn't let Manny's Music or Sam Ash on 48th Street grab it for cheap then sell it for beaucoup bucks to a Microsoft millionaire scumbag, some tech geek who'd seal it in a bulletproof glass case on his mansion wall like a museum piece, never to be played. Hell, no!

By afternoon he'd secured a loan. Terms were brutal, but Sean felt confident about paying Antonio back. He called Pablo. "One question. What's your cut?"

"A percentage when you eventually sell it, but I want ten large by next week. A finder's fee."

Sean considered his options. Record an album, play gigs with the Jimi guitar for a year, then sell it for a million. He'd have to part with his beloved Gibson 335 to not get fingers broken by Antonio's associates. He could do it. Rise to the challenge, bro.

"I don't have cash, but my '61 Strat is worth eight grand. Plus, a Martin D28." Sean's intestines roiled. "And if you make extra from selling them, keep it."

Pablo breathed through the earpiece. "Done deal. Meet me at nine tomorrow morning on 1st Street in Secaucus. By

Dunkin' Donuts."

Sean woke at the ungodly hour of eight, sucked on a chunk of frozen Tropicana, and chewed at a moldy English muffin.

A half-hour later, he stumbled down to his distressed Acura Integra. He looked terrible in the rear-view-mirror. From his late-twenties through early forties, Sean's center-parted, long rock star hair and symmetrical goatee had marked him as a righteous badass. At fifty, his hair resembled rust-colored wheat, dried-out and stringy, like a kind of pummeled straw hat decomposing around him. Sean first detected a thin spot in the back when caught in a freak storm, and the raindrops needled his crown scalp like Chinese water torture. Worse, to keep his facial hair the youthful dark shade of yore, he dyed it weekly, and in the harsh daylight streaming into the car, the beard appeared fake, drawn onto his chin with a brown Magic Marker.

Across the lane, neighbor Eddie gunned his 1970 Plymouth. Every morning, the elderly man woke Sean and the entire neighborhood, revving and revving a motor that never turned over into ignition.

"Goddamnit!" Exhaust fumes and cursing, a sputtering thrum, then a brief respite.

Eventually, Eddie gave up—his day's work done. No one knew where he intended to go if it ever started. Sean suspected humanity was bonded together through daily rituals with no clear purpose.

At nine, Sean parked near Pablo, waiting outside the Secaucus residence. He thrust a paper bag of cash toward the passenger-side window.

"Jesus, you brought your gun?"

"This could be a ruse." Sean palmed his hair back. "Guitar is the bait and a gang's inside waiting to rip off my ten grand. I used to deal. These innocent family exchanges are pretty common scams."

"Dude, you're barely awake and this paranoid? Your gun's not even loaded."

Sean flapped the cylinder out to display the .38 slugs. "You've got ten minutes to get back here or I come in like freaking De Niro in *Taxi Driver.*"

At twelve minutes, Sean felt panicky. He was a guitarist not a gunslinger. Even if you shot the criminals and escaped alive, you'd still end up doing time. In New Jersey, no good deed went unpunished. Not even the Pope—Bruce Springsteen—could save you.

Just as Sean's heart started beating at trip-hammer intensity, Pablo returned, smiling beatifically and carting a triangular cardboard box. Something only a beginner, a rube would carry any guitar in, much less a priceless treasure.

"Here you go." He slid the precious cargo flat onto the back seat. Sean took a quick gander to ascertain it was a vintage Strat, then squint-eyed the neighborhood like a getaway driver during a bank robbery.

Pablo knuckled the driver-side window. "Remember, two guitars for me next week."

Sean swatted him away and rocketed back onto the Turnpike.

Once home, Sean pulled the shades then locked the door. He unfolded the cardboard atop his coffee table, peeling the wrapping away slowly, like undressing a beloved girlfriend who'd passed out after drinking—delicately, chastely, and with respectful awe.

The sunburst Stratocaster was tattooed by stiletto-like etchings on its upper body. Flame marks revealing the natural wood beneath. A black pickguard made the three white pickups and tone knobs pop out. The toggle switch had turned a vintage cream tan with use and age, from Hendrix finger funk and genius sweat. Its metal bridge showed silver and rust and weird filmy soap stains hinting at untold gig stories. Beyond the bridge, the body held a slight greenish tinge, some patina of age, of weathering and outer space fungus glazed over the red-brown hues underneath. The mahogany neck felt extra slim, so easy to play that it was almost difficult, like a car with a hair-trigger accelerator pedal. You had to calm down and focus or your hand would run away, lose its grip in chasing after impossible riffs suddenly made obtainable.

Day melted into night as Sean jammed. Plugging through a Fender Deluxe amp, he strummed it with sweeping Stevie Ray motions, cocksure swagger, his pinky brushing against the newer whammy bar implanted into the bridge, all Electra Glide in blues tones. He felt young again, fully in command, at the zenith.

"Hey, it's getting late," came through the wall.

Ringing phones and outdoor car alarms ignored, time frozen as Sean attempted to inhale, to inhabit this purchase. Determined to become one with the guitar, he lit candles and incense, then turned the lights down low and rode the mystical vibe. Because if you couldn't get all woo-woo about a priceless Hendrix Strat that miraculously fell into your fucking lap, what exactly would it take?

The door thumped.

"I'll turn down." He fingered the volume knob.

"Sean, open up." A woman's voice.

He patted his sweaty face dry with a paper towel and slathered a dollop of Ajax liquid dish soap under each arm.

Debbie Schoenberg, his ex-girlfriend waited on the stoop. She was a vegan yoga instructor and turning forty had not diminished any of her charms. Sean felt a rustling in his pajama bottoms.

"Debbie? What are you doing here?"

Her face drooped upon entering his apartment festering with dirty clothes, food-encrusted plates, and trash.

"You look fantastic." Sean attempted a soulful embrace but she allowed only an A-frame hug.

"And you look like hell." Her nose crinkled. "Why do you smell of lemons?" She perched on the coffee table. "You know I'm an empath. Well, I got this bad vibe about you after hearing about that guitar."

Sean forgot any attraction as his stomach congealed. "Pablo told you, already?"

"My cousin's brother-in-law heard it from Mary, who heard

it from Nick in Pablo's band."

"Jesus, I just bought it this morning."

"I'm sensing it may be...cursed." She shook her wavy, shoulder-length hair.

Sean worked his lips together in discomfort. "I was really happy to see you outside, but now you sling this New Age crap?" He paced the floor. "That's why you came?"

"No." The way her eyes fluttered, he felt another tingle. "I'm looking for more work." Debbie scanned the interior. "Wondering if you'd hire me to clean? Once-a-week, then monthly when I get this disaster area under control."

Sean had no scruples, no dignity, nor pride. If that was his only shot to convince her to come back to him, then so be it. "Sure. You want to stay tonight and get started tomorrow?"

She cocked her head. "No, I do not. We'll set up an appointment. Answer your damn phone. I called five times before." Outside, Debbie hesitated. "But sell the guitar. It's bad news for you."

That night, Sean set the Strat beside him in bed—as Hendrix had done before fame and groupies intervened. Dozing off, he dreamed of Jimi. There he sat, cross-legged on Alice in Wonderland's giant bronze mushroom statue in Central Park, wearing a paisley kaftan and tan slacks, hair exploding outward.

"Jimi, how can I get your monstrous tone?"

"That's really beautiful, man, but you need to color your own rainbows, not just dig someone else's."

"I want to sound like you."

"Do your own groovy thing, so when the new rays of

dawn come you're not wearing a Jimi mask. Even I take off my Hendrix mask when I sleep, so I don't startle myself in the morning."

"You wake up before noon, Jimi?"

"Oh, man, morning, evening? It's a state of mind, not a number or street address."

Jimi put on his black ultrasuede hat, with buckle band and purple scarf attached, then slowly floated upwards until he merged with the clouds.

The next afternoon, Sean filled in with Blues Balls at an East Village studio. The quartet planned to record a CD before summer. His new guitar rang majestic through Sean's Fender Super amp.

"You sound amazing on that," bassist Buzz Phillips said. "Must be worth a mint. Heard rumors it belonged to someone famous."

"It's a 1963, so worth a few thousand," Sean lied. "Nickelback's guitarist owned it." Sean realized he could never tour with a Hendrix axe. Too valuable. Just record and rehearse.

They ran through the entire repertoire for their new drummer's benefit. The long-limbed Jeff Brodie approached Sean during a break. "They say you've played with the legends." He smiled. "David Bowie, right?"

"No, but I did sessions with Huey Lewis, Eddie Money, and Al Stewart."

"The 'Year of the Clown' guy?"

"Uh, 'Year of the Cat,' but afterwards."

Brodie didn't seem impressed. "Any other names?"

"And Miles in 1984..."

"Miles? Miles Davis?" Brodie looked stricken.

Sean got lucky when guitarist John Scofield caught the flu and he filled in for two weeks of Miles' New York gigs. Sean felt ecstatic upon being invited to one of the trumpeter's weekly recording sessions. Miles gave no musical direction, so Sean played his heart out, every riff he knew, wailing and screaming on notes and scales and modes, hoping to impress the jazz legend.

Afterwards, the other musicians ducked out, confident they'd return the following weekend, but Sean lingered.

Finally, Miles emerged from the engineer's booth and just stared. That forbidding face—both ancient and ageless—his wide white eyes peering into Sean's soul. Miles hobbled over on his bad hip and spoke in a whispery rasp. "In 1944, when I first sat-in with Billy Eckstein's band, Bird and Diz gave me advice I never forgot: Son, you got to blow all the bullshit out of your horn. It could take months, maybe even years." Miles went quiet.

"Nice." Sean nodded while grinning. "That's an amazing story, Mr. Davis."

Miles' eyes bulged. "No, man. I'm telling you what you need to do." The trumpeter gazed around the empty studio. "Now get a sandwich, go home."

After five more songs, manager Joey Beneducci burst into Blues Balls' rehearsal room. "Sounds great," he shouted. "I landed a summer tour, just need to discuss the deets with Sean." A compact man with a tight Brillo Pad of hair, Joey pumped the other band members' hands as a friendly way of telling them to get lost.

"So you'll be opening for Robert Craze Band."

"Robert Cray? Fantastic."

"Craze," Joey said. "He's the Weird Al Yankovic of Hackensack, does funny blues songs."

"Okay. And money?"

"$400 a gig."

"Per man?"

"Uh, no."

"Can't you negotiate a little higher?"

"I'll ask..."

Sean half-smiled, knowing he wouldn't.

At home in Jersey, Sean reheated leftover pizza that had been reheated the previous night. Tasted like a slab of burnt cardboard. After blazing a joint, he cradled the Hendrix guitar and watched the TCM channel with the volume muted. All those women in party dresses and dapper men in monkey suits made him laugh.

Footsteps sounded outside so he crooked an ear to listen. A scratching at the window. *Squirrel?* Sean killed the lights and humped around on his knees. No one visible through the blinds. His heart leaped when a fist knocked upon his door.

"Who's there?"

"Hunan Palace," a male voice said. "Your egg rolls and chicken-fried rice."

Sean's stomach groaned with desire, but he hadn't ordered them. "Wrong address. Try the neighbors." *A trick?* Head against the door, he heard the delivery guy shuffling away, bike wheels sprocketing along.

Sean relaxed before raising the blinds. Blaring headlights beamed into his dark living room. A giant SUV sat parked across the lane, their lights aimed directly at his window. The high beams eventually dimmed and the hulking black vehicle rumbled off. Everybody knew about the Hendrix Strat. *His* Strat.

Sean spent a restless night, any refrigerator hum or traffic noise amplifying his paranoia.

Next day in Paramus, he bought a Glock, pepper spray, and a Taser. Then Sean drove to Passaic and obtained security bars for his windows and a padlock.

After installing the door lock, he wedged the cross-bars into the window frames, but lacked the right screws to set them. *Tomorrow.* At five, his phone rang.

"Sean, it's Gloria."

"Gloria?"

"Yes, silly." She'd been his best weed client ten years ago in Manhattan. They'd pursued a casual affair, on and off for months.

"Oh, hey." He paused. "Listen, I don't, uh, distribute anymore."

"Not why I'm calling." Her voice breathy. "I wanted to hang again. Everyone's talking about you."

"What?"

"You've come into good times, riding a lucky streak."

A clanging of upended garbage lids came from the alleyway. "Great to hear from you, Gloria." He disconnected and tip-toed to his rear bedroom window. Sean's nostrils detected the tang of liberally applied Right Guard. Just the handyman. The phone rang again.

"No offense, Gloria, but I—"

"This is Cheetah." Sean's old drummer from Vinegar Stains. "Listen, I was hoping to get a small loan from you, bro. Ten grand?"

"What?"

"Okay, five to start." Cheetah chewed on something. "People at Bleeker Street clubs are calling you the Million-Dollar-Man, and since we were so tight..."

"We haven't spoken in forever. You called me an egotistical prick and a burnt-out has-been."

"Yeah, but I meant that in the good way." Cheetah coughed.

A light rapping sounded on Sean's door. "Let me get back to you."

"You fucking suck!" Cheetah yelled.

Sean tucked his Strat in the closet and gripped the pepper spray. *Aim for the chest,* they told him, *fumes rise into the eyes.* Just beyond the chain-lock, Debbie waited, looking fine.

"Thought about what you said." She moved inside, staring at the shag carpeting. "Maybe we give things another try." Her mouth wrinkled. "But could you, clean up? Maybe wash your hair."

Sean drank in her clinging jeans and plunging neckline. "Of course."

Debbie smiled wide. "I brought my overnight bag." She touched his goatee. "Scratchy."

Sean bolted for the bathroom. After showering, he did the unthinkable: shaved. He emerged in a fog of steam and soapy scents, a towel around his waist and another over his shoulders.

Debbie stroked his now smooth chin. "Wow, you look sort of younger but older at the same time."

"Um, thanks."

Their coupling was over in minutes. Sean apologized.

"Just like old times." Debbie massaged his shoulders then brewed a funky tasting lavender tea.

Sean nodded out, but spasmed into awareness thirty minutes later. He could hear Debbie talking from the living room.

"He has so many guitars," she was saying. "I'm not sure which one. It's a Stratocaster, right? I see two, and another in the closet. Which should I grab?"

Sean shook off the dizziness and dressed. Drugged tea? When Debbie squeaked a guitar case toward the door he tackled her. "This was all a set-up to steal my axe. Make some big bucks off your ex."

Debbie lay disoriented on the carpet. "No, no," she said. "The guitar's cursed, evil. I wanted to destroy it, so you don't get possessed. We'll burn sage later on."

"I"ll clear out the bad juju." Sean led Debbie onto the stoop, then tossed her bag after. "You're the curse."

At ten p.m., heavy paws or claws scuttled across his roof. Much bigger than a squirrel.

The blinding headlights showed again. Pissed, Sean tucked the Glock into his jacket and jogged over to the black SUV. He tapped the gun barrel on the tinted window, which eventually motored open.

"What are you guys doing out here every night?"

"Hey, hey, cowboy," said the dark-haired man inside. "Don't hurt yourself with that toy. Antonio told us to stick close. Remind you of your debt. We're going now, but we'll be back."

The vehicle grumbled off.

Sean tried to sleep after midnight. More scratching at his window. Someone ratcheting the unsecured bars, trying to get in. Wearing only boxer shorts, he found his weaponry in the darkness. When a hairy thing, some kind of Sasquatch beast or Jersey Devil forced the window ajar, Sean fired his Taser. The electric darts shot eight feet and implanted into the intruder. A loud sparking provoked an inhuman scream, then the smell of burning hair. Minutes seemed to pass before something heavy crashed to the alleyway fifteen feet below. Neighbors turned on their lights; motion sensor beams illuminated. When Sean leaned out, he saw an oversized and very dead raccoon lying sprawled on its back, smoke rising from singed fur.

Once the police left, the night quieted. Sean got little rest though, and received an unexpected visit from Pablo at ten a.m. "You here for the guitars I promised you?"

"No, man." His face looked ancient, haggard. "I was wrong. That wasn't a Hendrix Strat. Really sorry."

"You're just saying that, so I'll give it to you."

"Nope. Don't want it." Pablo laid photographs across the coffee table. "It belonged to him."

Sean squinted at a familiar balding man playing the exact same Stratocaster. "Goddamn, that's Phil Collins. He's no guitarist."

"Remember, he produced Clapton's records in the eighties? Took guitar lessons from Eric. Didn't pan out, so eventually he sold it."

"So it's worthless?"

"Nah, it's still a vintage Strat, dude. Probably six grand."

"That lady scammed us."

"I talked to your cousin," Pablo said. "He fixed everything."

"Antonio? You went around my back?"

"Take a chill pill. Antonio put the fear of life into the seller. She'll return your ten thou."

Sean shook his head. It was a cursed guitar.

A month later, a sports car's engine revved up outside. Sean walked down and found Antonio grinning inside a shiny Porsche. "Hey, my man. You ever need another loan, let me know. Your credit's good."

Sean noticed Debbie in the passenger seat wearing dark Ray Bans, hair piled-up high, Jersey-style.

"So I got my money back, you got yours, and everybody's

happy. Guitar get sold?"

"Not yet," Antonio said. "I kept it, and paid you that ten, so you could repay my loan. Didn't even charge you interest."

"Oh." Sean understood everything at once. "How did you get Pablo to turn on me?"

"You offered him guitars." Antonio glanced at Debbie. "But see, cash is king."

"But that wasn't a Hendrix guitar. Not worth close to a million."

"Definitely not. You are correct." Antonio nodded. "Remember those flame marks? Hard to decipher, but they were initials: SRV."

"Stevie Ray Vaughn?"

"Yup." Antonio feigned a sad look. "I'll be lucky to get a half-million for the damn thing." Debbie showed a resigned smirk before Antonio shifted gears.

Sean watched them drive west, fading away through a cloud of exhaust.

A dull pain of regret and remorse lingered, though he would endure. Whatever magic Sean summoned playing that Strat came from somewhere deep inside him. He could conjure the same voodoo on any one of his other axes. Sean had a recording session later. The only decision being, which guitar to bring into Manhattan.

EVER AFTER

In the open meadow at the edge of the forest where David had slept, the grass felt wet with dew. He gazed across gentle rolling hills that descended toward unseen houses and farther along to compact, tree-shrouded neighborhoods.

He ran away from home yesterday, his third attempt, and on this jaunt had traveled a mile and even made it through a night outdoors alone. The mild fall temperatures helped. After finishing a cold Pop Tart, David knew hunger would eventually drive him back. Not prepared to yield yet though. It could be a rehearsal for his next escape, where he jumped a train, or lived off the land like tribes he studied in school once did. Every day seemed intense for David and each moment mattered to the extreme.

He guessed it to be after nine a.m. but felt no guilt at missing school. He already understood that everything important in life, all critical learning, transpired outside of classes. Though his stomach churned and growled, he pledged not to surrender until dinnertime.

David turned his attention to nature. Maple trees and dogwoods showed October colors: red, orange, yellow. Closing his eyes, he saw flames, then black smoke. Hallucinations and inner voices visited him whenever they wished.

Just behind, tall pine trees rose in walls with small breaks for animal trails. A stream ran somewhere deep in the woods. He remembered counselors at camp claiming a person could survive for days without food, but wouldn't last long without water. David just needed to locate the chattering brook and drink from it. During the night, after the sirens faded, all manner of sounds came into focus: creaking branches, owls, critters rustling in the bushes. Any time he got nervous or frightened, he reminded himself he was twelve, no longer a child and soon a teenager.

He missed sleeping with his stuffed bear Oliver. His parents confiscated Oliver when David turned eleven and burned the poor creature in their fireplace. *Too old to play with dolls or his imaginary friends.* That was the first time he ran away. Maybe just so they wouldn't see him cry. When David returned six hours later, they locked him in his room without supper.

He scanned the humped meadows for people searching for him. No one. There was the rumble of heavy car traffic approaching from the near distance. Unusual.

Go hide, his friend Charlie told him, in a voice like the wind.

David followed a dirt trail into the shadow forest.

Sunlight spattered through branches. Various birds called or trilled, and the percussive sound of a woodpecker drummed in the distance. He didn't know where he wandered but home was less than a half-hour away. He listened for rushing water among the wind in the branches, the faraway car motors, and hum of machinery. Though he'd never hiked clear through, farms lay on the far side of the woods, with tractors and cows, crop fields and open pastures.

Something white fluttered ahead, but on the incline that rose above the trail. A flag? A garment? Who used this swath of forest beyond small foraging animals? David's only concern was discovery. Some pompous adult outraged to find an errant boy out of school. Determined to report him and ruin the lazy possibility of the day.

Instead, David heard music. Not a flute, but a wind instrument. A soft throaty thing. Straying from the trail, he followed after it, climbing past stumps, and the gnarled corpses of trees clutching one another in death—as if storm-tossed into an embrace. He felt dizzy gazing back down at the trail, but giddy too. The notes played louder. He clambered up a mossy rock outcropping to a ridge, the highest point of the forest.

David scanned the clearing with squat stones set in a circle. A meeting place. On the farthest stone sat a girl dressed in a long skirt and frilly blouse. Old-fashioned clothing. She ignored him and played a recorder, head cocked at an angle, so that only the bob of her hairstyle and chin showed in the clerestory light. David listened for a time, then cautiously approached—as one might toward a skittish deer. Music ceased.

"Finally," the girl said. "I've been waiting ages for you to join me."

"What?" David suddenly felt self-conscious, his clothes and brown hair mussed from sleep.

"I saw you last night, lying in the grass," she said. "I called out, but you must not have heard me."

"Really?" David squinted at her, looked away, then back quickly. Not a hallucination. Not Charlie or Brunnie, the imaginary friends his parents had sent him to therapists to dispel. He thought of his required daily medication. Thankfully, no pills for the last two days, and he felt so much clearer. "Who are you?"

She laughed, combing a hand through her long bangs. "Priscilla," she said. "But call me Pid."

David liked the name Pid. It reminded him of Pip from a Dickens story the school librarian read aloud last year. "Where are you from?"

"From my home, of course." She crackled over dead branches toward him, then studied David as if a museum display. "You smell smoky. Did you build a campfire last night?" Her eyes widened.

David shook his head. "No."

"That's strange." She plucked a leaf from his hair. "I thought I saw flames flickering in the distance."

He shuddered. At twelve, David hated girls in his class. They thought they were so smart and talked and talked—as if that was important. While boys might punch another boy, girls would insult and torment a boy with ridicule. Much worse. David *did* understand that at some point he was expected to marry one.

His singular hope lay in older girls, those teenagers charged with babysitting when his parents attended dinners or parties. They either listened to David's wild stories, or just let him do as he pleased while they watched television and ate snacks. Pid looked about thirteen, taller and calmer than his classmates. Assured but not a damn show-off.

"Is your house on the other side of these woods?" he asked.

"In a manner of speaking." She smiled. "Beyond, beneath, betwixt."

For an instant, David felt uncertain. He gripped her forearm.

Pid's expression showed a mix of amusement and slight annoyance. "Checking if I'm real? Ha, I was about to do the same with you." She beckoned him. "Let's leave now. This is where the Dark Watchers meet at sunset."

"Dark Watchers?"

"Tall, silent. They wear hooded black cloaks. You can never see their faces. Never ever."

She had to be kidding, but David scanned their surroundings.

"Come on," Pid said. "Time is flashing by. Let's go play while we can."

"You still like to...play?"

"That's all I ever do." She twirled her recorder as if a baton. "Mostly alone, so if someone else joins me, I'm absolutely thrilled." Pid descended from the high ground to a saddle below.

Follow her, Brunnie whispered.

David caught up. "I'm hungry," he said. "I was searching for water when I saw you."

"The stream's ahead. Want to go skinny-dipping?" Pid

giggled. "Just kidding."

She led him to the brook that snaked through the forest, widening into pools, spattering over rock upthrusts. David drank and drank, then washed his face. Afterwards, Pid showed him plants and berries to eat. He soon forgot his hunger.

She initiated elaborate games involving pirate ships, a settlers' cabin in the wild west, prisoners escaping a German castle, and plans for a bank robbery. Pid's imagination boundless. David only queasy when they played house and discussed their ten children. Time became elastic. He wondered had their shenanigans spanned three hours, all day? Whenever a break showed in the canopy of trees, he studied the sky. Light blue and no signs of night.

Their make-believe took place across large boulders, atop giant tree stumps, and even inside a dilapidated shack with a missing wall. Moss sprouted on the weather-stained wood and the corners were threaded with spiderwebs.

"I should probably go back now." David didn't want to leave. Home meant punishment, school, and therapy sessions. He *did* need to eat real food though, and not get lost in the woods after sunset.

"Wait." Pid squeezed his shoulder. "I've saved the best for last." She pointed to a wall of rocks with a slender opening.

"What's in there? A cave?" David had no interest in dark places filled with bats and dripping, slimy liquid.

"Yes," she said. "But more important, it's a portal."

David stared at her, mystified. "A portal?"

"A passageway. It's how I got here, the way back to where I come from." She smiled. "Come on. Unless you're chicken."

Insulted, David led the way. "Sounds crazy. Doesn't make any sense."

They walked through the cleft in the giant slab, then ducked to move inside the tunnel. It slanted downward and became pitch black.

Pid lit a candle she plucked from her skirt pocket. "It's just ahead."

"Good," he replied, sensing this adventure was a mistake.

They arrived at a wider space where old clothes lay scattered. Drunks or hobos perhaps spent nights there during heavy rain and snowstorms. In the center, David saw a pool, the water muddy—even oily. As he watched, bubbles formed and steam ghosted from the surface.

"What is it, a sulfur pit?" He didn't smell that gassy fart odor.

"Ignore what it looks like," Pid said. "That's just magic to scare strangers away. It's the portal I went through last night." She put her arms over her head and pantomimed a plunge.

"You come here a lot? And from somewhere else?"

"No." Pid looked sad. "My home is always the same. But the portal brings me all over the world. Usually to a forest. Somewhere away from people." Desperation flickered in her eyes. "Kids mostly run away, or think I'm strange. You're the only one who played with me all day." She turned toward the pool. "That's why I'm showing you." She nodded. "You have to go home now. But maybe, just maybe I'll return here tomorrow or the next day." Pid's face squinched.

"I'm not sure though. If you come back and find this pool, then you know we can play again."

"I'd like that."

"Again and again."

"Forever and ever." He wanted to believe it.

"And ever after," she said and sighed.

David poked a stick into the frothing pool. "You came up through there? It would burn you, coat you with mud."

"No." She bent down and dipped a hand into the thick waters then lifted it out. "Not hot and see, my skin is clean."

David saw no redness or dark stain on her. "Oh, okay." It confused him.

"You really have to go. They come out at dusk." Pid brought him back into the forest. Long tree shadows crossed their path and the sky overhead looked hazy, vaporous. "We're going to gallop like horses. The Dark Watchers are slow. They'll never catch us."

And together they ran the trail leading back south, jumping and splashing across the brook, under felled trunks, up the incline, and out of the woods to the hilly grasslands. David stopped, gasping for air. When he turned, Priscilla had vanished. "Pid!" No response. He thought he heard distant music, but felt uncertain of everything.

David staggered back the mile to his parents' house, imagining their lecture. He'd endure it though for a hearty meal. Tomorrow he could sneak out after school to find Pid again. With a flashlight and snacks.

Remember what you did?

Don't go home.

The medication kept his special friends at a distance, as well as erasing his short-term memories, but it had been days without pills.

Thank you, his stuffed bear Oliver told him.

Why did his parents always argue, throw plates and books at one another? Why did they hit each other, and when they were done, beat him, punish him? David started to remember. The older boys at the school playground talked about pranks to pull on parents to keep them occupied, to keep them from hassling their kids. Were they exaggerating, lying? David had listened intently.

Afterwards, he went home and extinguished the pilot lights, then turned the gas on in the oven and atop the stove. He closed all the doors downstairs while he heard his parents shouting and cursing upstairs. He used a long fuse that ended in the kitchen wrapped in old newspapers.

David paused halfway on his trek home. Did he actually do that? The real and the imaginary had no boundary within him. That's why the therapy sessions. What happened? Did he run away before doing it, or was it after? All his parents' fault, never allowing him to invite real friends over, isolating him. Of course he befriended Oliver, and then Charlie and Brunnie. They were all he had. Until today. Until Pid.

The sky held a muted, dusky light when he reached the hill overlooking his house. Even in the new dark he could see the ruins. Burnt black and brown, mostly crumpled, and still moist from water dousing the flames. Safety lamps shone out front by the driveway, but no one was around. Approaching, he noticed gouges where large vehicles had been parked in the grass and dirt earlier.

The back porch remained standing, connected to a solid back wall, the rest of the house devastated. David climbed over the yellow tape to lie down on the porch amid the smell of smoky wood and burnt wiring. Though only about eight p.m., he was exhausted.

David woke with a start sometime after dawn, shivering in the cold. He heard engines approaching. Big vehicles. In a panic, he ran and climbed the hill until he found a place to crouch in the tall grass and watch safely. It wasn't really his fault, but he knew the police wanted results, someone to take responsibility. With his parents not present, David was the only donkey to pin the blame on.

People walked around the ruined structure. They stared off in every direction, hands shading their eyes. One resembled the town sheriff, another the school principal, while others were firemen. David lay flat so that even with binoculars they wouldn't spot him.

He felt hungry, tired, dirty, confused.

You have to go back, Charlie told him.

Back to the woods, Brunnie added.

Find Pid, they said in unison.

David moved, first crawling, then eventually scuttling along, hunched over. He had traveled a quarter mile when he first heard the barking from behind. Dogs. They unleashed dogs to find him. Did they imagine he was dead, or alive and a menace? Even in his weakness, with voices caroming about inside his skull, David began to sprint as fast as possible. He searched for familiar landmarks. Maybe someday he'd look back on this as a grand adventure, his rocket-blast to a new life. *Pid will understand.*

Thank you for avenging me, his bear Oliver whispered.

Another five minutes and David reached the break in the forest wall, everything the same. He felt sick—though his stomach was empty—so he caught his breath while listening for the recorder playing. All he could hear was wind thrashing the branches, the brook running in the distance, and as he hesitated, the throaty howl and yawp of beasts on his trail. He estimated himself to be a half-mile out in front.

David dashed downward, tripping over roots, to eventually lose his balance and land in the stream. He barely noticed the scrapes or the bump rising on his forehead. A crackling sound nearby. He glanced behind. *The Dark Watchers?* Trees and their tangle of branches threw odd almost human-shaped shadows. *Find the cave.* It lay beyond the giant stump and past the decrepit three-walled shack. Finally he spotted the wall of boulders fused into a hillside and rushed toward the entry.

Being early in the day, more light penetrated the cave's interior. David found the hollowed-out center with the pool. He squatted down and squinted into its murky water. Then he dipped a hand in. Warm, very warm, but not scalding. "Pid," he cried out and it echoed. Something flew by his ear. *It's just a bird,* Charlie said, though David knew it was a leathery bat. He circled the pit and studied the slabs of rock, where he found a knapsack holding a stale sandwich, a child's hat, and a yellow hair ribbon that might belong to Pid.

Moving back to the lip of the pool, he gazed downward, hesitant.

It's a portal, Charlie said. *A passageway.*

She's waiting, Brunnie said.

"You close your eyes and hold your breath until you feel about to explode," Pid had instructed him yesterday. David thought he heard her recorder notes bubbling up through the pool. Then came barking and wailing, the hounds in the forest, drawing closer. Pressing hands together above his head, David dove deep into the brown soupy waters. The bottom of the pool funneled into a tight passage walled by stone. He kept swimming forward.

Pid sat with her parents around the dinner table. "I met the most interesting boy in the woods yesterday."

Her parents glanced at one another. "Really? Are you sure, Priscilla?" her mother said. "Another of your *friends.*" Her brow scrunched.

"Ha-ha, no," Pid replied. They never believed her. "I liked him. He was special."

"We think you are too." Her father's mouth twitched.

"Now eat your dessert," her mother said. "And look, you burned your hand. It's all red. Please stay away from the stove, Pid."

Both adults moved into the kitchen then shut the door tight behind them. Pid pressed an empty glass against the outer door to listen.

"Jesus," her father said. "We're getting old and she still looks thirteen. Should've gone to college two years ago."

"The doctors told us it was an extremely rare case." Her mother paused. "They might be wrong. She could start developing at any time. It's possible…"

"We've had to move, take her out of schools to avoid gossip and questions." Her father sighed. "Now we're on the outskirts of Danford Falls, totally isolated."

"Well, we can't stay in this town," her mother said. "Did you read the papers? A house burned down a few miles away. Possibly arson. And three children have vanished into thin air in the six months since we arrived."

"I don't know if I can take it much longer. We might need to put her into—"

"Remember what the doctor said," her mother whispered. "She may not make it past thirty."

Pid lost interest and wandered out to the porch. She had heard many variations of these conversations. Every day was magic time: passageways, portals, divergent realities. Tomorrow she would go back into the woods. Maybe David would be there, or maybe she'd lure a brand new friend into her world to play with, again and again, forever and ever. And ever after.

DINNER PARTY
EXIT STRATEGY

"So I *have* to attend the gathering?" Jacob Walden said. His wife snuggled with her gassy labradoodle on the living room couch of their Pasadena condo, so he maintained distance.

"Yes." Suzanne raked a hand through her dark hair.

Was it straight and she had it curled, or was it wavy and she straightened it, then curled it?

"You're finally getting promoted," Suzanne said. "Ridiculous that Armand Zucker is still running things. What is he, ninety?"

"Google lists different birth dates. Probably hired someone to muddy the water." Jacob shook his Martini. "I'd guess eighty-five."

"With a wife half his age." Suzanne sighed in disgust. "He looks a hundred to me."

"What does a hundred look like?"

"Like death. The walking dead."

Jacob gasped when the vodka gulp hit him. "So what are

you saying?"

"That you're going, but I'm not." She frowned. "I mean it's clear over in San Bernardino. Someone has to stay with Pizzles."

God he loathed that name. Something British royalty would name their pampered pets.

"Fine," Jacob said. "I'm curious to meet his wife Bianca."

"Bianca Auberge?" Suzanne shoved Pizzles off the sofa. The dog circled about in confusion before collapsing dejected in a corner. "She'll be there?"

Jacob nodded. "Didn't you read the invite? 'Your hosts, Armand and Bianca'."

"Nobody has seen her in five years. No photographs." Suzanne stood, as if the new information had raised the DEFCON level. "She retired from modeling at forty. Apparently developed an extreme skin sensitivity. Breaks out in rashes, hives." She flexed a cruel smile. "I *must* go."

Jacob drove east on I-210, the rear-view obscured by a back-up dress Suzanne had slung on a hangar. "Your clothes are fine," he told her. "The invite said casual."

"Look, you came from Ass Fork, Arizona where casual really means casual."

"It's Ash Fork."

Suzanne laughed. "They stuck a fork in your ass and said, get going, you're done here."

"It's autumn in my soul."

"Jesus, is that poetry? The world's too expensive to be a poet anymore."

Jacob winced. "Armand doesn't want to give up power, running things."

Suzanne sniffed. "He'll remain Executive Director or some bogus title so he can pretend to be in charge. Nothing kills a person faster than retirement." She grinned. "With a promotion and a raise, who cares who's the top dog?" She squeezed his shoulder. "We'll finally have our timeshare in Hawaii, and I can open a little French restaurant in Santa Barbara."

Sometimes Jacob felt as if riding a moving walkway at an airport. He could either stand still or try to pass other people ahead. In a recurring dream, he went against the flow—causing total chaos. "I won't ask Armand for the raise."

"That's why I love you, Jake. Because you take orders and just wait your turn in the corporate roulette."

Jacob concentrated on the manic Southern California drivers careening through the lanes. His wife's compliments always landed as insults.

"Respect," she said. "At Noblesse Academy, they taught us girls to do whatever necessary to get ahead."

He turned up the radio until he recognized it as "Taking Care of Business" by Bachman-Turner Overdrive.

"Remember, don't overstay our welcome," Suzanne said. "We eat, then you two smoke cigars."

"I hate cigars."

"Not tonight." She poked him. "We leave right after Armand's offer. No time to change his mind."

"Sure."

"Anyway, we need an exit strategy."

"Will you use Pizzles?"

She crinkled her eyes. "My poor little doobie-boobie, home alone."

Beyond San Bernardino's downtown, Jacob exited into the outskirts. Palm trees and strip malls: Whole Foods, Staples, Home Depot, and Target. At Mesa Seca Lane, he motored upward until they went through a security gate on a private road to "L'il Xanadu."

"Wow." Suzanne pointed. Roadside cages and pens displayed tigers, two gorillas, ostriches, and a zebra. The climbing route ended a hundred feet from the summit. Beyond the rise lay green foothills, the beginnings of the San Bernardino Mountains.

"I heard the house was huge," Jacob said.

While the two-story modern structure backed-up against the hill looked impressive, he guessed it held maybe eight bedrooms. Office gossips had mentioned dozens. Clearly just exaggerated second-hand reports.

They entered into the living room. Faux Roman columns rose to the twelve-foot ceiling, while statues of multi-armed Indian goddesses appeared as if they'd been spray-painted gold. Dusty antique tapestries covered the walls and a giant painting that resembled flayed sides of raw beef hung at room center.

Jacob and Suzanne wandered through the assembled guests. Strangers. Finally, Jacob recognized another coworker, a groveling two-faced, ass-kisser.

"Marcus." Jacob gripped his shoulder. "It's good to see you."

"Aha," Marcus said, his eyes goggling. "This is your wife? You described her as mature, matronly."

"I never—"

"No matter," he said. "Delighted to meet you, Susie."

She emphasized, "Su-zanne."

Marcus chortled. "Here to beg a few scraps from the table, eh?"

"Same as you." Jacob gazed around. "Where are our hosts?"

"Right. This is your first visit here." He laughed, all smarm and forced frivolity. "Bianca's never attended before, but Armand usually joins us at dinner."

"We thought it might be bigger," Suzanne said. "Considering his wealth."

Marcus allowed a flat smile. "Because of San Bernardino temperatures, Armand built most of the house within the hillside. Very cool in the air-conditioned interior. Tennis courts, an Olympic-sized pool, a gym, sauna, stables, the works." He yawned as if it had been oft-repeated. "This part is just the tip of an iceberg."

A deafening Chinese gong rang and someone announced, "Please be making your way into the dining area."

A long slender table with place cards awaited. Thankfully, Jacob was seated next to Suzanne, not near Marcus. Seatbelts dangled from the chairs.

"I can't wait to see Bianca," Suzanne said. "Probably in some beekeeper suit to protect her skin. Heavy makeup too."

As servants poured wine, a cranking noise of pulleys and gears sounded from the fifteen-foot ceiling. A few audible gasps came when a slim wooden and metal closet made its herky-jerky descent into the room.

"What is that?" Suzanne gripped Jacob's hand.

"An old-fashioned elevator, I think." He smiled. "What a dramatic way to make an entrance."

The chamber halted, hanging in space. The servers ignored the spectacle and brought salad plates to the guests.

Suzanne took one bite, then held a cloth napkin over her mouth.

Jacob asked, "What is it?"

"Organic meal-worm salad, with slices of gluten-free bark," the server behind him said. "An annual tradition here."

Guests cleaned their plates, grim faces set in endurance mode. Perhaps a test. Hoops you had to jump through to curry favor with Armand. As Jacob lifted a viscous fork-full, a fanfare of horns began.

The gathered froze in astonishment when a seemingly naked woman strode into the dining area followed by a uniformed marching band. Jacob noted she was unblemished, absolutely gorgeous.

"Don't stare, but don't look away," Suzanne whispered. "Maybe this is normal."

The woman circled the entire room before sitting by the head of the table. Jacob realized that she wore a sheer type of gown, so transparent as to seem invisible—except up close.

"Welcome, welcome. I am Bianca Auberge. My husband Armand will join us momentarily." She gestured toward the suspended closet. "I thank you for visiting our humble chateau."

In the nervous silence that followed, Suzanne said, "That's a very chic outfit."

"This old thing?" Bianca touched the gauzy material. "I have extreme dermal sensitivity," she said. "I can only wear certain silks and satin." Bianca frowned. "My wardrobe is custom made to not provoke hideous rashes." She gazed outward. "I so envy you ladies here tonight who can wear whatever you wish."

The women around the table smiled back with a Serengeti fierceness.

Jacob felt uncomfortable having Suzanne nearby, gauging his reactions. Their ten-year marriage a routine, a tax benefit, now reduced to a bi-monthly date night.

"Your husband is above?" Jacob pointed. "What's he doing?"

Bianca erupted in raucous laughter. "Armand's private elevator runs from his upstairs quarters to dinner." She restrained herself. "It's also a water closet..."

"A what?" Suzanne said.

"A loo," Bianca replied. "An indoor outhouse, if you will. At my husband's age, he feels it best to multitask, to combine an elevator with a bathroom for efficiency."

There was nothing to do but stare upward agog as servers removed the salad plates. They soon returned with steamy soup bowls.

Suddenly a mammoth flushing occurred, liquids sluiced through pipes snaking along the ceiling. A great ratcheting noise followed and the elevator dropped gradually, inch by inch, to finally land in the corner. Accordion gates slid open; a door swung wide as cloudy vapors emanated from the fogged interior. Two servants used peacock fans to dissipate the haze.

Out of the mists staggered Armand Zucker in a huge cowboy

hat; a once tall fellow who stooped at present, his body skeletal. "Greetings, friends," he spoke into a wireless microphone on his collar. "I finished my business, so now let's get down to yours."

Guests gave him a standing ovation, which he shooed away with a bony hand.

Armand's outfit was best described as a Texas gambler visiting Las Vegas—bolo tie and piping on both jacket and trousers. "Don't wait on me," he said. "Eat up while it's hot."

Guests looked pallid, hoping the eel head soup course had been forgotten. Jacob bravely took a spoonful, his stomach in immediate revolt.

A tremendous vibration shook the house, causing the chandelier to swing, empty chairs to topple, and soup to slop across the table. Lights blinked, while the foundation groaned. Then it stopped.

Armand cackled. "The San Andreas Fault runs right under San Bernardino. We get tremblers every day. Adds a little spice." He winked at Bianca. "Fasten your seatbelts."

Everyone buckled-up. After a course of breaded octopus, the dinner broke for dessert served in the living room. Guests split into groups and took self-guided tours of the vast house.

"Divide and conquer," Suzanne told Jacob. "We'll compare notes later. Remember, do whatever you have to. Hawaii awaits us."

Left alone in the living room, Jacob inspected the gory-looking painting. A familiar woman sidled over. "Francis Bacon. His work is so raw, so intestinal." She cocked her head.

"Lydia, right?"

"Yes, we dated just before you married...her." She struggled to smile. "I've always wondered. Why didn't you follow-through? You basically ghosted me."

"Sorry." He studied the petite attractive woman and wondered too. Stuck in a dreary marriage to a ruthless social climber, Lydia suddenly seemed very intriguing to Jacob. Then a familiar scent wafted up.

"Are you still teaching dressage at Malibu Stables?"

"Yes." She nodded, eyes curious. "Why?"

Lydia had been perfect: wavy brown hair, a nice figure, and a sarcastic but flirtatious expression. Except for the tang of horse manure she carried from work. No amount of showering and perfume could remove or mask it. So in a clinch, he smelled that odor and lost his resolve. However, months after their dating, whenever his nose detected actual horseshit, he imagined Lydia and grew aroused. Clearly this subject should not be broached now. Jacob could barely explain it to his last three therapists. "What brings you here?"

"I married your coworker, Chad."

"Oh, right," Jacob said.

Bianca Auberge, wearing a black silk kimono, interrupted. "Let me show you the den, Jacob, darling." She led him down a long dim hallway. Doors on either side opened, spilling guests into the corridor.

"I wanted to chat privately since you're headed straight to the top," she said in the den.

"Armand mentioned that?"

"People invited here either get fired or promoted," she replied. "You follow orders, never ruffle any feathers, so I'm confident in my prediction."

"Well, that's—"

"Shush for a moment." Bianca tapped her hearing aid.

"What?"

"A microphone's planted in Armand's jacket. I can hear his conversations."

Jacob stared at her.

"Don't judge," she said. "He's ancient. I monitor his health condition so I can prepare a public reaction of concern, shock, or sorrow."

"I see."

Bianca remained focused on eavesdropping. "Your wife's alone with Armand."

"Are you jealous?"

She rolled her eyes. "Of course not. Suzanne is basically offering herself. I love how ruthless she is." Bianca's face drooped.

"Well?"

"Suzanne just told your tragic story," Bianca said. "About the grenade clutched between your knees that went off in combat. Your manhood blown clear into the atmosphere."

"That's absurd," Jacob said. "I wasn't a soldier."

Bianca nodded. "She clarified, it happened during basic training for the National Guard."

"Unbelievable."

"No, it's perfect." Bianca's expression lit up. "Armand will have Suzanne and I'll have you." She fluttered her eyes. "Because of dermal sensitivity, no one can touch my skin. But you'll watch me, admire me as I... Well, you know."

Was he in too deep to run? "It's raining in my heart."

Bianca soured. "God, I hate poetry."

"May I talk to Armand now?"

She smiled evil. "Naturally."

A floor panel opened beneath him and Jacob slid down a metal heating duct. He popped out of the slanted aperture onto a plush sofa.

The chair at an antique desk swiveled about revealing Armand, massive cowboy hat and a cigar clutched in one hand. "Come on over, pardner."

Jacob obeyed, tucking into a leather armchair.

"You probably know why you're here tonight."

"Well, not exactly."

"No time for modesty." Armand's dull eyes became laser-focused. "I need you to run things. Going to put you in our penthouse suite."

Jacob felt stunned. "The Pasadena building?"

"No, the tall one you can see from Highway 101. Oxnard."

"I, uh, forgot about that holding."

Armand grinned. "You'll be the king of the castle, the Wizard of Ox."

"What are my new duties?"

"Maximizing cash upflow to top management."

Jacob leaned forward. "But how?"

"Theoretical optimization. You'll be proactive, a proactivist."

"A what?"

Armand sighed. "You'll develop new ideas."

"For us to market?"

"Hell no." Armand frowned. "You'll leak product ideas for other companies to develop in a rush to compete with us, then we swoop in, buy them out, destroy them."

"Really?"

"What part of Vulture Capitalism do you not understand?"

"I..."

"We have an obligation to our stockholders." Armand blew his nose. "Your good wife shared your painful history."

"I never fought in any war."

"Sure. It happened at a firing range, in the grenade grotto." He tamped out the cigar. "Your family jewels blown sky high. Very Hemingway."

Jacob sighed. "I still have them."

"Fine, fine." Armand's face brightened. "Because you'll need brass balls." The old man twisted his lips. "Part of the deal is Suzanne helping brighten up my golden years."

"What?"

"It was her idea." Armand looked Jacob over. "I can use Suzanne in my performance assessment branch."

"For job termination?"

"Relocation is the preferred term." Armand began flossing his thin teeth.

Jacob stared away. "It's the winter of our disconnect."

"Am I talking or are you listening?" Armand spit into a cuspidor. "My wife Bianca has taken a hankering to you. You're in good shape for near sixty."

"I'm forty-nine."

"See, I can't touch her. Damn dermatologists." Armand slapped his desk. "So you'll be her court eunuch. Hear her thoughts, type her screenplay, read her memoir."

Can I get away? Jacob wondered. *Could I survive alone in a mountain cabin or a shack out in the desert? I'd be lonely, but I'm lonely now, and disgusted. Is peace or freedom attainable in this life, or are they just imaginary conceits?*

"First assignment: downsize your entire department," Armand said. "You're moving up, so they have to go."

"Some are friends," Jacob replied. "I hunt and fish with Ted."

"We can go helicopter hunting together in Alaska." Armand winked. "No elk can outrun my pilot. Dynamite fishing is really something too. Boom! They float to the surface and you scoop 'em up in a big net."

The ground shook violently again.

"You'll get a 40% raise," Armand said. "I'll double your salary if you take it in cryptocurrency." He paused. "Triple it if you take it in Zimbabwe dollars."

"I need to think this over." Jacob rose to leave.

"Fine. Tell me by morning." Armand limped after him. "*Yes* means you get a Porsche Cayenne Turbo. *No* means a PT Cruiser." He laughed. "Either way, your wife's my new hatchet-girl."

Jacob exited into the dark hallway, encountering disoriented guests. "East or west?" one man asked. Faint yellowy light emanated from sodium lamps affixed to the walls.

"Jake, it's you." Suzanne embraced him. "The power went out after the last earthquake. Did you get your raise, can we leave?"

"Yes, but which way?" he asked. They reached a crossroads where the corridors split off.

"I'm not sure." Her voice trembled. "You go that direction, I'll take the passage to the left. We'll meet back here in twenty minutes."

Before he could argue, Suzanne vanished. Jacob tried various doorknobs along the hall until one opened. An ancient woman reclined on a poster bed, the flames from an unseen fireplace illuminating her features.

"Hello, ma'am." He approached her. "Are you Bianca's aunt?"

A groan emanated from the frilly nightcap and nightgown. "No, I'm Armand's first wife. His high school sweetheart."

"Really? You stayed on after your divorce?"

"We're not divorced." She drank something syrupy. "Servants call me Mother Zucker."

Jacob noticed the half-eaten wedding cake, then smoke. "Uh, Mrs. Zucker. The corner of your room is on fire." He pointed to the flames curling around a table and curtains.

"It's a controlled burn," she replied. "This house is made of stone and a forest of wood. We need to thin it out on occasion." When smoke began to gust over, she attached an old-fashioned oxygen mask to her face.

Jacob studied her and the room, started to say something, but instead left.

Moving on, he sensed the corridor slant downward until the

floor became slippery and wet, the air salty. Ahead, Jacob could see a single-file line of bedraggled people approaching. They clutched a long rope and looked both soaked and somewhat scorched.

"Stop. Where are you going?" asked their leader in a nautical uniform. "We're heading to the ship's aft to escape. The hull is breached, taking on seawater, and there's a fire in the engine room. Come with us, man."

"We're on a boat?"

The line of passengers gazed at him in astonishment then continued hiking upward.

Jacob could hear water sloshing about, so he turned right at another crossroads in the endless passageway. The floor leveled off. It was dank and windy with a feculent odor. Out of the darkness, a figure clutched Jacob.

"Take me with you," said a man encrusted in grime.

"Marcus? I thought you'd been here before." Jacob felt unexpected sympathy for the fool.

"I lied. First visit," he said. "Armand flushed me down a drain pipe. Means I'm being demoted." Marcus coughed. "Scuttlebutt is that you got promoted. Bring me along to Oxnard, please."

"You're not part of my team."

"I'll do anything. Don't let me be sent to Zucker's chemical plant in Juarez."

"Mexico?"

"*Yes,* hazardous chemicals and trigger-happy drug lords."

"I just want to leave this stupid gathering."

Another group appeared. Jacob didn't recognize them as

they hadn't been at dinner. Their formal clothes were soiled and torn, faces filthy, and they reeked of body odor.

"Is that you, Jacob?" a man in glasses asked. "We're lost. Do you know the way out?"

"Oliver?" Jacob said to the accountant. "I haven't seen you downtown in months."

"No." Oliver wiped his sweaty face. "My department came to the annual party and were to be relocated to a new branch. Instead, we've been wandering Armand's house since then. No office, no salary." His voice sounded raspy. "We found a food storage unit a mile further east. Need sunlight though."

Jacob realized that they had attended Armand's last party, a year ago. "Keep going. Eventually you'll hit the Pacific Ocean."

The besmirched group grunted, then continued on.

"Your only hope is to leave out the front door," Marcus said. "Alone."

"Without Suzanne?"

Marcus led him over to an antique nickelodeon machine and inserted a quarter.

Jacob pressed his eyes to the viewer. It showed weary guests traipsing through corridors, then Bianca trying on expensive nightgowns, and finally Suzanne in a harem costume dancing for Armand as two servants feather-dusted his groin. "Okay," he eventually said.

Using Marcus's compass, they walked due west for what seemed like miles. Whenever other guests tried to dissuade their direction, they ignored them. Eventually they reached a large oak door, and with both men using their shoulders, it opened into the empty dining room.

Marcus peered through the connecting door to the entryway and living room. "Armed guards everywhere. What now?"

Jacob noticed the elevator closet. "I'm riding that electric outhouse upstairs. Maybe we can escape from there."

"Sorry, I'm risk-averse," Marcus said. "But if you should make it, send help back."

"Will do."

Jacob worked the manual gears until the odd contraption rose. The second floor appeared empty. Peeking out a window, he saw the driveway outside lit up with Klieg lights. Security paced the parking area.

Instead, he found a skylight, and forming a pedestal of furniture, pushed his way out onto the roof. Stars shone overhead; the night air felt cool and refreshing. Jacob's phone had been lost during the last trembler, but he guessed it to be late, three a.m.

Rather than chancing capture by security, Jacob went east to where the house's roof merged with the hillside. From there, he hiked up the scrappy terrain. At the top of the mound, the ground leveled off into bushes before a gradual rise on foothills toward the Santa Bernardino Mountains. Jacob rested, eventually nodding off.

When he woke, the first colors of dawn showed to the east. A young girl of seven or eight, in pink dress with a bow, stood nearby. She dug into the dirt using a plastic shovel and pail.

"What are you doing?" Jacob asked.

"I'm planting seeds." She returned to work.

"Will plants grow in this desert climate?"

"Succulents will," the girl said. "And I have wildflower seeds. They're beautiful and live a short life, sort of like us."

Jacob couldn't argue.

"I need your help though." She pointed at the foothill. "Keep planting until you run out."

"What about back there?"

She frowned. "Your only chance is to keep moving, away."

He scooped seeds from the pail then filled his scuffed jacket pockets. Jacob concentrated, digging and planting, digging and planting. When finished, he turned. The girl was gone. Two rabbits scampered about, and farther away, a coyote watched them.

As a young man, Jacob had seen old movies that featured grizzled prospectors, mountain men living alone in shacks, bearded and mumbling to themselves. He had feared of someday becoming one. To be isolated, detached from the agreed-upon collective reality of schools, marriage, work, retirement. Now he no longer felt afraid. Everything ahead would be a challenge, with nothing guaranteed. And yet that was an improvement. Jacob smiled. He'd escaped; a new life awaited. At present, he just needed to find water.

SCRAPING THE BUCKET

She watched her husband drink his beer in the amphitheater as the loud music washed over them. So joyous in the moment. What a shame.

"I am so fucking psyched for this concert." He leaned forward as if listening intently. "Wow, sounds really different."

"He's sounded different for like twenty years." She studied him.

"I mean compared to the records I own."

"Those albums were done forty years ago, some even fifty."

"Maybe so." He scratched his head. "Album is a weird word. Sort of like stipend, or dumbwaiter or feckless."

"We may as well be speaking Latin, or any dead language."

"This is so cool." He peered at the stage through their binoculars. "But why do the band members have spotlights on them while he's standing at center stage in darkness?"

"He's a man of constant shadow."

"Glad tonight's concert was on my list. I just don't remember it being on there."

"It definitely was." She smiled with authority. This would be a tough evening.

"I wanted to see him, but he doesn't seem happy to be here."

"He's actually quite chipper tonight." She turned. "He hasn't spit once."

"Patti Smith spits in concert. I think it means she's really into it." He paused. "If she sprayed you, would you ever wash your face again?"

"I'd leave the concert right then and there. But that's just me."

"So these shows really go on for two or three hours?" he asked, stifling a yawn.

"Yup. You get your $115 worth in time with a legend."

"And it's all new or unrecognizable material?"

"No one ever accused him of being an entertainer." She squeezed his hand. *How could she reassure him?* "There's a good chance he'll play one big famous song."

That response made his face brighten. "So then the crowd stands up and we sing along together?"

"No. On the way home, one of us will say, 'I think the last song might have been his biggest hit.'"

"Oh, great." He gazed around.

She noticed some audience members sat rapt with attention, others slumped on the brink of dozing off, while a few couples resembled younger versions of them—perhaps attending for the same reason.

"What else is on my list? The *Star Wars* movies?"

"You completed that entry last year." She rubbed his shoulder. "You saw them all."

"Really? Even the bad ones?"

"You insisted."

He nodded, face showing an ancient weariness. "I didn't realize until afterwards that I only ever enjoyed the first three."

"Listen." She slapped his knee. "This song has a hook." *Try to cheer him up.*

"Amazing. He stopped writing hooks decades ago."

Around them the audience bustled with enthusiasm, the joy of vague recognition.

"How do you think he destroyed his voice?"

"Cigarettes, booze, coke, divorce," she replied.

"Divorce?" He turned toward her. "You mean an ex-wife got half his voice in the settlement?" When she didn't laugh, he continued. "Hook or no hook, I still don't recognize the damn song."

"That's not really the idea of this." She watched his jaw tightening, remembered he spoke of a dull pain in his back teeth. A gum infection?

"It's just a task to complete then."

"Exactly."

"Wait, something's happening."

"He's moving from guitar to piano," she said with excitement. "That signals the end of his lazy mid-tempo songs and the beginning of the slow ballads segment."

"Can't even see his face. Why does he wear that big absurd

hat?"

"He's over seventy-five. Maybe his hair's gone, or he doesn't like what he has, or he never washes it."

"I like to wear hats sometimes."

"They're generally very flattering on older men." She squeezed his arm.

"I'm just fifty-seven..."

She didn't reply.

"In the future we'll wear helmets and thick, padded environment suits so we don't feel things anymore."

She sniffed. "I'm on medication that achieves that effect right now."

"I think I started my list too young," he said. "Shouldn't we do them as close to death as possible?"

"By that time, most items on your list will be gone or dead."

"You mean like seeing The Ramones at CBGB or eating at Carnegie Deli in Manhattan?"

"Yes." She watched him tapping a foot along with the listless dirge but soon gave up.

"Fuck, what's next on my list?"

"Let's not discuss that," she said. "We're here to endure, I mean, enjoy the concert."

"But I'm not. No one is. He certainly isn't. Does he ever talk between songs?"

"Uh, that would be extremely unusual. He lets the music speak for him."

"Yeah, there's the problem. I tried concentrating but then felt a headache coming on."

"Hey," she said, feeling cautious enthusiasm. "This song was famous. Either the one about changing, or his later one about giving up and changing back."

"I own fifteen of his CDs and don't have a clue." He exhaled loudly. "Jesus, two and a half hours of this. Why didn't I see Springsteen instead?"

"You already went to Springsteen twenty years ago. That would defeat the whole point of your bucket list."

He grimaced. "Is he singing about Florida?"

"I think someplace near Jamaica," she replied. "Wow, is that yodeling?"

"It sounds like falsetto gargling." He sipped at their paper cup of flat $10 beer. "I'm astounded he can do that, that he even wants to."

"At least the band is great, and the horn section drowns most everything out."

"What's next on my list?"

She felt sad. "*This* was the last thing."

"So I'll add more."

"It was at the very bottom of the page, squeezed in with tiny handwriting."

"Then I'll make a word doc list on my laptop. It could go on and on."

"No, that's not a physical bucket list." She grew annoyed for an instant. "Do you write your shopping lists on a computer?"

"Okay, big picture, what does it mean?"

"After this show you'll have done everything you wanted to do before kicking the bucket."

"But I'm too young to tap the bucket, to even nudge the bucket, much less—"

"Once you're done you're done." She hugged him as if a dejected child. "I thought it was stupid to put this concert last, but it was your list, not mine."

"So now I just wait around to...?"

She sighed. "Other people put climbing Mount Everest during a storm, or skydiving without a parachute, or swimming off of Australia in shark-infested waters as their final entry."

"Great." His breathing became labored.

The night before he'd mentioned odd pains lancing his guts to her. How many sunsets did he have left? She studied his face. "Don't worry. When the time comes, I'll make sure Uncle Clarence doesn't give a racist speech or mention the ex-President. No Catholic bullshit either."

Onstage, the rock legend sang a plodding ballad about the Hundred Years' War. The song seemed to have countless verses and no chorus; if a melody existed, it had been ingeniously disguised.

"Is he gasping or wheezing?"

"Both, I think. Do you want to leave early?" She checked the time on her phone again. "Could be another hour left." Her ass ached from the cement seats in the amphitheater.

His back had bowed and his expression showed suffering. "No, I'm good. Really." He looked withered, dehydrated. A husk of a human.

End of the list. Final entry, she thought. Too bad. She needed to plan for after he was gone. Greg in Accounting seemed nice enough. They had rapport, traded witty banter. Just turned fifty and he hadn't even begun his bucket list. Smart man.

She felt sentimental watching her partner age and shrink into himself. For a moment, she hoped the meandering, tuneless song would stretch on forever.

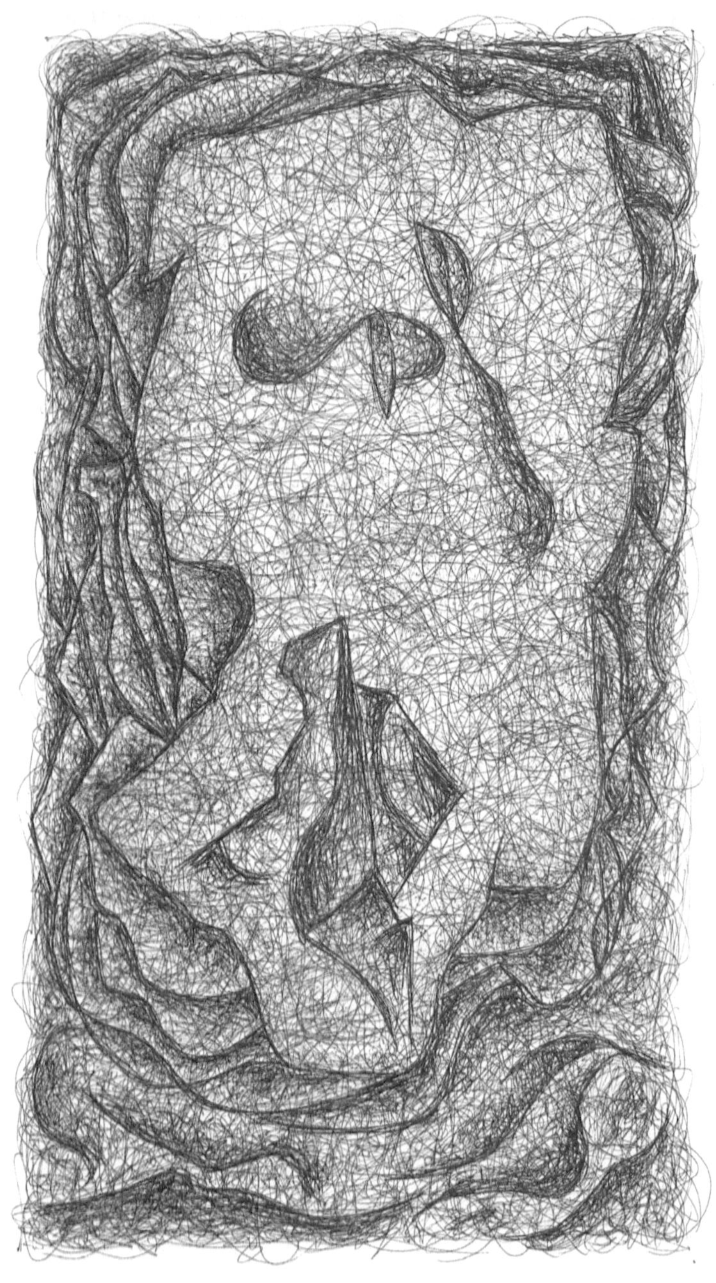

POISONED

My friends thought I'd gone mad. "I'm renting a cabin."

"In the Santa Cruz Mountains? It's the fucking wilderness up there," Steve said over a beer. "No movie theaters, buildings or shopping malls. Just Vietnam vets, old paranoid hippies, off-the-grid, redneck speed freaks, and the big, leather-skinned women who love them." He frowned. "I hear they're on solar power, and worse, propane gas. Expensive as shit."

"You're renting, Graham? That's just throwing your money away," texted Paul, my real estate agent friend. "For twenty percent down, you can buy a place and pay it off with three grand a month spread over thirty years."

Tina, my on-and-now-off girlfriend, looked at me as if I was a stranger over lunch. "Mud slides, fires, cyclonic winds, and winter rains. And by the way, redwood houses leak. Cell phone reception sucks up there. Have you thought about the mountain lions, wild raccoon packs, and the bears? Graham, they'll eat you alive, just like in that movie *Grizzly Man!*"

"That was Alaska."

"Close enough."

I didn't care what they thought. I lived quietly in San Luis Obispo in Central California, selling pianos and teaching music lessons. My grand dreams of youth had shrunk to a narrow reality at age forty-five. Through the death of various relatives, I had amassed a moderate bank account, which due to being single and childless, sat unravaged. There wasn't quite enough to buy a house, unless I chose North Dakota or Kansas as my residence, and the California women I'd been meeting rarely followed up on a first date for a net-worth under a million. My life had become so dull, so predictable, that when an opportunity arose to rent a cottage in the Santa Cruz Mountains as a getaway retreat from the retreat I'd already made from life, I jumped on it. I had seen the sunset over the Pacific and hiked over dirt roads that led past secluded residences of the misanthropic hermits I aspired to be like. Only a three hour drive north.

I hadn't gone insane.

"It's rustic and quaint, but homey," Carl, the burly owner of the cabin told me.

That usually meant the plumbing was broken, the space cramped, and it smelled bad. No matter, I paid a year's rent in advance to stave off any competitors' bids.

The place did look narrower each time I visited it, and adding furniture made the cabin resemble a double-decker storage container in which one had to perpetually turn sideways to navigate.

Once I'd rendered the interior basically livable, I began to muck about outside to improve the vistas. Dead trees sprouting a jumble of branches obscured the redwood-flecked mountains rising to the east. Huge growths of brush had blocked the distant ocean views to the west, while an unruly wood pile that incorporated metal sinks, a claw-foot bathtub, and discarded aluminum siding into its post-modern sculpture walled off a southern exposure through a lush canyon.

I assembled my saws, trimmers, shears, and rope.

Within thirty minutes I was bathed in sweat, so I removed my shirt and mopped my forehead. The dead branches had no intention of being sliced off by a tree-trimmer. They fought back, clawing at my face—the bastards having gained a new strength in death. Changing tactics, I sawed at their bases and brought troops of angry red ants charging toward my hands. Blood-thirsty flies began dive-bombing my ears. Standing back from the fray on neutral ground, I imagined cutting the brush would be easier. Wrong. I could only chop the high tendrils by climbing into their mass, until my hair and skin became peppered with insects. Thorns and cactus-like leaves raked my exposed arms mercilessly but I would not retreat. For amid this fierce battle with nature, I knew I was winning.

After three hours, definite progress had been made. Life had purpose. Forget my pale lay-about years of skulking in dusty, mold-ridden apartments. I was an outdoorsman. Sure, bug-bites rose on my face, my skin burned from the sun, and a headache was aborning in my skull, but those were mere technicalities. For once, my body odor smelled of triumph. In every direction, the view had improved. I made mental notes where I would cut more in the future.

The next morning, after I drove home to SLO to teach piano lessons, I began to feel itchy. It didn't seem strange, as I had scratched my arms, chest, and neck during the labors. Some temporary rash-like conditions had to be expected with my sensitive skin. Denial is an interesting state to linger in, but when the bubbles began to form on my neck, students pointed out the obvious.

"Dude, you've *so* got poison oak. Like literally, dude."

I'd either been exposed to ivy, oak, or the damnable sumac. By nightfall, small bumps formed on the back of my hands, all over my arms, and across my upper torso. I didn't panic. I'd endured it at camp along with most other kids. Those ugly growths stuck around for five days, itched like hell, and then disappeared. So I canceled my upcoming lessons and bought some Tecnu at CVS to get rid of the oils, as well as calamine lotion to dry the sores out.

"Hate it, hate it bad," the clerk said, nodding his head knowingly. "Basically, do not touch yourself or anyone else."

Once I'd rubbed the Tecnu on, I felt much better. The redness decreased, and driving home, I thought maybe I'd dodged a bullet. By the weekend, the whole incident would be a vague memory.

Forty-eight hours later I went to the local Urgent Care clinic.

Though the thermostat showed 83 degrees, I stood in the

waiting room clad in jeans and a long sleeve shirt. A military reservist from the South sat talking to everyone. A shock of blond hair sat atop a raw face like canned spam. "What are you here for?" he asked with a smile.

"Poison oak," I whispered.

"Poison oak? I remember skinny-dipping in a lake back in Georgia. When I got out, had to wade through some brush to get my clothes. The next day the stuff was all over my legs, all over my pay-nus. You ever seen a pecker covered with poison oak?"

"No, I, uh..."

"Neither had my Grandma. Hot damn, you son-of-a-bitch! And I'm in here just to get some moles sliced off my ass."

Juana, the teenage assistant ushered me into the examination room and studied me. "Mr. Peters, you're here for poison oak? Has it gone away? I can't really see it."

At that point, I removed my scarf and shirt to display the markings.

Juana dropped her clipboard to the ground and recoiled in shock, then collapsed onto the papered examination table meant for patients. "I'm sorry, I just started this month." She breathed heavily as sweat gleamed on her forehead.

Under the harsh fluorescent lights, each bubble in every rash stood clearly illuminated.

It looked like someone had spilled strawberry jam and grape preserves across my arms—the strident colors alarming in their richness. With a brown hooded robe I could have passed for a leper of Molokai.

Juana scooped up the clipboard and handed it to Dr. Stewart.

She appeared fiftyish, had a stone face, and studied my skin with cool dispassion, even boredom. I had brought in my over-the-counter remedies like offerings to the gods of medicine.

"Enough with this stuff." She pushed the containers into the finality of the medical waste disposal unit. "I want you to take four tablets of Prednisone a day for ten days to two weeks." The doctor put on her owl-frame glasses and scribbled out a prescription.

"That's a steroid. Aren't there side-effects?"

"Minor ones. Lack of energy, disorientation, insomnia, disturbing nightmares, bloating, constipation, sudden vomiting, breast growth, loss of appetite, oh, and some bad ones too. You might want to avoid sex."

"Not too difficult," I said gesturing at my angry rashes.

"Good. And you don't masturbate, do you?"

"Never. I mean, not every day. Well, not recently," I replied, but deep in my pants I felt an itching sensation, like the wild scratching needle of a lie detector.

"Fine, Graham. See you again in two weeks."

I carefully covered myself before venturing outside. A skin rash is no big deal, but purple sores strike fear in the common man. They hint at Medieval venereal diseases, cancer, and perhaps scurvy. They scream: stay away, it's contagious. Run for your fucking life!

After getting my medication, I slipped into a timeless void, a week where I rarely slept but barely rose from my couch. My eyesight became too blurred to read and I lacked the concentration to focus on television shows. Hallucinations abounded. Shadows of giant insects scuttled by at the periphery of vision, arias from Italian operas assailed my eardrums, and finally, Jesus Christ roller-bladed through my living room in a Speedo and halter top. Things went downhill from there.

A few days into the fog, Becca called out of the blue. "I need to see you, babe."

"It's been years, many years. What about Richard?"

"Who? Oh, can't you just let that go?" She laughed. "We only hooked up because I was on Ambien. Anyway, I'm off prescription meds these days. Just coke and booze. Greg, I miss you."

"It's Graham. I can't see you now, maybe another time."

"Still with that Mexican teenager?"

"She came from Spain and was twenty-six. Got another call coming in. Bye."

After seventy-two hours in the Prednisone half-world, I assumed I was on the mend. But when I faced the Picture of Dorian Gray that was my mirror, I called a high-priced dermatologist for an emergency appointment.

They ushered me in through the delivery door to not startle the wealthy Botox patients sitting in the waiting room. My chest had become emblazoned with a line of wet red welts that could have been the stigmata of a deep-sea diver returning from a chance encounter with a giant squid. I learned to walk in the shadows, to avoid crowds, to cover myself in oversized clothing that in the spring weather provoked sweat, further exacerbating the itching. Benadryl and Sudafed claimed to eliminate such itching, but despite my stockpiling amounts that had me tagged as a crystal meth manufacturer of Heisenberg proportions, the discomfort continued.

Dr. Mayfair recognized an extreme case. The kind that dermatologists dealt with in medical school and hope to fob off on neighborhood clinics so they can concentrate on the lucrative pampering of aging beautiful people.

"Let's double the Prednisone," Mayfair said, gazing at my chart. "I know it's a dangerous steroid, but we need to clean you up. I'll give you samples of a strong Cortisone cream and rolls of gauze to keep you from scratching. The good news is that it can't get any worse." He wrote a quick note in a case book while shaking his head, then looked at me with an expression of bottomless pity.

"If it does get worse, should I call you, Doctor?"

"I'll be in Pebble Beach this weekend for the tournament, but feel free to leave a message with my service…"

"What good will that do?"

"It's always beneficial to have a record of extreme, I mean, unusual cases. Thanks for coming in. The nurse will show you out the back door." He reached out a hand but changed his mind and jammed it into his white jacket pocket. "Keep your chin up." Mayfair flashed the kind of fake, carefree smile that generals of doomed military invasions have employed for time immemorial, then retreated from the room.

The Prednisone destroyed my common sense. I began calling friends I'd lost contact with years ago to ask their opinion.

John said, "Go skinny-dipping in the ocean under the full moon. Salt water will kill it."

That didn't work, though when I emerged mother-naked from the surf, I scared some stoners smoking a joint into running away from the beach. "It's the fucking Toxic Avenger!" one shouted.

"Rub white vinegar on the sores," Rachel said. "My mother's recipe."

Vinegar just made the rashes glow and coated me with a stink that conjured up dead rodents mixed with cat urine.

Like millions of Americans, I went to the Internet for advice and came upon a news report: *Climate Change has caused more poison ivy and poison oak growth. The sustained warmth in the western United States has spawned a super-virulent strain that threatens firefighters, forest rangers, hikers, and gardeners—especially in California.*

My blinds were drawn permanently and I found little to distinguish day from night. I slept a few hours with dreams so vivid they resembled reality, and upon waking, inhabited an opaque world that could have been plucked from a dream. Back and forth from slumbering to awareness I went in a sedentary position on the couch. Voices haunted me. Sometimes the television, or friends' words rising from my landline's answering machine. Other times, the voices emanated from my own throat: fragments, questions, and mumbled gibberish. The staggering doses of steroids I endured had reduced me to a Beckett character. Piano students who hadn't heard from me, either dropped lessons or switched teachers.

In another two days, the sores covered my entire body, and a light rash flecked my face, making shaving a painful and unnecessary function. At some point I broke down and called a fellow musician with knowledge of homeopathy and non-traditional medicine.

I confessed, "My condition is worsening and doctors can't seem to cure it."

Jason listened patiently then recommended Countess la Doyenne. "She helped me once with a lip sore that wouldn't go away," Jason told me. "She knows Santeria, Wiccan magic, voodoo, and is versed in spells and potions."

"Sounds crazy, but I'm desperate. Dude, please keep this on the down-low."

"She's the last person you'll ever need to visit, Graham."

On the treeless, burnt yellow hills above Morro Bay sit a series of large metallic holding tanks containing petroleum or similar fuels. They are fenced off, and besides some abandoned rusted vehicles nearby, the area shows little evidence of life. In a gully beyond one of the prominent tanks lay a warren of shacks: Countess la Doyennes's compound. She met me at night, which suited my need for concealment, as well as her own.

"Come in." The Contessa beckoned me into a garage-like structure. Her office. She appeared with head wrapped and her ample body draped in swaths of cloth. I tried to define her country of origin from what I could see of her face through the gauzy veil, but it proved difficult. She spoke in a deep accent that hinted of somewhere in Eastern Europe. "Please, you will to be stripping off your clothes now, and then will tell the Contessa how you are getting this?"

I had gone beyond modesty, beyond shame, so I complied, undressing until I stood revealed in the center of the chamber. She circled me slowly and studied every outburst that emblazoned my bare body, nodding and smiling sympathetically with understanding. After I told her of gardening at my cabin, she wrapped a sheet around me and bade me sit on a stool while she opened a cabinet brimming with vials, pill bottles, and herbs and roots wrapped in plastic bags.

"No more Cortisone. No more steroids, okay? It makes worse."

"What kind of poison oak is this?"

She looked me in the eye. "Not poison oak anymore. You attack mother nature, Gaia, and this is her revenge. There is only one way left." She sighed. "You must go back to Santa Cruz cabin. There you will be rubbing these leaves over your body and then eat the crushed roots. You must prove yourself the more powerful in the place of your first battle."

"And if I don't?" I said as I got dressed.

"You will be dead. Two, three weeks you have at most."

"The rashes will kill me?" I asked in a daze.

"No, you will be taking of your own life."

It sounded harsh, but I'd slid into a severe depression over the past days. My music students had disappeared, I couldn't face my few friends, and apartment rent would be due soon. I had already casually considered how easy it would be not to exist, and even speculated on what drugs I would need to snuff it.

I picked up the two bags she placed on the floor near me. "How much?"

"Expensive. But you will be paying later. Here, mark this map where your cabin is. Now go back up there. Save your money to buy gas for the trip. Leave right now."

Unafraid of infection, the Contessa took my arm, her long curled fingernails passing delicately over my extra-sensitive skin as she ushered me out into the cool darkness. She waved slowly as I drove downhill toward Morro Bay to gas up. Three hours later, I reached my cabin, rubbed the leaves on my limbs, and swallowed the brown powder. Exhausted, I slumped into my bed until near noon the next day.

The morning brought good news. The bright red and purple rashes had turned a dull brown. Undoubtedly drying up. I still looked bizarre, but the itching had ceased, and since I had no nearby neighbors, I could dress in shorts and T-shirt for the first time. The depression I'd been buried under seemed to lift too. I'd always been light-sensitive and the outbreak had initially worsened the condition. Now suddenly, I craved sunlight, to be outdoors and not cooped up in the shadows. I also felt parched, extremely dehydrated. Strange. A gallon of water went down my throat without any later need to urinate.

By the end of the day my skin appeared dirt brown in patches and light green in-between. Odd colors, and yet the globules had sunk back into the surface of my flesh. Beyond the obviously temporary coloring, my skin was smooth again. The Contessa had saved me and I'd gladly pay whatever price she planned to charge.

After applying her remedies again, I tried to sleep in my bed that night but felt constricted and short of breath. Instead, I slept under the moonlight out on the deck wrapped in a single sheet with a water bottle. Somewhere between night and dawn I woke beneath the full moon to remove the sheet and my pajamas, as they smothered me.

The blazing sun forced me into awareness earlier than I would have liked. Instead of resting on the wood planks of the deck, I stood comfortably unclothed in the bushes I had previously trimmed. Moreover, it felt perfectly natural to sleep in a vertical position.

That transpired hours ago. My voice is only a husky croak; my hands barely scratch words onto paper and they are my most animated parts. Some time during the night my feet sank into the soil, and now, looking down, thick brown roots encircle my ankles. I feel strong, centered, and am no longer hungry for food—just moisture. My skin is chipped and thick while my eyesight has fuzzed. I can just see the outline of the Contessa approaching with a pail. She waters me. I think she may have moved into my cabin. She sings folk songs and tells me that from where I'm planted the view is incredible: Santa Cruz Mountains, the Pacific Ocean, the cleft of a canyon. Just as I originally wished.

My friend Jason was right. I'd never need to see anyone else for a cure. I've beaten the poison. Forever.

THE DEVIL IS IN THE DETAILS

Emily prepared for the interview. A journalist meeting with a prisoner was rarely a relaxed or enjoyable experience. Not because of unexpected answers to questions, but due to the prohibitive restrictions placed on such meetings by prison authorities. In this case, Virginia prison authorities. Absurd time limitations, no unsupervised discussions in the same room. That kind of nonsense.

First, a journalistic request had been put in for a private interview, then when Warden Cliburn quashed that, contact with the prisoner's attorney led to the journalist being placed on the prisoner's visitor list. Rules dictated they would communicate on phones through a partition, and the conversation would be monitored by prison officials, but that didn't matter. A bestselling book could come out of the story. In the last years, lone gunmen opening fire on innocent people in malls, schools, and churches had become a regular occurrence in America. Isolated incidents? Nobody believed that cable news excuse anymore. So why? Perhaps Emily could find some answers. And this would be the book to truly get inside the mind of a shooter. Emily felt privileged to be involved. Money, acclaim, prizes. All of those were possible, if the series of interviews went well.

Emily's co-workers Charlie and Bernie had counseled her beforehand.

"These types are serial liars," Charlie said. "They'll tell you what they want you to hear, charm you, manipulate you. Do not be swayed. Some of them can be very convincing."

"Yeah," Bernie added. "Remember what happened with Perry Smith and Truman Capote? You saw that movie, didn't you?" Both Bernie and Charlie were veterans who'd been in these exact situations before.

Luckily, Emily had a photographic memory—since no recording devices were permitted for the meeting, nor laptops. Not even a pen and paper. Many modern prisons allowed open discussions at tables in a visitation lounge supervised by guards. But not in this 1950s era facility. Southern states seemed more determined to hold onto their past. The room smelled of cement and dust, of body odor barely masked by chemical cleaners with bleach. Emily caught a faraway whiff of cafeteria food: mashed potatoes, stew, oatmeal. Things that could be scooped out of large stainless steel pots with ladles. She pulled her chair as close as possible to the bullet-proof separation, picked up the bulky phone left over from another century to speak with Dante

Hodgson.

"May I call you Dante?"

"Yes, of course." Dante had a neatly-trimmed beard, glasses, short dark hair, and a high forehead. Not the forehead of a manipulator or a maniac, but of a thinker, even somewhat like a writer.

Don't be distracted by his appearance. Everyone's mother claims they were a sweet child.

"For my initial question," Emily started.

"You mean I won't be able to ask you questions?" Dante frowned.

"Since this is our first meeting, face to face," Emily said, "I thought it best that I do the questioning." *Stay in control.* "In subsequent interviews, I'm open to give and take, back and forth."

"I guess I'm at your mercy," Dante said. "But for this project to succeed, we'll have to work together. Actually collaborate."

"Granted." Emily pressed hair back from her face with her free hand. "Since we only have thirty minutes, let me get right down to it. You were college educated, Dante. What do you think causes these occurrences?"

"Gun massacres?" He gave her a quizzical look.

Why was he so different than all the rest? Remain detached.

"Yes," she said. "Some call it temporary insanity, others say it's evil, you know, a person being possessed by malignant forces. Though psychologists would consider that to be a chemical or mental imbalance. There are the copy-cat theories where the media's relentless coverage sparks people into taking similar actions. What's your opinion? What is the nature of evil?"

"You mean, do I think it's chemical or hereditary or conditioning or...satanic?" Dante gazed at her through the partition, a gleam in his eyes, the slight curl of a smile forming. "I was hoping you'd have theories. But since we'll be collaborating on the eventual book, I guess I should lay my cards, my beliefs on the table."

Emily heard clicking noises, the chatter of ghost voices inhabiting their phone-line, and imagined sweaty, overweight men sitting in a bunker-like room somewhere nearby monitoring the prisoner-to-visitor conversations. *Stay focused.* That's what Charlie told her. *Keep the upper hand.*

"Your last name is Duvel," Dante said. "Is that French?"

"Belgian," Emily replied.

"Were you born there?"

Emily smiled with impatience. "Can we get back to my question?"

Dante looked away for a moment, his forehead strained in thought. "The media sometimes says that lone shooters are born evil," he said, "like it's in their blood. Or that it was inherited from their parents' teachings and influence. Some go along with the idea that killers are possessed by spirits, whether it's violent insanity or evil forces that are spiritual in nature." Dante paused. "I come from a religious background. The desire to go to heaven and the fear of eternal hell were very real for me growing up."

"And where do you believe you're going, Dante?"

"With my history?" He laughed. "I don't think there's too much doubt." His eyes turned harder. "But seriously, you're the first woman…"

"To meet with you in prison?"

"It's always been men before. Always."

Emily shuddered. She felt Dante manipulating her and the interview with his guile. She hadn't expected him to act normal, and worse, to look attractive. She caught a glimpse of her spectral reflection in the hard translucent surface. *No, don't picture yourself on Dante's side of the partition. Do not identify with him. Keep a critical detachment.* Emily squeezed her eyelids shut as she imagined Charlie and Bernie's counsel. They were hard-asses; they would guide her through this. Emily opened her eyes.

Dante stared at her, his face taut and constricted, then he relaxed. "Sorry, we can work up to that angle later. Let me continue with my theory," he said, and Emily nodded. "I don't believe people are born evil or possessed by the Devil. You see, our actions—good or bad—are controlled by chemicals in our bodies, as well as synapses sending electrical signals that influence brain functions. The only rational way to look at it, to explain these incidents, is through the prism of science."

"Is it? And you see it as chemistry over behavioral science." Emily paused. "So you believe you were rational then and are rational now?"

"Me?" He seemed surprised. "Yes, definitely."

Lawyers didn't want to hear that answer. Maybe that's

why recordings were forbidden in these interviews. Temporary insanity would be the only way to beat a death sentence in a gun massacre case. A sympathetic jury? Impossible. Emily squinted to see deeper through the thick fiberglass partition with its scuff marks and dull surface. What was it like on the other side? Could she survive a single day in that regimented order, in a world forever poised on the brink of violence?

"Many believe that the Salem Witch Trials were a result of ergot poisoning," Dante said. "Therefore, the women were not witches or infused with evil, but the ergot they ate changed the chemical makeup in their bodies. It caused them to act wild, to do things they would never have done ordinarily."

Gates clanged open and shut in the distance while distorted intercom voices made announcements in faraway areas of the prison. Emily studied Dante. She'd expected a fool or a zealot filled with ideological fervor and a warped viewpoint. Not only was Dante intelligent, but he spoke dispassionately, like a science professor discussing data from experiments in a university classroom.

"Anyway, that's why the idea that Hitler was actually Satan, or that Charles Manson was possessed by demons seems laughable to me," Dante said. "Our brains and bodies are intricate and delicate systems. If one chemical lessens and another increases through dilation brought on by drugs, or by anxiety, or by adrenaline levels spiking from a threat, then a stable personality can completely change in an instant. In other cases, the chemical balance alters slowly but incrementally. A paranoid person becomes anti-social, then progresses to believe that they're somehow threatened. At that stage, they may arm themselves in defense, until they finally reach a breaking point where they need to take action, go on the offense. Unfortunately, that leads to tragic consequences. As we've seen over and over again." Dante looked at Emily with an almost ancient sadness. "Does any of this ring true?"

"In my studies of other shooters?" Emily asked, but he didn't reply. "Your theory has validity, Dante. But I'm wondering, is that the argument you wish to put forth? Is that your defense?"

"I thought we were collaborating on a book," he said. "I don't need a defense, and we're not meeting today for *you* to defend me. That's what lawyers are for."

Yes, lawyers. Linguistic magicians who could turn murderers into disturbed people not responsible for their own actions. Emily said nothing. Dante was trying some transference trick on her. He clearly held a near genius IQ. She'd have to prepare more, be more unrelenting in their subsequent meetings. Charlie and Bernie had been right about everything. It was a chess game and Emily wasn't winning this match. She could imagine them chattering away. They'd critique her first interview later on.

"Sorry, I didn't mean to snap at you." Dante removed his glasses and wiped the lenses.

Emily stared at the ground. The media and mass murderers, wrapped up in an unholy matrimony of reckless desire and needless carnage. Was Emily an accessory to Dante's crime, or was he an accessory to hers?

A buzzer sounded and a prison guard moved through the telephone visitation area to signal the various guests and inmates that their time was up.

"I really hope you'll let me ask questions next time," Dante said, glancing over his shoulder. "I mean for the sake of the book and because you're the first woman." He frowned. "It's always men. Usually young, isolated white men." Then Dante looked happier. "That's why this book, our book is going to be a best-seller. You broke the mold. People are curious."

A male and a female guard escorted Emily out.

"I guess it's back to my office with Charlie and Bernie," she said. "Are they waiting to pick me up?"

"Sure, whatever," the male guard said.

"You'll have the upper hand next time," Charlie told Emily, appearing vaporous beyond the gate of the hallway. "You let him talk too much. Ignore those dazzling blue eyes; Dante's not your friend. He's using you."

"You can't let him fuck with your mind again," Bernie whispered into Emily's other ear. "Don't you know that journalists and writers are the lowest of the low? They trick you by saying whatever they have to. They will lie, cheat, or steal to get the story the way they want it to be, not the way it really was."

"Fiction is their preferred drug," Charlie said, "and they only resort to facts when it suits their narrative."

The guards led Emily downstairs into her solitary confinement cell. They locked it and left.

She had been placed there for her own safety. Shooters who massacred a number of random people disturbed the other inmates, and scaring potentially violent prisoners rarely went well.

When Emily tucked into her hard cot, both associates continued to counsel her in breathy whispers. She nodded and told Charlie and Bernie, yes, yes, yes. Then, pulling the thin, itchy blanket around her, Emily became just an amorphous balled-up shape wedged into the corner of her cell.

It didn't matter. There would be another interview with Dante to correct things, and another visit after that one too. A lifetime filled with possibilities.

IDENTITY LIQUID

Daryl James relaxed, surrendering to the moment in the private room. He felt the man touch his chest, stroke his back, and squeeze his ass. Then the stranger fondled his crotch. Daryl turned toward the muscular man, and soon they locked in a tight clench, kissing with abandon.

"I scanned the incidental collection," the man said, pulling away, "but I didn't see any signs that you—"

"Hoped it would speed things up," Daryl replied. "Business meeting in Monterey."

The uniformed agent slid the gray curtain open. "So that's our new TSA enhanced pat-down. What do you think?"

"Intimate," Daryl said.

"Are you originally from South America, or Mexico?"

"Neither."

"Then you have a beautiful tan."

"It's not a tan. Am I free to go?"

"Yes. Will I see you again?"

"Maybe. I fly out of LAX for business."

"Got your information on file. I'll text you."

Daryl shuddered inside. "Need to board now."

Why did I just do that? Ever since his doctor prescribed Nirvanarol, a cheaper Xanax substitute to treat anxiety, Daryl had felt odd desires, acted without thinking, and even experienced fugue states. Anything to fend off a sudden panic attack.

He rushed from the screening area toward his flight.

"Daryl James?" The gate attendant's smile became an unsettling grimace.

"Yes."

"We recently changed our boarding policy. You're in Group 0."

"Zero?"

"Yes, you board first." Her lips quivered. "But you'll exit last."

"I'm okay with that." He grinned. "Direct flight and just my carry-on bag."

The woman walked him to the jet bridge door.

Daryl hunched and squeezed himself into the Air Canada jet. Inside, he saw no passengers besides a harried flight attendant wearing heavy makeup.

"You're our last Economy Minus. Follow me."

"I'm a business traveler," he said. "Never heard of Economy Minus."

"Brand new program. Maximizes space." She led him through the empty cabin until they reached the bathroom.

"Dead end," Daryl said. "Where's my seat?"

The attendant slid a panel open on the rear wall. Behind it, the passageway narrowed, allowing four rows with one passenger on each side.

Daryl stooped down to fold into his slender seat. "It's the tail of the plane. Literally."

The attendant sealed the panel, leaving Daryl isolated in darkness.

Beyond the absence of windows, his seat had no cushion, and the seatbelts were thin polyester straps. "This is awful."

"But we boarded first," a man across the aisle said. "And a ten dollar credit for my next flight."

As he adjusted to the dim enclosure, Daryl observed the other travelers. A woman's hat sprouted drapes shrouding her head, while her face was mummy-wrapped in bandages and embellished with dark sunglasses. A tiny bald man mounted on platform shoes paced the aisle speaking Russian into a phone, and a middle-aged Korean couple squabbled and slapped one another.

During takeoff, the seats shook, the violent juddering causing loose plastic bits to rain down on the passengers.

"Relax," the neighbor told him. "Please stop breathing so hard. Not much air back here."

"Can we use the front bathroom?"

"No, but there's a chemical toilet behind us."

Daryl squinted. "That tiny thing?"

The neighbor nodded then passed him a used Wash'n Dri. "To clean your hands." He smiled. "You boarded Section Zero last. You'll learn to arrive early for these perks."

The pilot made announcements to the main cabin, but the words came muffled and incomprehensible.

In his cramped position, Daryl tried to nap. A man chanting like a muezzin atop a mosque at sunset prayers kept him in a state of drowsy awareness.

Soon, they descended at a severe angle, straining the flimsy seatbelts. When the aircraft landed, bumping and jolting, their seats pressed together like a compacting accordion. Fifteen minutes later, the wall panel opened. A blinding gash of daylight entered.

"Everyone out." Two tall private security men glared at them. "Maintenance crew needs to clean the cabin."

Disoriented under the dazzle of sunlight on the tarmac, Daryl got his bearings. *Something's wrong. Airport's too big.*

A female baggage handler with dreadlocks scrolled her phone, ignoring the luggage-filled cart.

"Where the hell are we?"

"Monterey got fogged in," she answered without looking up. "Your pilot chose San Jose. Don't worry, Monterey is only seventy miles away."

"I was sitting in Section Zero. We didn't hear."

The woman frowned. "I've worked this airline for five years. There's no such section."

Daryl attempted to fist bump her, but she just stared, unresponsive.

Inside the terminal, he traversed the line of rental car kiosks—Enterprise, National, Budget—without any luck. The final desk had no company insignia and a disheveled clerk.

"Welcome to Last Ride." The man coughed. "Lenny Balz. What can I do you for?"

"Overnight rental, your cheapest car."

"They all are," he said. "We rent beaters." Lenny eyed Daryl. "Thirty bucks a day..."

"That's great for California."

"And a seventy dollar deposit until you return it. Cash."

Daryl winced. "I have thirty, but I'd need an ATM machine."

"Tell you what." Lenny wiped his sweaty face with a rag. "Drop me home downtown and I'll waive the deposit."

"Really?"

"Yeah, my ex-wife took our Ford Focus in the divorce." He grimaced. "She once said I looked sexy driving it. Can you believe I bought that horseshit?"

Daryl motored the 1995 Hyundai deep into San Jose, while Lenny slumbered.

"My phone's GPS says we're here," Daryl announced as he parked in a sketchy neighborhood. "Wake up. I have business in Monterey—now."

"Monterey?" Lenny said, one eye widening. "There's a ten dollar charge for crossing county lines."

Daryl fished a bill from his wallet. "Okay, get going."

"Whoa. Hostile, dude."

Daryl descended from sun-blanched hills of Highway 17 into a steel wool fog by the coast at Moss Landing. Minutes later on Highway 1, a cop car drove alongside Daryl, then slowed to follow before flashing its lights.

Daryl pulled over and meditated, letting the anger coloring his face drain away.

The young cop with a hand on his holster did a double-take at the window. "Hey, I thought you were…"

"Thought I was what?"

"Uh, nothing." He scowled. "Your middle brake light isn't working."

"Overnight rental."

The cop nodded. "I'm only issuing a warning. Have a nice day."

Daryl soon reached Monterey. He hadn't visited in ten years and the outsized hotels sprouting like displaced big city high-rises over the funky two-story structures of Cannery Row surprised him.

The Excelsior Inn's lobby looked amazing. Glass and stone and gleaming metal with a dark wood front desk where a smiling man awaited.

"I'm Daryl James."

"Aha." The desk clerk winced as if he'd just bit a bone in a piece of fish. He clicked and scrolled on his computer with mystification.

"My boss, Ben Farnsworth, guaranteed me a fantastic ocean view room," Daryl said.

"Mr. Farnsworth?" The clerk's scrunched face relaxed. "Oh, yes. Mister James, we have a special downstairs suite."

"The basement?" Daryl felt the collected rage of the day boil up. "Jesus Christ, is this because you think I'm—"

"What? No." The clerk pressed his face close. Everyone in

the lobby went quiet. The clerk smiled—showing teeth and gums. "I get it," he whispered. "That's how you identify." He raised his fingers in air quotes. "My parents came from Japan, but I identify as a Portuguese sailor."

"Yeah, well I'm an American, born in Oakland. So why am I getting a shit room in the cellar?"

"The Captain Nemo Suite is our finest accommodation. An ocean view, and a secret passageway allows free entry to our neighbors, the Monterey Bay Aquarium."

Daryl exhaled. "I'd hoped for the top floor."

"Fog, that's all you'll see up there."

A young porter escorted Daryl to the sub-basement in an elevator. They walked a dank hallway, the percussion of dripping in the distance. The porter unlocked the suite, then turned on lamps.

Instead of a window, a circular porthole was embedded in the wall. Pulling the curtain, Daryl peered into the dark, impenetrable void of the Monterey Bay. He found a switch for an outer light that illuminated the waters, but lured several curious sea lions to press their snouts to the glass, obscuring any view. A thundering foghorn sounded, causing items to vibrate on tables. Daryl detected a constant pinging noise like the sonar of a submarine.

"Can we turn that off?"

The porter shook his head. "Our owner installed sensory prompts for an authentic experience." The vent system blew gusts of sea air mixed with a rotting kelp odor into the room.

Before Daryl could argue, the porter scuttled off into the

elevator. When he followed, Daryl found no call button to press. He downed a Nirvanarol capsule and phoned Farnsworth.

"I'm in Monterey, on Cannery Row."

"California?" Farnsworth said. "You were supposed to be in Monterrey, Mexico!"

"The LAX flight took me to San Jose." Daryl sighed. "Not my fault."

Farnsworth shouted at his assistant. "Who's the motherfucking skid mark who reamed me with a grenade-launcher on this one?"

"Sir?" Daryl asked. "What should I do?"

"Spend the night. See the aquarium tomorrow. I'll set up a meeting within driving distance." He mumbled to himself, cursing. "We didn't just hire you for the quota thing, but because you're good with all types of people, making them agree to what my company wants. And let me tell you, Darnell—"

"Daryl."

"Advancement is coming. I'm talking promotion, and at some future date, possibly a raise. Keep your phone nearby 24/7."

A week earlier, Emma Selby made her way into the San Francisco office of Humongous near the Shipyard at Hunter's Point. Sweating already. A strange foreboding inhabited her.

Emma arrived fifteen minutes late for a departmental meeting on getting products to customers faster. Humongous fashioned itself a distribution network, a mini-Amazon. Their massive warehouse of items situated east of Oakland was now run primarily by robots. Emma had prepared notes: local deliveries by driverless cars and trucks, regional same day delivery drops by drones, free 3-D printers for book, calendar, and art-related orders so files could be sent instantly upon credit card verification.

She raced toward a central elevator but a lobby receptionist intercepted her. "Emma? You have a private confab. Conference room #5 on the gallery level."

The gallery level? Humongous used that floor to entertain guests, journalists, and tour groups. "But my meeting."

"That's rescheduled." The woman gestured toward the side elevator, her eyes sinister and magnified by thick glasses.

Emma's shoulders slumped as she marched over.

A bland, handsome man sat waiting upstairs.

"What's this about?" Emma asked.

The man half-smiled. "You are being transferred, effective immediately."

"Transferred?"

"Transitioned."

"Transitioned where?"

"To the free market, outside of this company."

"But..." Emma shuddered. "Why?"

"When you joined the Humongous team you clicked 'accept' on the company's online conditions and regulations form." He loosened his tie. "Sadly, many employees treat that like a Netflix membership and accept without reading. Anyway, page seventy-seven, sub-clause 3b, states that if an employee is ten minutes late four times in one year, they can be terminated immediately." He frowned. "Emma, applicants from across the world are fighting for jobs here."

"But my rent, my bills?"

The man passed her a folder. "Today's classifieds from the *San Francisco Chronicle,* along with the craigslist website address."

"I have it."

He slid a plastic cup over. "Cod liver oil?"

"No thanks."

"I can spike it." He showed the silvery flask nestled inside his jacket.

"Really, no."

"Are you on LinkedIn, Emma?"

"Yes. Will that help?"

"Probably not." He drummed his fingers on the table. "How old are you, thirty-seven?"

"Twenty-nine."

"Really?" He removed his glasses, squinted, then put them back on. "You know, there are exciting opportunities in the custodial field. It's a valuable rite of passage for millennials."

"A janitor?"

"Janitor implies scrubbing toilets. A custodian has power: a key ring, access to offices and closets."

"What about my things from upstairs?"

"Right here." He scooped up a garbage bag from behind and jostled it over to Emma.

She noticed the man wore a frilly red tutu under his suit jacket. Hallucination? Side effects?

Emma left the building dazed. A rough week for her. Or a "bad patch" as her mother would say. She had discovered her older boyfriend William habitually visited a site that matched up middle aged white men with Asian men in their early twenties. That was a thing in San Francisco, but she had never suspected William was bi or whatever.

Emma stamped out of William's apartment last Saturday. When she tried calling him Tuesday, the number was no longer in service.

She drove to her Oakland building overlooking the constant traffic noise of the Nimitz Freeway. As Emma approached her apartment, she saw landlord Claude Bucci waiting outside.

"You're six days late on rent." He fingered his dark mustache. "About to post an eviction notice."

Emma felt short of breath. "I just got let go, fired."

Claude nodded, then an eyebrow raised. "Maybe we can work something out."

No, not that.

"My wife kicked me out." He scratched at sparse hair on his scalp. "Now, if you let me stay a week, until I can settle things with Gladys, then we'll forget this month's rent."

"In my apartment?"

"I'd take your bedroom, you'd sleep in the living room." He folded his arms. "Strictly business."

"I guess so," she replied. "Let me shift stuff around."

"Fine. I'll move in tonight." Claude headed for the elevator.

A housekeeper entered Daryl's hotel suite at 8 p.m. and wandered about until she noticed him. "Oh, excuse me," she said. "I can clean later."

"That's okay."

The woman looked young and attractive, with high cheekbones and an innocent face. Except for her wide, haunted eyes, she resembled an angel.

"Are you Polish?"

"Ukrainian," she said. "But I'm no mail-order bride."

"No, of course not."

"I'm Irina." She approached and examined him. "I like Israeli men. Curly dark hair and a gorgeous tan." Her hand lightly stroked his face.

"Uh, yeah." Daryl didn't argue.

"Though scientists say modern humans all originated from Africa."

"Maybe so." Daryl felt movement in his pants. Irina's long auburn hair was mostly tied up, so he touched the strands that descended around her neck.

She sighed and collapsed forward onto him, her lower torso pressing his.

"This is crazy," he said. "We just met, but I want you."

"I know, me too." Irina pulled back. "I just got out of a horrible relationship. Not looking for another." Her sulking mouth turned upward. "Just fun to help me forget."

"I can live with that."

She pulled away and blushed. "It's probably best to tell you. I'm bleeding."

"I've been with women before who have been."

Irina peeled off the top of her brown uniform and faced Daryl. "You have?" There were gashes on her shoulders that bled.

"Uh, not exactly." His erection flatlined.

"My wings were clipped," she said. "I'm a fallen angel."

She's nuts. Totally psycho. He grabbed for the room's landline. "We need to get you bandages, a doctor."

"Don't do that." Her voice rose to a shriek and she rushed outside.

"Yes?" the desk clerk asked through the phone.

"Just a moment." Daryl followed her but the hallway lay deserted. "Listen," he said. "Irina, your Ukrainian maid needs a doctor. Maybe a therapist too."

"What?" the clerk said. "Housekeeping works mornings, not at night. Furthermore, we don't employ Eastern Europeans. Our staff is primarily, uh, Mexican."

"But she—"

"No pronouns, sir. Some of our workers are..."

"Huh?"

"And you seem to be identity-liquid."

Daryl set the phone back on its cradle. *I need another Nirvanarol.*

After a room service dinner and an HBO movie, Daryl dozed off.

He woke before dawn feeling damp. Never a good thing. Daryl crawled through a tunnel, sea water sluicing through it. His legs felt constricted and the tunnel was too slender to turn around in, so he continued. A wave slapped him, spume frothing his face, but a hatch like on a submarine lay just ahead. Daryl twisted the handle and pushed through into a large, brightly lit pool. An amphitheater of packed seats surrounded him, and the people laughed derisively while pointing at him. He looked down to see his legs encased inside a mermaid's tail, yet his genitals—shrunken from the freezing Pacific Ocean water—were exposed. Above, a smiling woman stood by a bucket on a diving board and shook a bell. *The aquarium.* Daryl stared in disbelief as she kept ringing the bell. An urge to perform a trick infused him. She threw a pungent sardine that smacked his forehead. The ringing continued, growing louder and louder.

Daryl spasmed into awareness. The hotel room phone rang by the bed. *Just a nightmare.*

"Hello?" He shook his head to clear it.

"Farnsworth here. It's 7 a.m. Wake the hell up."

"I am, now."

"I Fed-Exed a briefcase. When it arrives, drive to a land plot off the 101, and give the briefcase to Raoul—personally. He's running a crew there, needs the information ASAP."

"Couldn't you just call him?"

"Raoul needs the documents in my handwriting, which you'll destroy after he reads them. You know how we do land development business. Under the table. No e-mail traces, no phone records."

"What about this call?"

"A throw-away phone. If you can't complete my simple assignment, don't bother coming back." Farnsworth disconnected.

Daryl received the package at ten, then took Highway 101

until the 156 East exit. He drove across beautiful rolling hills of the San Juan Valley, time traveling backward to a simpler, undeveloped world.

Unable to deal with her landlord moving in, Emma stayed with her mother for a week. She returned on Friday, hoping to find Claude gone. Instead, two teenage girls sprawled on her couch texting while listening to Taylor Swift.

Claude shuffled out wearing only boxer shorts. "Listen." He yawned. "Things didn't work out with Gladys. Finding a new place might take me a while."

"Who are they?" Emma gestured toward the oblivious girls.

"My daughters. I figured you ladies could camp out together in the living room." Claude winked. "I have company now, so please, no interruptions." He returned to the bedroom.

"Who's he back there with?" the blonde asked her brunette sister.

"Some skank from downstairs who couldn't pay her rent."

Emma exited to stand trembling in the hallway, a stranger in her own life. Since her mother had loaned her five hundred, she decided to take a road trip south.

Emma felt much better once driving. The Ford Focus was the only thing she got out of her divorce from that loser Lenny Balz. After San Jose, Emma veered east to travel the back roads. She was in no hurry and wanted to see nature, not an endless freeway.

Deep in the San Juan Valley, beyond a grassy field littered

with empty construction vehicles, she found a rustic gas station with two pumps and an adjacent diner. Something from a black and white movie. Emma felt overdressed in the knee-length skirt and heels her mother gave her for job interviews, but had nowhere to change. The swarthy work crew massed at the diner's counter leered at Emma, so after buying a sandwich to go, she munched it inside her car.

Daryl sipped iced tea in Victor's Diner while contemplating his future. Several construction workers ate potato chips and drank Corona beers. Waiting. Daryl had seen their massive bulldozers, an earth grader, and an excavator lying abandoned by the edge of a field. Amid the ancient oak trees sat old migrant shacks and fallen-down structures. Undoubtedly, some disadvantaged people lived in them illegally.

Disobeying Farnsworth, Daryl had opened the briefcase in his Hyundai. Instead of documents, he found a Post-it note saying: *Yes. Go ahead.* Three words, and easy to predict their impact. The complete decimation of the bucolic scene: birds chirping, laundry drying on a line in the breeze. Daryl shredded the note and tossed the briefcase in the back seat, then removed his suit jacket and tie—the signal for Raoul—and entered the diner.

He had just sunk into a booth when a mustached man sidled over.

"*Eres tu, Daryl?*"

"I don't speak Spanish." By feeling anger or embarrassment,

Daryl could temporarily alter and darken his skin.

"I am Raoul. Your boss, he sent you with a message?"

"Nope," Daryl said. "I'm Tyrone. On vacation to Oakland."

Raoul scowled. He spoke rapid Spanish to two men at the counter, occasionally glaring back over his shoulder.

Daryl exited and put his jacket on. No use returning to Los Angeles. Walking across the construction site, Daryl felt like an untethered astronaut—adrift in space. A woman in a white shirt and business skirt exited her car to follow him.

"Where are you going?"

"That way." He pointed east.

"Can I join?"

Daryl sighed. "I don't have any particular destination. What about you?"

She glanced back west. "I just want to get as far as I can from what's behind me."

"Sounds reasonable." They strolled beyond the site and over low green rises. He shortened his stride so she could keep pace. Daryl frowned. "You know, I can't protect you out here. I'm kind of lost now." His mask must have cracked, revealing truth.

"Well, I can't save you, and have nothing to give either," she said. "I'm done with men."

"Yeah, I'm done with women." Daryl's iPhone pinged with texts. Nude photos of the TSA agent. "And I'm done with men too." He hurled the phone against a granite outcropping; it impacted with a satisfying *thwack!*

"Your face got much paler," she said. "You're a chameleon, like a Zelig."

"Survival mechanism. I can't always control it. Instinct."

"Got it." She nodded. "What's beyond the horizon?"

"I think there's a hill, then another hill. We should get there by dusk."

She adjusted her shoe in the shade of a displaced stand of Monterey pines and shivered.

Daryl halted. "You okay?"

"I will be." She opened a canister to swallow a familiar-looking pill. "Just needed my stress medication."

SANITY CLAUSE

Barry Shipman waited on the corner slapping his gloved hands together and stamping his feet. The hood of the sweatshirt underneath his coat helped, but his nose went from numbness to feeling pain. Could someone get frostbite of the nose? He'd seen photos of Mount Everest hikers who'd lost toes or fingers on their frozen treks, but couldn't remember any blackened noses.

He shivered as he stood on 27th Street and Park Avenue in Manhattan listening to the bell jingling in the distance. It served as a kind of clock or timer counting down the moments until he acted. The tinkling grounded him and reminded him why he had come.

Christmas season didn't strike Barry as the ideal time to

murder someone. Though it was not a scenario he'd dwelt upon, having never killed anyone before. The Monday before Christmas retained happy memories for him. The spirit of goodwill, the sharing of niceties, and the promise of humanity putting aside their selfish pursuits for a moment—whether authentic or forced by a collective, commercial tidal wave. He felt those things too, but needed to make a moral exception this Christmas.

In a few days people would get manic with last-minute shopping. Not to mention the social tensions of pleasing family-members, of being thrown together with relatives both loved and those despised. If Barry had been given a choice when to kill, he would have picked after the holidays, during that bleak trough of early January when the next year arrived newly born and barely sentient. A dark, depressing time.

Barry planned to skip town before then. Unless something went inconceivably wrong, he'd be rolling south toward palm trees by dawn. He hated winter in the tri-state area. Most years, the conditions became intolerable around New Year's. In December 2018, unfortunately, an Arctic air mass gripped the region by the family jewels early on and it had remained at record low temperatures ever since.

"Excuse me," said a grouchy pedestrian dodging around Barry's stationary form. "Merry fucking Christmas."

"Same to you," Barry replied. He heard the sidewalk Santa's jingling bell and again went over his plan, again imagined his escape to Florida. Last winter he traveled to Phoenix, Arizona—but that hadn't proved warm enough.

A week ago, Barry was summoned from his miserable apartment off the New Jersey Turnpike to meet with Ron Marino at his Paramus office atop a pizza parlor. Just across the Hudson River from Manhattan but a world away. On the face of it, the request was no big deal. Ron served as an "associate." Not a made man, but a facilitator or helper for the big boys. He had suggested places for Barry to rob in the past and even recommended partners for two-man jobs. This time however, Ron had sent muscle in a car to make sure Barry accepted the invitation, and that perturbed him.

Barry tried to pry information from his driver-escort Phil, but the man's grayish slab of a face could have been carved from stone, and his communication skills ranged from grunts to the occasional, "let's go" or "come on" when spoken language became absolutely necessary. Barry was a wiry, nimble guy, perfectly suited to climb fire escapes or squeeze through narrow entry spaces. He avoided fighting other people—especially if they stood taller, weighed more, and carried weapons. So he shut-up when Phil told him to and stared out the window of the brown Lincoln in silence. They drove the eastern slice of Jersey that people warned of, that comedians joked about. Even within the car, a sulfur gas odor mingled with the windblown garbage stench from the hundred acre Kearny landfill.

Inside the upstairs office above Best Paramus Pizza, Ron got up from his desk grinning. "Barry, my man." When he embraced Barry, the smell of tomato sauce and nicotine, of cologne and musky B.O. washed over him. A complicated aroma that Barry had inhaled much of his forty-nine years of life. That hug, followed by Ron waving Phil away, both relieved and relaxed Barry. If he had been in serious shit, Ron would have skipped the pleasantries. The suggestion of a meeting just a ruse for a final haunted ride to perdition.

"Sit." Ron gestured at a plush leather chair. After pouring them both a shot of Maker's Mark on the rocks, he sat back down and slumped forward, resting his elbows on the desk. "We've got a kind of situation, Barry, and we need help resolving this thing." Ron palmed the sparse dark hair back on his scalp.

Barry knew who "we" referred to.

"You and I have always helped each other, so I know you'll want to do your part to make things right."

"Of course." Barry leaned in to show enthusiasm even if he only felt confusion. "Is there a job you need me on? I'm in. And you know I'll do it gratis since you got me plenty of scores in the past."

"Good, good." Ron cracked his knuckles. "Don't know if you heard about the robbery a month ago at a Fast Loans nearby in Passaic..."

"Uh, no, I didn't." Barry kept his eyes steady on Ron and allowed no facial twitches.

"Sloppy, amateurish job." Ron winced. "Not your style. The two dipshits involved were too stupid to realize it was a front, money laundering and such. They were stealing from my employers." He sighed while shaking his head. "Only took twenty large. Not a huge amount, but a major show of disrespect."

"Sure, I get it," Barry said. "A pair of dick-brains. Want me to ask around for their names?"

"No." Ron approached Barry's chair. "One of them was Sam Jacobs. Name ring a bell?"

"Sam?"

"Yeah, the guy you did a job with four years ago. Remember, before you pulled an eighteen month stretch in East Jersey State?"

"Oh, right, right. *That* Sam." Barry kept his expression rubbery and casual. "Any leads on his whereabouts?"

Ron's smile appeared created with great pain. "We found him. Unfortunately, my man Phil—" he pointed toward the door, "—was over-enthusiastic and we lost Sam before extracting his partner's name." Ron perched on the edge of the desk. He stared at Barry, his brow scrunched in contemplation.

Thinking among criminal associates rarely led to good things so Barry interrupted the oppressive void of silence. "I'm happy to find the other dude."

"I'm ninety-nine percent certain it was his cousin, Justin. Another stupid prick who gets caught and locked-up every few years."

"I met Justin while I was doing time," Barry said. "Total dumb-fuck."

"Yeah." Ron rubbed at his lips with two fingers. "So I need you to eliminate him fast, like within the week."

The turn of events seemed both beneficial and troubling. "Ron, I want to help," Barry said, stuttering, "but I'm a porch climber, a second story man." He wiped at his damp forehead. "You know I'm not hired juice. Never done that type of work."

"Sure, sure." Ron again smiled without joy. "See, if I present two deceased schnooks to my employers, it ends there. If they investigate—and they will—they'll torture Justin and he'll give out names. People he worked with, guys in the slammer, people he wants to finger. Your name likely, since he knows you from prison and from your jobs with his cousin Sam." Ron clipped a thin cigar but didn't light it. "If you don't handle this, we're all in trouble. Especially you."

Phil reentered the office with a black leather satchel and unzipped it. Inside lay a selection of knives, along with a hook and a pike.

"Your target is running scared after Sam got popped, but he's definitely been spotted in downtown Manhattan." Ron's voice became a whisper. "No guns. Too loud. Stab him or slit his throat. You know the deal. You offed a guy once, right?"

Barry nodded. He'd sliced someone's arm when they tried to rip off his wallet outside a Bronx bar, but then he exaggerated the story into a brutal execution by stabbing to keep him safe while in prison. So Barry could shower with impunity. "But, I..."

"Don't worry, we'll know Justin's exact location over the weekend. You'll go into Manhattan at night, do the job, and head out—far away."

"Well, I planned—"

"Don't tell me the destination." Ron pulled an envelope from a desk drawer. "Five hundred should get you pretty far.

I'm not paying for the job itself because it's what you call life-preservation."

"Understood."

On the half-hour drive back home, Barry watched the marshy terrain around the Meadowlands Sports Center flash by. Phil the silent driver sped from I-80 onto 95, merging with the Jersey Turnpike near Secaucus. Along the foul Hackensack River, Barry saw black smoke gushing from factory chimneys, the flames rising atop gas towers above the Turnpike, and considered his dilemma. He really had no choice. Murder the only option. Today's meeting had been the first he'd heard of Sam's demise. He assumed the guy was hiding out somewhere. Sam Jacobs, his partner in the robbery of Fast Loans in Passaic. No wonder no one else had hit that joint before. A mob front. If Barry didn't take out Cousin Justin, his own guilty ass was cooked.

On Friday, Barry met Debra at the bar inside Palisades Grill on the cliffs overlooking the twinkling sparkle of Manhattan and the colored lights of ships cruising up and down the Hudson River. He had flirted with her before, but those times she'd been seeing someone.

Debra lowered her long fake eyelashes in confession mode. "I'm recently single," she said in a hushed voice, as if admitting to a rare disease.

"That's no crime," Barry replied. He knew Debra was the type of person who couldn't survive alone for long, the type who preferred a bad relationship over waking up solitary in the world, having to face oneself, without direction, without appreciation. "So what are you doing for the holidays?"

"Drinking." She laughed. "I hate this time of year. My parents are both dead and I don't speak to my sisters in Pennsylvania."

"I'm going to Florida, next Tuesday or Wednesday."

"Really?"

"Yeah, I can't stand the cold and all the false Christmas cheer," he said. "I mean Christ, I'm nearly fifty."

"But you could pass for late forties."

Barry didn't reply. Instead he studied his drink and surreptitiously ogled Debra's shapely figure, imagining her in a bathing suit stretched out on the beach. "Why don't you join me, spend a week down south? We could hit Miami or Palm Beach, then even the Florida Keys."

Debra's head hung loose from the alcohol but she twisted her neck to study him. "That sounds great, but I'm pretty broke and still getting over Ray-Ray."

"Ray-Ray?" Barry held an innate suspicion of people with two identical first names. "Listen, I'd be covering travel and lodging." He still had seven grand leftover from the Fast Loan job and the desire to spend that dirty cash fast.

Debra leaned close to him from her neighboring bar stool. "I need a vacation and warm weather, I really do." She gave him a cock-eyed glance. "Would we be sharing one room?"

"No, I could get you a separate room nearby. I'm not expecting—"

"How about a two-room suite?" she asked. "I don't plan things in advance. I like to decide my sleeping arrangements on the fly." She nestled her head of big Jersey hair on his shoulder. "You're not bullshitting me?" she whispered.

"Hell no." He felt as honest as someone with a criminal background could feel, and noticed the arousal when she brushed a hand up his leg then chest in slow motion.

"I'm not going home with you tonight but I will go to Florida, if you call me." Debra snorted. "I don't believe you will though."

"Pack your sexiest bathing suits."

"Bikinis but no thongs." She wagged a finger. "Stopped wearing them after thirty."

"Same with me."

She gave Barry a few sloppy kisses on the lips and cheeks then staggered outside when her Uber pulled up. The bartender handed him napkins to wipe off the bright red lipstick smears. He couldn't explain why, but he felt an odd love for Debra. The sense of not really knowing someone so you could fill in the blanks, imagine them as exactly the person you needed.

Standing on Twenty-Seventh Street of Manhattan in the frigid cold, Barry could no longer focus on Debra. A distraction. He'd meet her after midnight as planned. First, do the job, then get cleaned up at his hotel room, then haul ass to Penn Station for their Amtrak train ride to Florida. He'd been born in 1969, the same year his favorite New York movie with Jon Voight and

Dustin Hoffman came out. Seeing it at age eighteen on VHS and again later on DVD, Barry realized he fit into that late sixties era. Poor hustlers and small-time-crooks eking out a living in the harsh landscape of a filthy and dangerous Times Square. He couldn't relate to the modern day city where everything was expensive, shiny, and out of reach.

Over the last hour, Barry circled the block several times attempting to hand out cards. New Yorkers moved in a hurry and walked even faster during icy weather. They were especially adept at sidestepping around a hooded stranger wearing ragged clothing and offering cards for a nonexistent massage parlor in Brooklyn. To add to his created character, he talked aloud: muttering, spitting, asking questions. Just as Barry's target stood nearby hiding in plain sight, he too was stalking in plain sight. If anyone described what went down to the police later, they would peg him as a mentally disturbed, homeless man.

New York was the city that never slept, but on the Monday night before Christmas, car and pedestrian traffic thinned out after ten. The bell-ringing from Santa became sparser, less spirited. The cue for Barry to make his move.

Ron had explained over the phone on Saturday. "Yeah, we tracked Justin down in Manhattan. He worked Times Square dressed as a Pirate of the Caribbean for tourist photos, then scored a job with the Salvation Army as a sidewalk Santa in the Grammercy Park vicinity. So you need to do the thing we spoke of—soon."

Barry had psyched himself into the act out of desperation. Life or death. *His.* Still, as he walked in a shuffling stagger from

Park Avenue South toward the chiming bell, he decided to make sure this Santa wasn't some hapless fool in the wrong place at the wrong time.

Santa had retreated into an alcove formed by a descending stairway on one side and a jutting four-story brownstone on the other. The spot shielded him from the bracing evening wind and kept him—for the most part—out of sight, about thirty feet west of Lexington Avenue.

Since Barry had circled the block numerous times in his disguise, Santa showed no apprehension when he approached. Not until he got up close.

"Hey, beat it," Santa said. "I've got no money for you. Done for the night. Step off."

Barry feigned moving three paces away and checked the street for a break in car traffic. When the cross street lights turned red, he lunged at Santa, knocking him off balance against the iron gate of an alleyway that separated the two buildings.

"Justin?" Barry tore the bogus white beard off the startled man's face. "It is you."

"Fuck, Barry, is that you? I didn't expect you to be disguised."

Barry had no time for small talk, only action. He jabbed the blade into Justin's stomach but instead tore into the massive padding used to create Santa's girth. Before losing his nerve entirely, he brought the knife up and sliced at Justin's neck. A sharp scraping noise sounded. Justin wore a protective metal collar, as if expecting an attack. *What the hell?*

Justin kneed Barry in the groin and his knife went skittering across the pavement. The fist extruding from Justin's red Santa sleeve gripped another larger knife. "Thanks for making this easy." He slashed at Barry's side tearing away layers of clothing.

Barry felt the cold air but no pain so he dodged away. "Making what easy?" He retreated as the knife whistled through the air, just missing his chest.

"You delivered yourself right to me." Justin smiled, his scarred face extra ugly under the sagging red cap and pom-pom.

"I delivered?"

"You don't steal twenty large from *them* and walk away."

Total realization struck. Barry had been set up—the target of this hit, not the hired juice. Hell, Ron was cackling back in his Paramus office, betting that they'd both take each other out.

An adrenaline rush of fear helped Barry grab Justin's right forearm and bend it back to the point of pain. He hammered it against the iron gate until the knife dropped. Before Justin could recover, Barry took the pike from his pocket and using all his weight pounded it into the guy's heart. Justin's eyes went wide with fear before glazing over. His hands flopped around as his fat Santa body trembled and shook until he collapsed to the sidewalk.

"Mommy, Daddy, that man just killed Santa Claus!" a young girl shrieked from the corner of Lexington Avenue.

Barry panicked. Unable to retrieve the impacted pike, he left it lodged in Justin's chest and hustled west toward Park Avenue.

"Somebody stop that guy," a man shouted.

Barry brushed by pedestrians, but glancing back noticed them taking photos, maybe even videos. *Fuck, fuck, got to make it to the subway.* His side ached like he was getting a stitch, but when he rubbed it, the flesh felt wet and warm. That asshole Justin had cut him. He just didn't register it immediately in the bitter cold.

Barry heard a siren. It could be for anything or it could be for him. Park Avenue was only a half block away, then another block south to the subway entrance. People stood massed ahead of him, pointing and shouting. *How had this thing escalated so quickly?* He registered the street construction, a large hole in the asphalt surrounded by safety lights and fencing, then darted off the sidewalk toward it. Without thinking, he plunged into a low tunnel running just below street level. In one direction, seeping hot steam clouded the passage, so he moved back east toward Lexington.

In about fifty yards he found a metal ladder leading downward. *Don't get caught, don't get caught.* He descended into a pitch black subway tunnel and waited until his eyes adjusted to see the faint shine of rails below. Water dripped from above and chunks of granite lay across sections of tracks. Barry knew the Lexington Avenue line yawed west below 42nd Street and subsequent stops were on Park Avenue. He must be on a leftover spur from the moribund Third Avenue Line. Manhattan was spider-webbed with abandoned train tracks.

Flicking a lighter, he got his bearings and began moving north. Just six blocks to the Penn Station vicinity and he'd find an avenue of escape back to the surface. The dank tunnel smelled of entombed death. A chilling breeze came from somewhere ahead along with the phantom rumbling of distant invisible subways on other lines. Barry hurried along the tracks but sloshed through puddles. Coming out of a deep one he studied his unfamiliar-shaped boot. A large gray rat sat atop it gripping the sides. "Shit," he shouted and stamped his boot down on dry ground until the creature scampered away.

When his vision adjusted further, he could discern other people—carrying on, living their lives. The urban legends were true. They groaned or laughed as he passed by them. Some smoked cigarettes at the edges of the tunnel where they'd built ramshackle shelters. Overhead, the faint sound of carolers on the street singing "Fa-la-la-la-la..." filtered down.

The tracks Barry followed veered left and crossed another set before dead-ending in a mess of broken rails and rubble. He sparked the lighter and decided to follow the neighboring tracks north. A grimy hand grabbed his elbow. "Stay here. Don't go." He shook loose, having no plans to join their subterranean civilization. Another three blocks and he was safe. Barry had never identified with Ratso Rizzo, the sickly loser, but with Joe Buck. He imagined arriving in Florida and changing into short-sleeved shirts, ditching his winter clothes like Jon Voight had.

He smiled wide, almost delirious, and picked up the pace, ignoring hissing voices saying, "Stop," and "Come back." God, he was tired but needed to move faster. Outrun time. Once above ground he'd make his way to Hotel Metro on 35th Street, take a shower, put on fresh clothes, bandage his side and get to Penn Station by 12:30 to meet Debra. All the hard shit lay behind him: robbery, murder, a bleak Christmas. Barry ran and ran, picturing Debra sprawled across his Florida hotel bed tipsy and naked, her tan lines showing and the moist heaven waiting. Their love would blossom then grow under a wintry sun.

His head felt woozy, maybe he was catching a cold, but who cared? From somewhere he heard Harry Nilsson singing "Everybody's Talkin," except the words had ceased and Nilsson was mouthing, "Waugh... Waugh-wah-wah-waugh." Just one more block. Barry could already hear Debra saying she loved him as he descended while she held him. And it was so goddamned cold in that tunnel, but in the midst of the smell of ash and soot and all the dust that a corpse eventually decays into, he felt something good. The sun rose behind him, heat growing, as its light illuminated the darkness beyond. Barry laughed so hard that tears streamed down his face. *Florida, here I come!* And the sun got warmer and brighter on his back, the tunnel rattled and vibrated, so Barry let himself go. Total relaxation. He may have even pissed his pants like Ratso Rizzo did on the Greyhound bus, but it didn't matter. Nothing mattered.

He could hear the Greyhound's horn. *Merry fucking Christmas.* Shrieking noise, a shuddering vibration, and the light grew brighter, and Barry got to his destination in an instant.

FALLEN ANGELS

Fort Ord had closed in 1994. The military base on Monterey Bay stretched from the coastline miles back—halfway east to Salinas. A small university, CSUMB, started up, followed by new housing units and strip malls. All that sprouted near Highway 1 and the bay. Some acreage became a park system with meandering trails, but most of the vast sprawl remained hardscrabble land after twenty-five years.

Deere scanned the stark surroundings. "It looks haunted."

"You don't believe in spirits or monsters," Sven said.

"No," Deere replied. "The monsters are all within us."

Hazardous chemicals lingered in the soil, and fenced-off danger zones with unexploded ordnance remained. Those issues were whispered about from Seaside to Marina—places that bordered the base. Decaying barracks and empty officers' homes remained in facsimiles of village squares with abandoned outbuildings that once served as canteens or social halls. Ghost towns. The hollow encampments stretched eastward to where paved roads became dirt treads. Amid the scrubby grass and dwarf pine trees, surrounded by dung-colored hills, the Pacific receded into myth.

Fort Ord is where they found themselves, a half-mile back from any traffic or signs of life. And that's where they found her.

"Looks like she's been dead awhile," Deere said to his partner. The young woman was illuminated by their powerful flashlights, a small island of clarity in a foggy soup of darkness.

"Yup." Sven bent down to examine her. "Keep your beam steady, JoJo." She appeared to be wearing only a bathrobe.

Deere's white light took in the corpse but also caught Sven's western hat, casting a giant ominous shadow.

"No sign of blood," Sven said, a frown etched into his face.

"She wasn't stabbed or shot?"

"Not what I meant." Sven showed a mildly annoyed expression. He removed the outsized hat to rub his brow. "Extremely pale and puncture marks. I'm guessing she's been drained of much of her blood."

Deere moved closer and squinted. "Melted candle wax on her too. Is this where you're going to say a vampire done this?" He picked up bird feathers near the body.

Sven snorted. "I don't give credence to such movie creatures—at least on this planet." He stared upward into space as he was wont to do at times of deliberation. "However, there are people who drink blood, for whatever fucked-up reason. They get high off it. Doesn't make them young or live forever. Probably makes them puke eventually. But they do, for ritualistic reasons."

"No wonder we got summoned," Deere said. "Always for the weird shit."

"And so it goes, JoJo."

Deere exhaled. "Could you stop calling me JoJo?"

"Remind me, what's your legal name?"

"John Joseph Deere."

"No way in hell I'm calling you John Deere." Sven cough-laughed. "And Joseph? Sorry, no. Anyway, I didn't come up with JoJo."

"No, that near deaf criminal did," Deere replied. "Asked me my name and I said, Joe. He said, 'what?' and I said Joe again. He said, 'Okay, JoJo' and ever since that name's stuck."

Sven shook his head. "We never get the nickname we want."

Deere turned. "Someone's coming."

"Oh, Jesus, him again."

"You know who it is?"

"Same guy with different names." Sven grunted in disapproval. "The local constabulary."

A police officer entered their area of light. "Point those things downward," he said. A small woman followed behind. "I'm Sergeant Jimenez and this is Officer Kim." He cleared his throat. "Heard you guys were nosing around, stepping on our jurisdiction."

"And what jurisdiction would that be?" Sven asked.

"The City of Marina," Jimenez said. "A chunk of this base is our property, within city limits."

"True," Sven replied, "but I probably don't need to remind you that we're on Bureau of Land Management territory here. Government turf. Washington D.C. called us in." Sven flashed ID cards at Jimenez's disgruntled face.

"So you're going to take this one away from us?"

"Hell, no. We'd love your help. Got information on anyone who's been draining their victim's blood?"

Jimenez went pale. "I haven't encountered that."

Sven offered a silver flask to soothe the policeman. "I bow with one arm extended."

"We don't drink on duty."

"Tragic." Deere intercepted the flask. "No reason to waste this good stuff."

"I'll request an ambulance, bring her to the city morgue," Jimenez said as if asking permission.

"Yes, you do that." Sven studied the victim again. "Any theories about her, and why out here?"

"No. An officer from Seaside called this in, being north of their city limits." Behind Jimenez, Officer Kim looked unsettled. "This is twisted, serial killer stuff."

Sven frowned. "No, a cult murder."

"Is that why you two were called in?"

"Yup." Deere handed the flask back to Sven. "In a filthy world of human garbage preying on innocents, we're the clean-up crew."

"You think there's a connection to that other death?" Officer

Kim's index finger pointed northeast.

Neither Sven nor Deere replied.

A week earlier they were tipped to the alleyway behind Lucille's Ball, a drag bar in Castroville. Situated ten miles from the victim on Fort Ord. What they thought was a woman, turned out to be a Latino transvestite. The corpse lay moldering at the bottom of a green metal dumpster. Nothing unusual about the lipstick and makeup, the dress or the big curly wig. It was the man's face. When Sven opened his closed eyelids with tweezers, Deere saw the eyeballs were gone. Just ugly red sockets and connective tissue.

"That shit ain't right." Made Deere think of calamari first, then about hurling dinner.

A sheriff from nearby Prunedale clomped around in the grayish haze of a foggy sunset. "This place should've been closed long ago."

"You think a customer did this?" Deere felt his brow scrunch.

"Maybe," Sheriff Rearden said. "But a drag bar attracts haters. People threatened by trannies, who want to stop them, send a warning."

"Nah," Sven said. "You beat someone up or maybe burn the place down as a warning. No regular angry dipshit kills then removes their victim's eyeballs."

The sheriff seemed unsteady. "Could seagulls have pecked them out?"

"Nope." Sven lit a cigarette.

"I thought you were quitting," Deere said.

"I am. Part of the cure involves continuing smoking." Sven turned back to the sheriff. "This was done by a human."

"Where you guys from again?"

"Texas..."

"Really?"

Sven stubbed out his cigarette while Deere squatted down to examine the ground around the dumpster. "Bird feathers."

"Hey." Sheriff Rearden pointed upward. "It's the Goodyear blimp." His expression showed wonder. "Reminds me of being a kid, imagining riding in one. Haven't seen it for years."

Neither of the agents bothered to look. "Yeah, a helluva thing," Deere said.

"We need names of everyone who visited Lucille's Ball over the last three nights." Sven smiled. "That's all."

At Ford Ord, Sergeant Jimenez made calls inside his car with its lights strobing. Officer Kim remained outside with them.

"Need to talk to whoever is in charge." Deere stared off. "Over there."

"Over where?" Kim asked softly.

"The East Garrison," Sven interrupted. "Military personnel remain on duty there. They might have heard or seen something."

Kim acted reluctant.

"We follow every possible angle," Deere said. "We're older than you and slower, but thorough."

"Part of that is true," she said. "Okay, I'll contact the Major." Kim walked toward the distorted police radio jabber coming from the Sergeant's car.

In the twilight of the following day, they knocked on a clapboard cottage's door. Deere watched men wearing important hats and tan uniforms move outside between a larger central building and the smaller residences.

"Major McAnus?" Deere said loudly.

"It's McAnnis..." A man with a stiff posture and sour expression opened the door.

"What's this all about?"

Sven came forward. "Didn't Officer Kim—"

"Oh, you're the investigators." He frowned at Deere's Hawaiian shirt. "I guess you prefer plain clothes." The Major ushered them inside. "Can we make this brief? It's dinner time over at the commissary."

A boiled cabbage smell and a burnt rubbery meat—like Salisbury steak—flavored the air.

"Now that the base is closed, what goes on here?" Deere said.

"National Guard units." The Major's mouth flexed, animating his mustache. "My Army team draws maps, and prepares for any unexpected aggression."

"From whom?" Sven asked.

The Major led them to an outer deck with a powerful telescope. "Directly west," he said, "is China. We don't expect imminent hostilities, but remain vigilant."

Deere restrained laughter. China could be a threat someday to Taiwan, but to Central California? And what would officers without any artillery do to repel them if they parked their submarines in Monterey Bay?

"At present, we monitor earthquakes on land and sea. Anything that might trigger a deadly tsunami." The Major nodded. "We're a small defensive force, not an active military presence."

Deere sniffed. "Clearly."

"Let's cut to the chase." Sven collapsed onto a deck couch that groaned in protest. "A woman was murdered under odd circumstances about a mile southwest. It's rather quiet here, away from highway noise. Have you heard anything suspicious over the last week?"

"Cries for help or screams?" Deere added.

The Major paced the deck, as if trying to physically locate the words. "Events occur every week or two out there."

"Events?"

"I don't understand, being older, but young people hold these outdoor parties. Suddenly lights flash and they blast this terrible robot music. Lasts an hour."

"I think they call them raves," Deere said, but the Major ignored him.

"We complain, but it takes a few tries to get police response. By the time anyone arrives, they've gone. Just their junk left out in the dunes. Glow sticks, food wrappers, drugs, Halloween masks. Hate it, but my hands are tied. Not Military property anymore."

"College kids?"

"No, mid-twenties to thirties, from what I've seen." He signaled toward the telescope.

"And the last one was?"

"About a week ago."

Sven dug into a carry bag. "I have moon cycle charts."

The Major sneered. "Okay..."

Sven scrutinized them. "Last week must have been a sign party for the sun moving into Taurus. And tomorrow night the moon goes full. Bingo."

"They never use the same spot twice," Major McAnnis said. "Leaves you a thousand acres to cover." He looked upward. "You hear that droning noise? A Goodyear blimp has been flying over lately. Haven't seen one in ten years."

Sven didn't reply.

"Are we done?" The Major stamped around turning off lights. "If you have any other questions, don't hesitate to contact our desk sergeant, not me. Ever."

Outside, Deere and Sven wandered beyond the garrison until they reached dirt trails. "Think he's clean?" Deere said.

"Likes to watch. Maybe a voyeur." Sven frowned "You have the signals, JoJo?"

Deere planted four flares in the ground over a large rectangular area. They flickered and sparked a pink-red light.

"That should alert Mother Trucker," Sven said. "Give her plenty of room to park."

For the next two nights, they patrolled the grasslands and scrub brush, the sandy dunes and flats in a jeep loaned by the East Garrison's desk sergeant. On their third attempt, Deere wore night vision goggles and sat on a chair-back in the rear while Sven drove slowly across the vast base.

"You get those from your time with the NSA?" Sven asked.

"Maybe."

Sven knew Deere didn't like speaking about those days. He came off all peace, love, Bob Dylan and Ken Kesey—with a Jimmy Buffet wardrobe—but clearly had been involved in some dark shit way back when.

"Can you roll us a little smoother, chief? Killing my ass on the bumps."

"You're aware of my driving skills?"

"Sure, you got a tractor license at sixteen and are winging it on anything else."

Sven chortled. "Last night of the full moon. Has to happen."

"Unless it's a movable feast." Deere slid down to the seat. "Different parkland or beach each time."

"They'll come back." Sven let the jeep rest in a gully while they sipped from thermoses of chicken noodle soup. "Not bad for 7-Eleven."

"Yeah, we're still breathing." Vapors rose into Deere's face.

Sven huffed and puffed his way up a hill of soft clay dirt to a near 360-degree view. He focused on the southwest.

Eventually he saw movement and faint green a mile away. Not flashlights, but possibly glow sticks, as a line of people in a soft parade moved east. Sven let Deere slurp his soup until he was certain. Flickering torches were lit to form a semicircle.

Sven hustled downward to the jeep. "Something's starting up. You drive us over."

"A wise decision." Deere tightened his thermos cap.

"But with the headlights off, JoJo. Whoever is in charge, I want them."

"Sure, boss, but that may not be our psycho killer."

"True. He'll know something though."

"Weapons?"

"Only for self-defense," Sven said. "Didn't they teach you karate and judo in the NSA?"

"I cannot confirm or deny that I was taught anything, that I was a member of said organization, or that I even exist on this plane of reality."

They motored forward, the jeep's frame jostling and shuddering in the darkness—the full moon their only guide. About two hundred yards away from the now throbbing lights, Sven tapped Deere's shoulder. "Let's walk from here."

Deere nestled the jeep into a copse of pine trees and killed the engine. The sound system played a droning, Eastern thing. Not dance music. The people in attendance hummed or moaned along, like an "Om" chant but more nasal, more eerie.

When they got within forty yards, both men lay flat on the rise of a dune. "Pass me the goggles," Sven whispered.

About thirty people sat around a roped-off stage area. Sven studied their costumes. Big furry rabbit and bear masks, wolf heads atop figures in brown robes. Not laughable Disney images, but old handmade masks from pagan rituals. There were goat men and witches with gnarled pointy noses, a prancing unicorn man, and various women in skimpy clothing—faces painted a monstrous green, and vampirish teeth descending from blood red lipsticked mouths.

"A freak-show ceremony."

"Should we be getting scared?" Deere asked.

"No. Just watch the performance area."

"Pass me the flask."

"Afterwards."

A tall robed man wearing a ram's skull mask led a cloaked figure to the brightly lit staging area and the crowd grunted in approval. A generator ratcheted away nearby. He removed the cloak to reveal a young naked woman with wide drugged eyes. Her quivery expression was half ecstatic and half-terrified. The Ram man laid her out atop a long slab table on the stage.

The others began groaning and humming, issuing animalistic noises. The music's volume increased until bongos and congas began thumping.

"Sounds like voodoo drums," Deere said.

"Get over there on my flank. The shit's about to hit the fan."

"Do you think she's out there waiting?"

"I sure as hell hope so."

Onstage, the high priest painted a bright yellow circle below the supine woman's left breast. He howled, then mumbled Latin phrases into a microphone. Sven sent a text on his phone. No reply. Damn, they might have to rush in. Not good.

The leader picked up a jagged bone knife and held it high

toward the light. The audience went wild, dancing or thrashing about, groping each other, hooting in approval. Cheering him on.

"It's a fucking Mayan sacrifice." Sven lumbered toward the spectacle.

A megaphone voice called out from the west, beyond the stage. "This is the Marina Police. You are breaking the law. Hands up and don't move. You are surrounded!" Shots fired into the air.

Torches crashed to the ground as the spectators panicked and bolted northeast. The nude woman rose off the slab and staggered away from the lit-up stage area. Their leader looked furious, slicing his bone blade through the air.

Sven heard Deere fire warning rounds as participants neared him. They turned and ran directly at Sven. He pressed his hat tightly down and lunged forward. Two people collided with Sven, bouncing off his bulk. He swatted another guy into the scrub brush. "I want the Ram Man," he shouted.

A black SUV roared over to the stage and the high priest jumped inside. Then it drove fast toward Sven, hitting and throwing two followers into the dirt.

Sven ducked behind a tree. He tried to photograph the expensive vehicle's plates but someone struck his head with a club.

"Ow, that fucking hurt." He wrestled the masked man into a choke-hold then raised him up off the ground, legs kicking wildly. "Do you know how much my hat cost?" When the assailant passed out, Sven dropped the fool and cuffed him. The others had dispersed in a dozen directions.

Deere appeared from the darkness with an unconscious figure in a gorilla mask folded over his shoulder. They loaded the suspects into the jeep and rumbled over toward the police car idling by the stage area—its blue and reds flashing.

Officer Kim stood outside, all five foot two and calm, holding her gun on two masked participants.

"Thanks for coming," Sven said. "We saved a life tonight."

"Three nights of waiting," Kim said. "Glad something happened."

"Sergeant Jimenez didn't want to—"

"Didn't want anything to do with your hunches. I brought my brother." In the passenger side of the prowl car sat a bored young Asian man playing games on his phone, a police bullhorn nestled on his lap.

"And the woman?"

Kim gestured. A shivering figure covered in a blanket lay across the car's back seat.

"Damn, you're good."

Kim half-smiled. "I know."

Sven scrutinized the four prisoners' features under his facial ID detector beam. "Take this dude and woman for questioning, along with the sacrifice girl. Keep them detained overnight. They'll break down when the drugs wear off."

"And the other two?" Kim's forehead was pinched.

"They're in their mid-thirties and have records. Must know something. I'll bring them to your station tomorrow."

"That's highly irregular."

"Imagine they got away and we retrieved them for you. Then everybody's happy."

"No torture." Kim poked a finger into the mass where Sven's chest and stomach met.

He giggled as it tickled him. "Of course not. Just questioning."

Deere laughed. "They'll wish they were tortured after Sven tells his hat story."

Officer Kim showed reluctant agreement. She herded two prisoners into the back seat, then drove toward the distant car headlights cruising on Highway 1.

Brendan came back into consciousness slowly. He sat in a booth with Naugahyde-covered seats around a wood slab table. Four booths, a frosted glass barrier, then another row alongside a bar. A woman with a lumberjack's weather-blown face tended bar, drying glasses. A banner hung above her: *Mother Trucker*. Then Brendan noticed Jared, head lolling about. Across the table sat two men, big and broad, near twice his age. Stern-looking motherfuckers.

"Is this that retro diner in Santa Cruz?" Brendan asked.

The silver-haired man in a Hawaiian shirt chuckled.

The big hat guy sipped at scotch or whiskey. Cleared his throat. "Brendan Lorber and," he kicked the other man, "Jared Rank."

"Sure smells rank, Sven," his partner said.

"Welcome to our lounge," Sven continued. "Deere and I

serve strong drinks and passable food. We just need information about that ritual sacrifice."

Brendan remembered. "I heard there was a pop-up rave," he said. "Wanted to dance, get buzzed. Meet women."

"Wrong answer," Sven said.

"Why are you hassling us?" Jared asked. "Just innocent spectators."

"Innocent?" Sven slammed a fist down hard. "Both of you clowns have records. Brendan: two robberies and aggravated assault, plus resisting arrest."

"My record's clean for the past three months."

Sven ignored him. "Jared: two aggravated assaults and an attempted rape charge. Part of a gang-bang thing in Palo Alto last year."

"I never touched her," Jared insisted.

"Because the cops stopped it before you got your turn, dipshit."

"What authority do you have? I demand to see a lawyer."

Both older men laughed, then drank, then laughed some more.

Sven displayed a western-style five-point badge emblazoned with a Buddha face showing three eyes. "We are the Omni-Authority. Past, present, and future converging on you now."

"What are the charges?" Brendan asked.

"Accessory to an attempted murder," Deere said. "Possible accessory to the Fort Ord and Castroville murders. And general fuckery."

"That's crazy," Jared shouted. "The sacrifice deal was a

surprise. We planned to distribute X and Ketamine to the ladies. Have a sex party. I freaked when that dude flashed his knife."

"So you're not murderers, just guys who drug women for sex." Sven smiled anger. "I have much more respect for you now." He leaned across the table. "Who's your cult leader and where can we find him?"

Jared trembled. "Can't tell you. Don't want to die."

"We all have to go someday." Deere chewed on beer nuts.

Sven grabbed Brendan's shirt collar. "Where is that ram-headed fucker?"

Jared leapt up and ran the length of the lounge side. Finding no escape, he rushed around the frosted partition and back toward a curtained doorway.

Sven cut across to block the doorway with his mass. Brendan watched Jared careen into Sven and recoil. He rammed him again, then thumped his fists against the large man's chest. Sven stood unperturbed, smoking a cigarette.

Deere cuffed Brendan to a metal handle set in the wall. *What the hell were the handles for?*

Jared turned, seeing something. He sprinted toward the far end of the lounge to an emergency exit door.

"Don't go out that way," Sven bellowed. "Please, for your own safety."

"Fuck off, fatso." Jared turned the circular wheel, unlatched the locks, then pushed out through the opening.

"Aaaaahhhhh!" Jared's scream went on and on, slowly fading into the distance.

Deere raised the thick blinds on the wall. When Brendan

saw only clouds, he almost fainted, a tickle of vomit rising. "We're...up in the air."

"A thousand feet." Sven's face was stern.

The bartender closed the hatch, whistling to herself.

"What is this?" Brendan gazed around.

"We travel by blimp," Sven replied. "With the Goodyear logo, we're hiding in plain sight. People look up, register it, then ignore us."

"So Jared, he's..." Brendan slumped forward onto the table.

"I really need to talk to Jared about his landing." Sven squinted. "He just didn't land right."

Brendan dreamed of topless women in animal masks dancing around a campfire, until one approached, then slugged him. He woke to the older men jostling him, slapping his face. "Stop."

"We're out of time." Deere pressed in close. "Talk, or first stop is Marina jail, then Soledad or Lompoc."

"For what?"

"Accessory to murder," Sven shouted. "Where were you three nights ago, and a week before that?"

"On a solo camping trip in the Big Sur mountains."

"Alone, with no witnesses?" Deere said. "You plan to drive around the country and sell that bullshit alibi door-to-door?"

"But I didn't kill anyone."

"We don't care," Deere said, then gazed at Sven. "It's useless. Let's dump him." Both agents perp-walked Brendan over to the emergency hatch.

The bartender cackled while opening the latches. Both large men pressed him along.

"I-I don't know the leader's name, but he's a rich dude," Brendan said. "Wait. He works for or is an investor in this church in the mountains. Run by a pastor who supports the pagan rituals."

"Above Santa Cruz?" Deere asked.

"The Church of the Fallen Angel, near Felton."

Sven and Deere lifted him to the exit hatch and tossed him out.

Brendan's scream got cut short when he face-planted into dirt. Looking behind, he saw the blimp had landed—somewhere in the back country of Fort Ord. Being alive held little joy. Brother K would kill him for squealing.

Sergeant Jimenez was so delighted with Sven and Deere delivering suspects, and letting the Marina Police Force take credit, he loaned them an impounded Subaru Outback. The only rational explanation for Jared Rank's death was an accidental plunge from a defective hang glider. Neither Jimenez nor Kim seemed eager to search Monterey Bay for glider wreckage.

Deere motored north to Santa Cruz on Highway 1, then veered uphill on Highway 17. Though only ten minutes from a California beach town, Felton held a rustic seventies vibe. Sort of a base camp to the Santa Cruz Mountains. Historic lodges and weathered local bars sat on a main street; beyond lay rises and pastures, farmlands and tree-dense parks. Old hippies passed them in VW buses and Volvos, ranchers and farmers drove pickup trucks—some with horse trailers. Redwoods sprouted in every cleft of the hilly terrain. Forests held dark mossy secrets and off-the-grid cranks living in leaky cabins fueled by propane and rusted visions of freedom.

A mile above town, they found the small church, painted purple and orange. Deere and Sven climbed the outer staircase. Inside the empty chapel, annoying modern dance music blared.

Sven shouted, "Pastor?"

A dark-haired man emerged from the rear and turned down the sound. He wore a white shirt and black pants, but nothing about him suggested clergy.

"I'm Pastor Gorman." His baby face smiled.

"Hello, uh, Father," Deere said. "Are you old enough to be a father?"

"I'm thirty-three but still get carded," he said. "Please, it's Kevin. My friends call me KG."

"Church of the Fallen Angel?" Sven said. "Satan was a fallen angel."

"True, but there were others," the pastor said. "I study all religions and preach a blend to my flock. God and Satan are just representations of good and evil. I prefer religions that predate Christianity."

"So you teach both good and evil?" Deere cocked his head.

The pastor snorted. "I don't teach. I accept them. Both exist, always, balancing us through life. Can't have one without the other."

"You sound like Robert Mitchum as the preacher with *Love*

written on one hand and *Hate* on the other."

"Who's Robert Mitchum?" He frowned. "Are you cops? What brought you to Felton?"

"We're government men," Sven said, "investigating pagan rituals going on around Monterey Bay."

"The government cares?"

"Okay...*Father*," Deere said. "Enough. Two murders and another attempted one in the last two weeks. We're in a hurry. Tell us about the tall guy who works here. He wears a ram's skull at ceremonies and has a thing for blood and hearts and eyeballs."

The pastor's face paled. "Do I need a lawyer?"

"No, you're going to need a medic." Deere approached him.

"You would strike a man of the cloth?"

"I'm an atheist," Deere said. "And we researched you. Former priest drummed out of various churches, bounced around from Castroville to Aptos, and now gone rogue up here. Basically defrocked."

"No, I'm still frocked. I left the constraints of Catholicism to speak my truth."

"We don't give a frock," Sven said. Both agents closed-in on the skinny man.

"Y-you want Brother Kenneth," Gorman said. "He's from a wealthy East Bay family. He bankrolled me, bought this decrepit church, helped me attract a following." He began crying. "He'll kill me for telling."

"Maybe," Deere said, "but we would have made you wish you were dead."

"Why the sacrifices?" Sven tilted his brim up.

The pastor sniffled. "For years we've had a drought. Tough on the farmers in the valley and brutal on our vineyards. We have to pay a price. The Earth spirits and mountain gods demand it. Brother Kenneth isn't killing, he's trading blood for enriching our soil. His parents own a winery in Bonny Doon."

"What a saint." Deere felt disgusted. "Can't you clowns do a fucking rain dance instead?"

Sven gripped the pastor's arm. "Where is Kenneth, right now?"

"I-I..."

"Let's book Father Pretty Boy," Deere said. "He'll be popular in men's prison."

"No, wait," he said. "Kenneth holds meetings in an abandoned chapel. It's been condemned. Structurally unsafe."

"Where?"

"On Fort Ord."

They went to the base with Officer Kim and found the black SUV first, in a University parking lot, without plates. "Tear it apart," Sven told Kim. "Then make arrests."

"We'll trace the VIN number," she said. "You don't want credit?"

"We solve problems," he said. "Clean up the mess and leave town."

"And you work for?"

"IBOT. Internal Bureau of Troubleshooters."

After Kim towed the vehicle, they toured the abandoned military barracks and boarded-up stores, through mud flats and puddles. Mangy dogs barked at the Subaru as they passed a second church on the brink of collapse. Broken fencing with "Danger" signs encircled it. They parked a block further by two junked cars and a VW van. Their engines still radiated heat.

"We've got an hour of daylight left," Sven said.

"What light?" The bay fog had obscured depth and distance with a gray flatness. Deere noticed himself shivering.

"Let's take the side door." Sven looked grim. "It's gonna be hairy."

"Yup." They both had denim bags slung over their shoulders; Sven held a baseball bat and Deere brought a .45 along.

Inside, the chapel was dark and deserted. Cracked support beams above and smashed stained glass littered the ground, while noisy crows nestled in open windows. Sven put a hand up and both froze to listen. A vague hum from beneath. They found a stone stairway to an even darker cellar. Smells of decaying animals, rotting wood and stale urine, moldy food and sex lingered. Deere affixed his goggles then pointed toward an aperture. They pushed through a clot of pelts and garbage, old clothes, dirty curtains, and damp blankets—the reek near unbearable.

Within lay a candlelit chamber the size of the upstairs chapel. Dead feral cats and wild dogs hung from a low ceiling. Defiled statues of Jesus and Mary were marked with blood and stained by excrement. The goggles helped Deere see the filthy naked people writhing entwined on the floor. He spied Ram

Skull reading at a dais, oblivious to them, while five followers sat cross-legged listening. Braziers burned frankincense and fouler herbs, clouding the room.

"One of you shall become immortal in death," the leader said. "How I envy your sacrifice."

"This is where it ends," Sven said in his booming Orson Welles voice. "You've already killed two. Time's up, Brother Kenneth."

The ram skull looked up. "You meddlers. I'm trying to save the land, help the people. You talk about murder. Ha! This is a trade. Insignificant lives for the greater good." He banged on the pedestal.

A shirtless man in an executioner's mask came from behind a curtain toward Sven. He clutched a spear. Sven swung the baseball bat against the underling's skull. He dropped.

More followers approached them so Deere tossed a tear gas concussion grenade. The basement shook as dirt and pumice rained down from above. The acolytes collapsed, rubbing their eyes. Brother Kenneth seemed unaffected. Deere and Sven advanced on the pulpit. Deere noticed a hole in the floor where vapors rose from. "What the hell is that?"

Kenneth laughed. "Some kind of hot spring running below, the waters poisoned by Fort Ord's foul legacy." The air smelled sulfurous. "I have dumped body parts and animals down there. And tonight, a person. The Devil's cauldron. I feed it and we'll be repaid by winter rains, a blessed spring, and a bounteous harvest by summer's end."

"More like Satan's sphincter." Deere climbed the platform

holding handcuffs.

"You won't stop me." Kenneth stabbed a dagger into the muscle of Deere's left arm.

"Fuck," he shouted. Deere took a hatchet from his bag and hammered it into the goat skull. The mask split in two, revealing Kenneth's frightened face. "You're just a spoiled rich kid from Stanford playing high priest."

"I'm thirty."

"You'll do thirty, at least."

Kenneth pulled a revolver from the lectern, but Sven brought the bat down, crushing knuckles. Deere fired his .45 to keep the acolytes back while Sven grappled with Kenneth. They pitched this way and that, until Sven clapped both fists against Kenneth's ears. The cult leader lost his balance and fell sideways, tumbling halfway into the steaming rift.

"Brethren, help me out," he cried.

Sven aided Deere, yanking the blade from his bicep. One of the torches had toppled and a curtain started burning.

The followers approached Kenneth, only his arms and head visible above the floor. "Thank you, Brother K. Your sacrifice will insure a successful crop." They began stamping on his hands.

"No!" he screamed, then plunged into the hot springs below.

Sven took Deere's arm. "Let's brass it out. This shithole is coming apart." The rafters moaned and more stones and wood rained down from the ceiling. The fire was spreading. After squeezing through the foul aperture, Sven hustled them back to the Subaru.

Resting on the damp ground, Deere watched flames rise and illuminate the church against the blackened night sky. "It's finished. Let's get back home before we have to explain anything."

A day later they enjoyed the sunset from the gondola of the blimp, outside the lounge. Their view stretched north across the Monterey Bay, beyond Santa Cruz and even Half Moon Bay, to where a mass of low clouds and fog enveloped San Francisco.

"You have to go away for awhile?" Deere said. "Up there?"

"Not really up or down. More of an out there."

"Far out."

"Exactly." Sven observed him. "How's the wound, JoJo?"

"Only hurts when I'm awake."

"Uh, you're an insomniac."

Deere nodded. "I'm heading back to Manhattan."

Sven chuckled. "Remember those albino alligators we tangled with?"

"If I had a dime for every chrome lizard..." His words trailed off. He felt suddenly sentimental. "Tell me that New Mexico hat story again."

"Really?" Sven rambled on, though Deere barely heard until, "So I paid him $600—"

"For a single hat?"

Sven ignored him. "I tried it on and the damn thing slid down to my nose. Supposed to be custom-made. Guy said I needed to sit out on the high mesa overnight in the rain. Three days later it finally stormed. I ate several peyote buttons."

"Part of the magic shaman shit?"

"Nope, just to help me get through the long hours. Fell asleep at dawn and when I woke in sunshine, the hat had shrunk. Fit my head exactly. Besides the body aches and fever—"

"Wait. Let me get my meds." Deere went inside. The Percocet alone wasn't cutting it. He grabbed his hooch and last skunk bud then wandered back out. "What was that guy's name from Sky City, in case I ever need to spend a fortune on a hat that don't fit?"

Deere stood alone on the gondola in the new dark. The firmament of stars above looked spectacular. So he raised his flask to the night sky and toasted Sven.

ART

Max Talley is a writer, painter, and a musician, who was born in New York City and lives in Southern California. His stories and essays have appeared in numerous journals, including *Vol. 1 Brooklyn, Atticus Review, Santa Fe Literary Review, Litro,* and *The Saturday Evening Post.* He won the 2021 best fiction contest in Jerry Jazz Musician for "Celestial Vagabonds," later nominated for a Pushcart Prize. Talley's first novel, *Yesterday We Forget Tomorrow,* was published in 2014, his curated anthology, *Delirium Corridor,* appeared in 2020 from Borda Books, and his short story collection, *My Secret Place,* was published in 2022 by Main Street Rag Books. www.maxdevoetalley.com

Borda Books
www.bordabooks.com

Hurricanes & Swan Songs, April 2019
Dames & Doppelgangers, October 2019
Delirium Corridor, December 2020
Silver Webb's All Hallows' Eve:
The Thinning Veil, October 2021
The Fifth Fedora, Fall 2022
A Flash of Darkness, April 2023
When the Night Breathes Electric, Fall 2023

Santa Barbara Literary Journal
www.santabarbaraliteraryjournal.com

Volume 1: *Andromeda*, June 2018
Volume 2: *Cor Serpentis*, December 2018
Volume 3: *Bellatrix*, June 2019
Volume 4: *Stardust*, November 2019
Volume 5: *Wild Mercury*, September 2020
Volume 6: *Saturn's Return*, June 2021
Volume 7: *Oh, Fortuna!*, August 2021
Volume 8: *Moon Drunk*, December 2022
Volume 9: *Space Sirens*, June 2023